THIS TIME FOREVER BOOK 2

RENEWING
Forever

KELLY JENSEN

RIPTIDE
PUBLISHING

Riptide Publishing
PO Box 1537
Burnsville, NC 28714
www.riptidepublishing.com

Renewing Forever

Cover art: Natasha Snow, natashasnowdesigns.com
Editor: Carole-ann Galloway
Layout: L.C. Chase, lcchase.com/design.htm

ISBN: 978-1-62649-841-9

First edition
November, 2018

Also available in ebook:
ISBN: 978-1-62649-840-2

THIS TIME FOREVER BOOK 2

RENEWING

Forever

KELLY JENSEN

RIPTIDE
PUBLISHING

For Loris

TABLE OF
Contents

CHAPTER 1

A s a writer, Franklin Tern held a specific disdain for dark and stormy nights. They were nature's taunt—an opening he was supposed to take advantage of, and fought against. No one, not even a prize-winning journalist, could surmount such a cliché.

Such nights were also unwelcome when he was driving.

Phone pressed between his shoulder and his ear, Frank turned the wheel just enough to guide his sleek black BMW Z3 away from the lake forming along the side of Route 447. More than an inch of standing water might swallow them whole.

Lightning flashed overhead and thunder boomed. His friend Simon shouted through the phone. "The story was great!"

"The story was depressing. The whole trip was depressing, which, as you well know, is not my thing. I am not hard-edged. I'm fluff. Pure and simple."

"But that's why the article was so effective. I could feel you, Frank. Your horror, and how out of place you were."

"Gee, thanks." Feeling the phone slip, Frank hitched his shoulder up a little higher. "I'll have to send you the full piece when I figure out how not to sound horrified."

"I was trying to tell you I thought it was good."

"Whatever."

"Are you still going down to Texas to cover the church bombing?"

"What? No. What would make you think I'd do a story like that?"

"Something you posted on Twitter."

"You're on Twitter?"

"Charlie signed me up."

Frank ground his teeth—his instinctive reaction to any mention of Simon's partner, with a little desultory weather hate slipped in on the side. "I haven't posted to Twitter in weeks. Keeping my phone charged quickly became secondary to . . ." *Not cringing at the devastation humanity could heap upon a natural disaster.* Pushing those thoughts aside, "Can you believe I willingly flew coach to get out of there?"

Also, what had his idiot PA been posting on Twitter?

"I can't believe you went to Puerto Rico," Simon said.

"Neither can I."

Where the hell had the road gone? He tapped the brakes, slowing from a crawl to a near standstill, and guided his precious around the river now spilling across the blacktop. The turnoff to Bossen Hill must be coming up soon.

"Listen, the storm of the century is blowing through the Poconos right now." Mild compared to the tropical storm that had recently ravaged a still-recovering Puerto Rico, but enough to compel him to concentrate. "I have no idea where my earpiece is, and I need to focus on the road."

"What are you doing in Pennsylvania? Is it bad up there? Wait, didn't you land just a few hours ago?"

"Personal business. Maybe a story." Because everything was a story, wasn't it? "I'll call you next week?"

"Come down on Friday. I'm learning to grill."

The car jerked as Frank's foot gave the brakes an involuntary tap. "You're going to cook outside?"

"With hot coals and all."

Frank swallowed the question about whether Charlie would be there. Of course he would. Simon lived with Charlie now, in an extremely cozy house with a ready-made family. "I'll bring wine. And pictures of hell."

"I promise not to say they're great. Drive safe, hmm?"

"Will do." Frank tossed the phone onto the front passenger seat and gripped the wheel with both hands. "C'mon, baby. Just another few miles and we'll get you out of this storm."

In response, rain lashed the windshield, blurring the road. Leaning forward, Frank peered through the fevered swish of the wipers.

Had he missed the sign? A flash of white peeked out of the wet darkness. He didn't need to read it to know what it said: *Bossen Hill Family Resort. Turn right 1000ft.*

The disquiet of his thoughts calmed a little as he remembered the day they'd planted the sign. His older brother, Matty, had made it in shop class—chiseling the letters into a plank before painting them black against white. Then he'd invited Frank to help him measure the distance back from the turn and dig a hole for the post. That had been a good afternoon and typical of summer in the Poconos.

Sudden thunder boomed, vibrating up and in from the road and the air. The car shook. Frank could just make out the turn ahead and flipped on his blinker to warn all the other idiots out on the road that he was going to attempt a right turn without hydroplaning or ending up in the gully that swallowed the forest on this side.

Except, no one else was out this late during a monsoon.

Not a monsoon, Frankie. You've seen what a real *storm can do.*

He managed the turn with a minimum of fuss and powered his way up the narrow and winding road. That the drive would have been any easier tomorrow morning was debatable. Returning home to claim a legacy left by his dearly departed uncle didn't fit into such categories as easy or moderately difficult. It was what it was.

The forest lining each side of the road flashed into stark relief as lightning and thunder crashed together. The storm had moved right on top of him. Frank pressed his foot down, knowing it was probably the wrong thing to do. But he really wanted to be out of the rain. The pitch of the engine rose, and the rear wheels spun against the road before grabbing hold and propelling him over the crest of the hill. Lightning flared again, blinding in its intensity.

When the world faded back to reality, something large and bristly lay across the road in front of him. Frank blinked a few times, unsure if the sparking obstruction was an afterimage or something actually blocking the road. No, that was a downed power pole, and if he didn't stop or turn or both, he was going to—

If not for the river flowing down the road, he might have safely avoided floating across the center line while white-knuckling the wheel, lips clamped together over the yell pushing against his vocal cords. For a moment, he thought he *was* going to make it. The world stilled and the thunder of the storm seemed to rumble more quietly. Time slowed, catching the flash of sparking electricity in single bright frames. His urge to shout was under control, not going to happen, so not going to happen . . .

Then the wheel jerked from his aching fingers and the car slid sideways. The shout cut loose. Watching himself flail and panic was like having an out-of-body experience. A terrible grinding scrape shuddered through the floor. Metal shrieked and the car came to an abrupt halt, sound cut in half by the dying of the engine.

Adam Levine endeavored to fill the pause, detailing what lovers did. Frank stared dumbly at the radio. His heart was beating too rapidly for the song, and the sound of his yelling and cursing echoed in his ears. But he was alive. That was good, right? And the storm continued *outside* the car, which could mean any number of things. It took a while to pin the most obvious: he hadn't wrecked his baby too badly. The fact he was looking at the top of the trees rather than the middle of the trunks probably meant he was wedged halfway down a ditch, but he was breathing and thinking and still listening to Maroon 5.

"Jesus."

Much as he did not want to venture out into the storm, he had to assess the situation. The door groaned horribly as he pushed it open. Doors only groaned on old cars, and his precious wasn't even a classic yet. They had five years to go.

Rain pushed into his eyes the second Frank poked his head out. A minute later, standing in the gully, assessing bodily harm both to himself and his car, the rain finished drenching him and moved on to the worthwhile task of spilling through the open door. Frank eased it shut, wincing at the corresponding moan.

Long story short, he wasn't going to be driving anywhere tonight.

Short story long, the rear end of his baby was buried in a rapidly filling creek, while the front end barely crested the verge. He'd slid backward off the side of the road into a gully the depth of his car. *Fantastic.*

At least the thunder and lightning had moved on, still clashing against each other, but not right over his head.

Frank patted his front pocket, fingers absently seeking the outline of his phone before he remembered tossing it into the front passenger seat. He opened the groaning door and leaned across the center console to feel across the seat. The phone wasn't there. He'd cry over what he was doing to the leather upholstery but his face was so damn wet, he wouldn't feel the tears, and tears should never be wasted.

Head tucked under the front passenger seat, ass soaking in the wind, he finally found his phone, and of course he had no signal. Not even a measly 1x. How was one supposed to call a tow truck at . . . 8:37 p.m. on a Friday night in the Poconos? Hmm?

Frank whacked the phone against the dash a couple of times before tucking it into his pocket. He could feel his throat moving, meaning he was muttering. Stuff and nonsense. Curses. Something between a whine and a moan. A plea to the God he didn't believe in to show himself and offer to put Frank on an ark with two of everything.

He couldn't be more than a mile from the resort, and without a working cell phone his only option was to walk. Frank wrestled his carry-on out of the cramped back seat. Later, he'd thank the missing God that he hadn't put it in the trunk. Now, he'd thank his own foresight for the fact the small suitcase was of the hard-shell variety.

He'd only repacked it a few hours ago; dumping ripe laundry from Puerto Rico into the laundry bag for his service to deal with, replacing it with lightweight "summer in the Poconos" linen and wool. All hopefully dry within the bright-blue shell. He shouldered the well-worn leather satchel he used to carry the essentials and splashed through the gully until he found a place to climb back up onto the road—avoiding the downed power pole which had, thankfully, stopped sparking.

Head down, though it made little difference—he was soaked in an utterly proverbial way—Frank pushed into the rain. After the tenth collision between case and knee, he dropped it to the ground, pulled out the handle, and wheeled it through the storm. Yes, he probably looked like an upmarket hobo.

He'd have to throw these shoes away. Leather did not suffer repeated soakings. His pants would survive, though they'd undoubtedly lose the tailored look he liked so much. The shirt—linen and rain did not mix, and he suspected his jacket, which also suffered under the effects of the storm, was leaving marks around the collar and cuffs that would not wash out.

He had greater concerns than the state of his outfit, but preferred the head-down method of coping. His reason for drowning along the road to his long-lost childhood could remain unexamined until he'd found a fireplace, a towel, and some quaint flavor of tea only served in dusty old family resorts.

The road dipped, prompting another memory: clutching his middle as he bounced off the back seat of his uncle's car—Robert Tern laughing as everyone complained about leaving their stomachs somewhere below them. One more bend and the road widened slightly as the familiar driveway came into view.

The storm must have loosened the sign, but the fence was still there, still ridiculously rustic—a curve of stacked slate to either side of the drive, rising toward an arch. The sign welcoming visitors to Bossen Hill Family Resort hung from one end of the arch, blowing in the wind, the letters obscured by rain and age. Frank ducked around it and started the long trek down the rutted drive. He couldn't see the sprawling lodge or make out any of the surrounding buildings. The power must be out.

As he drew closer, the ghost of the lodge separated from the night, an indistinct bulk of stone and slate. He could make out a single light flickering in a window to the left of middle. That would be the office. Was someone up? Or had the generator kicked in, powering the only light left burning in an otherwise dark building? The rest of the place looked empty and . . . empty. Vacant. Hollowed out and lifeless. Frowning, Frank crunched across the unkempt circle of gravel in front of the lodge. The wind picked up, blowing him up the wide steps to the porch. He stood shivering, cold and wet, air sucking at and ruffling his hair and clothes in an entirely unsensual manner. In the fractional pauses, he could hear the distant rumble of a generator.

Frank tried the door and found it locked. He rapped his knuckles against the damp wood. After shivering on the porch for another few minutes, he kicked the door with his ruined shoe. Another interminable minute passed. Frank stalked to the wan light of the office window and tapped on the glass. A shadow moved behind the curtain, jerking up, turning, and finally waving in the direction of the front door.

Frank splashed back across the porch to await salvation. The door swung open, revealing a dimly lit lobby and a slight figure beckoning him out of the rain. Frank hurried inside and reached to push the door closed behind him. Then he glanced at his rescuer.

It was as though time itself twisted, the storm plucking him out of the Poconos like a storied tornado. The light was bad, but he'd know that mop of hair and those dark eyes anywhere. It was Tommy. Thomas Benjamin. His best and only childhood friend. His first love. The first person he'd kissed.

The guy who'd repaid him with a broken nose.

Frank dropped his suitcase. "What the hell are you doing here?"

CHAPTER 2

Tom tried to catch air with his mouth open, but nope, it wasn't working. Frank had always had that effect, somehow robbing the space between them of oxygen.

Messages fired along Tom's synapses, most of them still coded by the time they hit the cortex. His brain wanted to skip back, forward, and a little sideways. It was a freaking merry-go-round in there . . . and his mouth was still open. He could taste the musty atmosphere of the lodge on his tongue.

He'd known Frank and his sister were coming up this weekend. But now that the reality of it stood in front of him, Tom found himself unable to cope.

Oh my God, it's Frank.

"Verbose as ever, I see," Frank said.

Words. He needed words.

"Ah . . ." *Good start. Now, say something sensible.* "You're here."

"Obviously. On foot no less. I don't suppose you have any dry towels? And what is that smell?"

"Damp."

Frank's brow creased with displeasure. "Yes, I am rather."

"I meant the smell."

For someone who resembled an overdressed otter, Frank smelled pretty good. Like cedar and birch. He looked pretty good too. Age had sharpened his features, banishing the smiling boy with pink, freckled cheeks and riotous orange curls. This Frank—this older, wetter, not-smiling Frank—was taller, slimmer, serious and . . . really, really wet.

"Towel." Tom sounded like an idiot. Not talking at all would be better. "Getting you a towel."

He abandoned the dimly lit lobby, navigating the hallway by memory and the square of light from the open office door. The power had failed about an hour before, and with no guests in residence, Tom had started only one generator. There was no need to have the place lit up like the Fourth of July when there wasn't anyone here to appreciate it.

He groped through the darkness, past several closed doors until he reached the laundry, where he stepped from gloom to no light at all, and felt his way along the shelves until he located a stack of towels. Leaning forward, he gave a quick sniff, hoping the dank atmosphere of the lobby hadn't penetrated this far. God, was the roof leaking? He'd have to check all the guest rooms in the morning.

Light pierced the darkness. Flinching, Tom turned and made out Frank's shape behind an illuminated cell phone. He watched as Frank reached for the light switch and flipped it up and down.

"Why is there no power in here?" he asked. "I can hear a generator."

"It was meant to be just me tonight, so I only started one of them. I can connect a few more circuits if you want."

"What I want is a goddamn towel. And to know what you're doing here."

Tom snatched a towel and tossed it across the room. Frank caught it and immediately mopped his face. The light from the cell phone bounced around the walls, then cut off as Frank tucked the phone away.

"I'm the manager," Tom said. "Didn't you know?"

"No. I didn't. Can we talk somewhere where I can see you? I don't suppose you have coffee or tea or something?"

"In the office."

The parade back toward the light was short and not particularly sweet. Frank muttered into his towel, and Tom could feel each indistinct word as a pinprick against his skin. He'd messed up. Again. And, as always, he wasn't quite sure what he'd done wrong.

In comparison to the lobby and hallway, the office was well lit. Frank paused in the doorway, one foot half raised as though he was unsure whether the floor would hold him. Distaste lined his forehead and pinched his mouth.

"God, what happened in here?"

"What do you mean?" Tom followed Frank's gaze, wondering if one of the property's cats had managed to drag a dead chipmunk inside, but he saw only the cozy confines of a room he considered his safe space. The office was his favorite part of the old lodge. Generous windows peeked out onto the long front porch, providing a perfect view of the circle and driveway. Tom liked waking up to that view from the couch against the wall opposite. Liked the idea of facing forward while wondering what the day would bring . . . which hadn't been much for a while, but ever since Robert's death, that had suited him.

"It looks like someone's great old aunt started nesting." Frank plucked the blanket from the couch and tossed it aside. "When did he paint the walls red? No, the better question might be why? And why aren't any of the pictures straight? You know what? Never mind. You said something about coffee. I could also use another towel. Is there any light in the bathroom across the hall? I need to get out of these wet clothes before I wrinkle permanently and have to live forever with folds of wet fabric adhered to every crevice."

Frank finished his inspection of the room and faced Tom. For an instant, the ill-tempered lines across his forehead dipped toward something akin to the emotion sitting heavily in the center of Tom's being. Then Frank blinked, and any trace of the grief he might be feeling over his uncle's passing disappeared. He turned away, muttering again, and left the office. Tom stood there—the odd disconnect between thought and action still hampering his every move—and listened as Frank collected his suitcase from the lobby and wheeled it into the bathroom.

Was the light in the hall bath connected to the generator? Tom leaned a little to the left and peered out into the hallway. Light drew a line along the underside of the bathroom door.

Right. So. Coffee.

It was in inspecting the Keurig that Robert Tern had loved so much that Tom's thoughts finally broke free of gridlock. The weight in the middle of his chest pulsed and the familiar burn crawled through his sinuses until his vision blurred.

Jeez, get ahold of yourself.

It'd been a week since the service. Two weeks since Robert had passed. Frank barely looked aggrieved, and here Tom was nearly sobbing over a coffee maker. Frank hadn't been to visit his uncle in close to a decade, though, while Tom had never left. He'd feel guilty about stepping in and being around when Robert needed someone, but he'd needed Robert too—as a mentor and a friend.

God, Frank was here. Really here. Would he want decaf this late at night?

Rather than make a decision, Tom went to get another towel. The bathroom door opened just as he returned and he handed it over. "Decaf or regular?"

Frank grunted as he took the fresh towel. "Decaf sounds good. Though anything hot would be good right now." He flipped off the light, wrestled his suitcase and an armload of wet clothes out of the bathroom, and followed Tom across the hall. In the door of the office, he paused again. "And thank you."

Nodding, Tom selected the appropriate K-Cup and snapped it into place. He added water from the stack of bottles on the floor, tucked a mug under the spout, and pressed Go. When he turned back around, Frank had folded the blanket, set it on the arm of the old sofa, and sat somewhere close to the middle in a weary sprawl.

Tom pulled a chair out from the desk and perched cautiously on the edge of the seat. "I wasn't expecting you or Annabelle until tomorrow."

"I figured I'd beat the Saturday-morning traffic. Not the most intelligent plan, but the rain wasn't that bad until I'd passed through the Gap." Frank crossed his legs and picked at a wrinkle in his pants, drawing attention to the fact that he had not changed into sweats like any normal person might when finding themselves wetter than wet after hours. No, he'd opted for dark-gray dress slacks, a pale-violet oxford shirt with the top two buttons open, and a pair of leather shoes. Loafers or something.

In comparison, Tom was wearing sweatpants and a T-shirt with more holes than fabric. Not because he'd been caught out in the rain, but because he'd been close to sleep when Frank tapped on the window.

"Sometimes the storms seem to hit the Gap," he said, "roll back toward the Poconos and get stuck somewhere in between." *Between* being Stroudsburg and East Stroudsburg, the foothills of the gloriously named Pocono Mountains. They were hills. Big hills.

"How long have you been managing Bossen Hill?" Frank asked.

The Keurig gurgled and Tom rose to extract Frank's cup. He handed it across the small space and settled back into his chair before answering. "About seven years, I guess. On and off."

"On and off?"

"When Robert"—his throat tried to close over the name— "needed the help. He had a full-time manager up until 2010. Ah, then, um, things weren't going so well with the bookings. Weather, the economy."

Frank should know all of this. What he wouldn't know was how much Tom had needed the job. How much he still needed it. Now wasn't the time to ask after Frank's plans for the resort, though, and not because it was late. Not even because Tom's thoughts were threatening to mount the merry-go-round again.

Mostly because a future Tom couldn't see was usually better for all concerned.

Frank sipped his coffee and made a face. "Was the pod machine your idea or my uncle's?"

"I bought it for him last year. Birthday gift."

"Huh." Frank looked around the office. "Was the red paint your idea too?" When Tom didn't answer, Frank continued, "I didn't see any cars in the circle. Are there no guests for the weekend?"

"Where did you park?"

"About a mile down Snow Hill Road."

"Why would you park on Snow Hill Road?"

Frank drained his mug and waved it through the air. "Power pole hit the road in front of me, and I slid off the side into what passes for a gutter up here."

Tom jerked forward in his seat, feet falling flat on the floor. "Jeez. Are you all right?"

"Fine. Only wet. My car, however, is another matter."

"I'm sure we can get it towed tomorrow. Ken's is open Saturday mornings."

Frank's smile had the fleeting nature of a rare bird. "Ken's still in business, huh?"

"Yeah."

"So, the guest situation."

Tom licked his lips. Telling Frank they were closed would put him out of a job—not that he was doing much more than managing a crumbling pile of stone. "There was a bit of activity back in March. The late snow? Slopes all stayed open until the end of the month and we got a few overflow bookings. But no one comes up here just to stay *here* anymore. Not to Bossen Hill, anyway."

"That's depressing."

Tell me about it.

"I had no idea things . . ." Frank glanced around the office, brow furrowed. A truncated sigh left him, pulling his shoulders down. "Then again, I've been out of touch." He cut a sideways look at Tom before seeming to find interest in the empty mug in his hands.

"We can talk about it tomorrow when your sister gets here."

"Yes, let's do that. What time were you expecting her?"

"Probably not before the afternoon."

"All right. Are any of the rooms made up?"

"206 and 207."

Frank glanced at the wall separating the office from Robert's bedroom, the only bedroom on the ground floor, then at Tom. His eyebrows twitched together and his mug became a precious article, cradled and stroked. For a moment, he looked more like Frankie— the boy who'd stolen Tom's heart, a good portion of his soul, and maybe the livable portion of his life. His hair was shorter now, clipped close, and a sedate strawberry blond. Paler at the temples. The lines around his mouth and eyes were friendly, his mouth the same: small and intense. His eyes that lighter shade of brown some folks called hazel.

Frank had aged well, though Tom had always liked the way he looked.

The emotional puddle in the center of Tom's chest rippled, and he broke the connection between their gazes to study his bare toes. There was little point in apologizing now. He was three decades too late. But in this moment, he almost wanted to. No . . . he didn't want to apologize; he wanted to explain. Or both. Say something that might throw a line across the chasm yawning between them.

Instead, he pushed off the edge of the chair. "Help yourself to a key. I'll go make sure the lights are connected to the generator."

"You needn't bother. I'm probably going to sleep pretty soon. Do you live close by?"

Forcing himself not to glance at the couch, Tom answered, "Um, yeah. But I've been sleeping here since . . ." He motioned toward Robert's empty bedroom. "To keep an eye on the place."

"Oh, right. Sorry, I'm not at all sure what a manager does."

"It's negotiable."

"Well, if you want to stay . . ."

Tom let his gaze wander toward the couch. If he wanted to stay, Frank had given him the perfect excuse. But even he couldn't deny that after tomorrow, the future would need to be contemplated, welcome or not. It wouldn't take Frank long to figure out the lodge was all but closed. Might as well get used to staying elsewhere. "It's fine. Now that you're here, I guess I can get going."

"You know what? That's ridiculous. You should stay. You were going to stay. I'm sure my uncle . . . I'm sure Robert would have appreciated your diligence." A wry smile flickered across Frank's small mouth. "You were always better than me when it came to things like this."

"I—"

"Stay." Frank rose from the couch. "We can talk more tomorrow."

"I've got another job from eleven to three. So I'll probably see you after that."

"Oh. Well, okay." Frank corralled his suitcase and bundle of wet clothing. His brow furrowed again in what was becoming a familiar pattern. "It's good to see you, Tom."

Tom answered with a short nod.

After Frank left the room, Tom slipped out and back down the hallway toward the laundry. The generators were in the shed behind. The wet night misted his head and shoulders as he crossed the small pad of concrete and hauled open the door. He grabbed the flashlight from the wall mount and played it over the circuits until he found the upstairs hallway and lights for the front side of the lodge.

After flipping a couple of switches, he checked the propane level in the main tank. Enough to last another thirty hours or so with the current load.

Satisfied, he returned to the lodge, grabbed another towel for his wet feet, and retrieved his blanket from the arm of the sofa. For a while, he listened to Frank moving around in the room overhead. Then the bed groaned and settled. Silence followed. Still, Tom didn't sleep. He lay there trying not to look at the ceiling, trying not to remember, and failing at both.

CHAPTER 3

Summer 1978

T om ducked down behind the prickly bush, taking care not
to snag his new shirt. The camouflage pattern was the wrong
green for the forest, but if he stayed still, he should blend with his
environment. Heavy cotton clung to his back, damp with sweat.
His neck and wrists itched within the confines of the collar and cuffs.
Tom bore the discomfort as a soldier should.

Voices floated gently through the densely packed trees, born
on a breeze that could be stronger. A lick of air on the back of his
neck would be welcome about now. Tom hunched in a little closer
to the bush and poked one finger inside. Carefully avoiding thorns
and leaves, he bent a slender branch downward and peered through
the gap.

The enemy didn't even try to hide themselves. Dressed
impractically in suits of scorching orange, purple, and blue, they were
alien to the landscape. Hikers from somewhere other than the Pocono
Mountains, exploring one of Penn's many woods. To Tom, they were
scouts from the enemy camp. Unwelcome guests to his corner of
Pennsylvania.

Not that he owned these woods. Whoever had posted the signs
every twenty feet or so on this side of the creek did. He hadn't been
prosecuted for trespassing yet, though, and if the enemy did capture
him, they'd never break him. There hadn't been a torture invented that
could put down Corporal Thomas Benjamin of the 25th Infantry.

He waited until the enemy patrol rounded the next bend in the
trail before moving to follow them. The prickly bush didn't want to

let him go, but Tom insisted. He shouldered his pack and ducked across the narrow trail, taking cover in the cool shade on the other side. Then, threading his way through the trees, he tracked the patrol to their camp.

Or where they'd decided to break for lunch.

His stomach rumbled as he watched them unpack several plastic containers from one of their packs. That the containers were color coordinated with their outfits did not escape his notice. The enemy had interesting customs. And whatever they were eating smelled really, really good. Was that fried chicken? Potato salad? And two kinds of pie?

Tom pulled out his peanut butter sandwich. The enemy was making so much noise that he didn't even have to move slowly or worry about the rustle of plastic as he unwrapped the limp white square, crusts cut off. He eyed his drink. The scratched-up label advertised the liquid inside as Mello Yello, and the lid wasn't a good fit. But he'd been carrying the same bottle for three weeks now, washing it out and refilling it with anything from tap water to lemonade he made from lemons acquired on his last mission.

It wasn't stealing if he found a bag of lemons lying around.

A twig snapped somewhere off to the right, followed by loud chatter from farther down the trail. More enemy soldiers? He needed to report back, but could he cross the trail unseen? Make it over the creek without alerting the sentries? He tried not to panic as the second patrol drew closer, talking and laughing among themselves. Tom pressed his back to a massive tree, breathing hard.

A hiss came from above. He peered into the canopy—was his mission about to be complicated by a timber rattlesnake?—and saw a face peeking back down at him. He couldn't make out any of the features, just a shock of hair the color of a Duracell battery and a beckoning hand.

Quickly, Tom decided whoever it was was on his side. A forward scout from another regiment. He grabbed a knot on the side of the tree and started climbing. Between lumps of sap, broken branches and, finally, some lower limbs, he found his way up in quick order, and by the time the second patrol had turned into the trail below, Tom was pulling himself over a wide branch and into the dense cover of leaves.

Now that he was high enough, Tom could see the planks wedged between two divergent branches, forming a wide platform above him. He reached for the edge of the closest plank and tugged, checking the stability, then climbed up over it, dropping his pack onto the platform before daring to look down at the ground.

The hikers passing below the hideout were dressed less loudly than the first group, which would make them more dangerous if they knew how to be quiet. Some patrol they made.

Leaning back from the edge, Tom turned to confront the fellow soldier. His first thought was how someone so big had managed to climb this high without breaking every branch along the way. His second thought ran along similar lines, allowing for the fact the boy wasn't actually huge, just kind of chunky. The halo of curls, round and freckly cheeks, and equally round and freckly knees poking out of a pair of dark green shorts gave more of an impression of bulk than was true.

Of course, everyone was bigger than Tom. At nine, he still had the build of a seven-year-old, which could be an advantage, but wasn't. He was a runt and he knew it.

The boy seemed to be giving him equal appraisal, and Tom wondered which of them would speak first. If it was up to him, it'd be the other boy, because one of the best ways to stay unnoticed, aside from his size and camouflage shirt, was to stay silent. He continued studying his rescuer's face, looking beyond the freckles to discover a pleasing symmetry of straight nose, even eyes of a light brown, and a surprisingly small mouth with lips that seemed a little too pink.

Finally, after what felt like a hot and close hour, the other boy broke the silence. "How are you wearing long sleeves and jeans when it's melting out here?"

Tom inspected his new shirt and was dismayed to discover a loose thread on the lower hem. He tucked it into his old jeans and wiped his sleeve across his forehead, mopping up some of the sweat.

"A soldier's will is stronger than the elements." He told himself he was whispering to avoid being heard by the enemy.

"Huh. I'm Frankie and you're trespassing."

"Tom. And my orders are to patrol these woods." No, jungle. He was supposed to call it a jungle.

"You're weird."

"Well, your hair is orange."

Frankie tugged at his curls with a mournful expression. "I know." Scowling, he gestured downward. "I was watching you. Why were you following the hikers?"

"It's an enemy patrol."

Frankie frowned. "Are you on something?"

"On something?"

"Yeah, you know, drugs. Weed. My brother smokes weed."

"Huh."

"So?"

"No. I was . . ." Heat crawled over Tom's cheeks, making him even hotter than he already was. He shrugged. "It was just a game."

"Like war?"

"Yeah."

"My mom says war is dumb and soldiers are brainwashed dupes."

A hot flare completely unrelated to the weather swept through Tom's middle. "Soldiers fight so the rest of us don't have to."

"Put a lid on it. The war is over."

Biting his lip, Tom looked away.

A slice of watermelon wobbled into the periphery of his vision.

"Want some?"

Tom took the wedge. It was warm and sticky, but all the sweeter for its suffering. Frankie offered him a can of cola next, as warm and sticky as the watermelon, and a crumbling cookie after that. He had a cache of food up here. Also, he was talking.

". . . so my sister said she'd tell if Matty lit up outside her room again, and he paid her two dollars to stay quiet. Two measly dollars. I'd have asked for ten. He earns at least that much on Friday nights at the gas station."

"What?"

Frankie glanced up from his handful of cookies. "The weed. Weren't you listening?"

"Sorry."

"Anyway, I snuck up to his room to see if he had any more, but if he has, he hid it pretty well. Ever had it?"

"What?"

"Weed. Are you special or something?"

"Special?"

"Man, you're weird. I'm not sure if this friendship is going to work out."

"We're friends?"

"Don't you want to be?"

Tom had to think about that. He hadn't expected to make a friend today. He hadn't expected to make a friend at all. Could he expand his game of war to include a friend? Maybe Frankie could be another scout.

"You can't be a sergeant."

Frankie's eyebrows were lighter than his hair. They twitched together in a brief motion, then straightened. "Okay, what can I be?"

"A private, first class, or a corporal."

"What's the difference?"

By the time Tom had finished explaining the ranks of the US Army, they'd eaten all the cookies. Having such a full stomach was an odd sensation. Made him sleepy. Not a good situation when caught behind enemy lines.

"Was your dad in the army?" Frankie asked.

"Mmm."

"What does he do now that the war's over?"

The cookies and watermelon and cola swirled around in his gut, fighting for room. Tom wiped sweat from his forehead and scrubbed the back of his neck with the same grimy sleeve. He was ruining his new shirt. Maybe he could wash it in the shower before his mom saw it.

"I asked—"

"He's dead. He was killed in Vietnam."

"Oh. I'm sorry."

Tom shrugged. He rarely knew what to say when people told him they were sorry. Words didn't fix the reality of growing up without a father. He only had his mother's words. *I'm sorry, baby. You can't meet your daddy. He never came back from Vietnam.*

"I never met him," he said now.

"Huh."

Frankie offered him another can of soda and Tom shook his head. "I don't feel so good."

"Too hot?"

"Yeah."

"Want to go swimming?"

"I don't have anything to swim in."

"You've got something on under your jeans?"

"Yeah."

"Then you've got something to swim in."

Tom helped clean up the platform by sweeping crumbs over the edge while Frankie sealed the lids on a set of orange Tupperware. Then he took point, slinging his pack across his shoulders before picking a path down the tree trunk. He waited at the bottom for Frankie and watched in surprise as the larger boy descended with ease and agility.

When they were both on the ground, Tom's eyes were level with Frankie's chin. Just.

"You sure are short, Tommy."

"Tom."

"How old are you?"

"Nine."

"Hey, me too. What school do you go to?"

"Chipperfield."

"You live in Pocono Court?"

More heat stung Tom's face. "How did you know that?"

Frankie, with his round cheeks and endless supply of cookies obviously lived somewhere nicer than a muddy circle of trailers.

"I've seen you crossing the creek."

"You've seen me?"

"That's not the only fort I've got in these woods."

"Oh."

Voices sounded to the west and Tom snapped back to his mission. "Another patrol is coming!"

Frankie gave him an odd look before smiling. "We better make a break for the creek."

"Good plan. This way."

"I know where the creek is."

"Fine. I suppose as the newest recruit, you should lead. I'll take the rear guard position."

"Sure."

Still smiling, Frankie took off at a jog, dancing delicately around tree trunks and over lower bushes, proving again that he could move lightly and quickly. Following, Tom decided that this was fun. Having a friend could work out. Frankie glanced over his shoulder, and then he seemed to drop from view, letting out a sharp cry as he disappeared.

Banishing panicked fantasies of pits infested with sharpened stakes, Tom skirted a tree and nearly tripped over the same root that must have caught Frankie. The ground sloped away from the base of the tree, exposing several woody vines, and Frankie had rolled to the bottom of the small hill and lay curled on his side, both hands wrapped around his ankle.

"Ah! Dang it." He hissed before uttering an entirely unmilitary whimper.

After scrambling down the slope, Tom knelt at his side. "What is it?"

"My ankle. I tripped over the tree and came down wrong. Is it broken? Can you see any bones sticking out?"

Tom's stomach rebelled, sending a hot surge of cookies and cola up to visit his esophagus. He swallowed, wincing at the burning retreat, and leaned forward to look at Frankie's ankle. There didn't seem to be any blood. "Here, move your hands. I can't see anything."

"It's broken, I know it's broken!"

"It might be a sprain."

Should he go get someone? Abandoning a soldier behind enemy lines was the opposite of heroic, but he couldn't exactly call for a medivac out here. Tom pulled Frankie's sock down to expose the ankle. Still no blood and no bones, and he couldn't tell if the puffy appearance below the red indent left by his sock was normal or not.

"Let me see your other ankle."

The injured one *was* puffier. And turning sort of red. Tom looked Frankie up and down. He'd stopped whimpering and hissing, but was obviously in pain. What should he do? A head taller and lots of pounds heavier, Frankie wasn't going to fit over his shoulder.

"Can you stand?" Tom asked.

By the time he was upright, grim determination had hardened the soft lines of Frankie's face. Tears beaded his pale lashes, but he hadn't broken down.

Tom inserted himself under Frankie's arm like a crutch. "Okay, let's see how this goes."

The journey back up to the hiking trail was torturous, leaving them both a sweaty mess by the time they reached level ground. Tom could almost feel Frankie's pain. They'd been limping along the path for several minutes when Tom heard someone ahead of them. His first instinct was to duck away and hide. But even though Frankie's injury could be tied into the game, Tom didn't want to play anymore. He was tired and worried. He'd twisted an ankle before and it had never hurt for this long.

A man and a boy came around the bend, maybe a father and son.

"Frankie?" The man strode forward, all of his face wrinkled up with concern.

The boy—a taller, slightly skinnier, less orange version of Frankie—ran past the man, skidding to a stop at Frankie's side. "You okay?"

Frankie only grunted, so Tom spoke up. "I think his ankle might be broken." He pointed in the direction of the creek. "We were running down to the creek and he fell."

"Near the big tree?" the man asked. "I really need to pack some more dirt around those roots. Add it to the list, would you, Matty? Okay, Frankie, let's get you sitting down a minute so we can take a peek at that ankle of yours."

Frankie made a needy whine as Tom tried to ease out from under his arm. Matty—the weed-smoking brother?—immediately picked up the slack on Frankie's other side, and together, all three of them helped Frankie sit on a boulder beside the path. The man crouched down to inspect the now very swollen ankle.

"Sure looks broken. Can you move your toes?"

"Hurts," Frankie hissed.

"I don't wonder. Let's get you back to the house and Matty can call up your dad."

Tom took a step back, assuming his part was done. But the man turned to him. "Son, think you can keep on being Frankie's other crutch while Matty runs on ahead?"

Ducking his head, Matty did just that, disappearing back around the bend in the trail.

Frankie gave Tom a pleading look, and Tom sidled closer to Frankie again and offered his shoulder. That was what friends did, right?

The man supported Frankie from the other side and together they lifted him off the rock. With Tom being so much shorter than the rest of the party, they made a lopsided group, and he wasn't bearing all that much weight. The man seemed to be doing most of the work. But when Tom tried to edge away, Frankie gripped his shoulder.

Ducking his head, Tom renewed his efforts by slotting himself more firmly under Frankie's arm, jostling him. Frankie moaned in pain.

"You're doing just fine." The man peered over Frankie's head. "I'm Robert, by the way. Matty and Frankie's uncle. Who might you be?"

"Tom."

"Well, Tom, I'm glad to make your acquaintance. Frankie's lucky to have such a steadfast friend."

But we only met today, and he was on my patrol—

"You live around here?" Robert asked.

Tom swallowed. "Over the creek, s-sir."

Instead of accusing him of being where he shouldn't be, Robert nodded his head. "Right close, then. You like wandering these woods?"

"I . . . er, um." Tom dipped his chin and muttered, "I didn't see the signs." Which was only sort of a lie. He hadn't seen the *No Trespassing* sign until the first time he'd crossed back over the creek. So he couldn't say he hadn't known he wasn't supposed to be here now. Would Robert blame him for Frankie's fall?

"We were playing war," Frankie put in, squeezing Tom's shoulder again.

"Were you now? I remember playing war with your dad." Robert's face took on a wistful expression.

Ahead, the path took another turn, bringing them closer to the edge of the forest than Tom had dared venture on his own. The trees were starting to thin. Beyond lay a sweep of deep-green lawn, with a barn and stables off to one side and a riding circle hemmed in by a split-rail fence.

"How're you doing there, Frankie?" Robert asked.

"Okay." Frankie sounded like he was in pain, but was being brave about it.

"What about you, Tom?"

Tom turned away from the sight of lush grass, sleek and polished horses, and a barn that promised a thousand mysteries. "I can head home now, if you like." They wouldn't want him, the trespasser from the trailer park, muddying up their lawn.

"Nonsense. I need your help to get Frankie up to the house. Then I'm sure Madge will have some cookies for our brave soldiers. Maybe a pitcher of lemonade." Robert smiled warmly.

After all he'd eaten that day, the last thing Tom wanted was more food. But maybe he could pocket some of the cookies for his mom. She was working late tonight and wouldn't be up to cooking dinner when she got home.

"And might be I could talk to you about a job," Robert continued.

"A job?"

"I need someone to tell me where all the holes are on these trails. Where folks might fall and break themselves. Think you could do that for me, seeing as you're familiar with the woods and all?"

Tom glanced up at Frankie, who was nodding vigorously, even with his face all twisted up in pain. "And you have to come visit me in the hospital, until I can walk again."

"I'm pretty sure your dad can set your ankle for you, Frankie." Robert's eyes were twinkling. "But you're going to need help getting around. So what do you say, Tom? Want to make yourself useful?"

Despite the bewilderment unfurling in his chest, Tom found himself matching Frankie's nod. Up and down, fast enough that all that green grass blurred. "Yes, sir," he said. "I'd like that very much."

CHAPTER 4

Present Day

Unfamiliar ceilings were a regular occurrence in Frank's life. Cracked plaster and water stains were not, recent travels aside. When had the lodge fallen into such disrepair? Pushing up to his elbows, Frank squinted at the ceiling, following the crack from over his head to the window. Cosmetic or structural? Until the roof fell in on him, he'd have no idea. Simon was an architect, though. Surely he would know.

Frank groped across the nightstand for his phone and checked the time. The display dimmed and darkened as he tried to make sense of the digits in bold white type: 11:47 a.m.? He never slept that late. He didn't often fly in from one continent, repack a suitcase, and drive to another—because right now, Northeastern Pennsylvania could be a continent apart—in a single day, either. Then there had been the storm, leaving his beautiful car in a ditch, and the hike to the resort.

And Tommy.

Frank selected the green phone icon and let his thumb hover over Simon's name. He could say he was calling for architectural advice and it would be true in some sense—if one expanded the definition of *architecture* to include persons in contact with the buildings. Simon would go for that. For all his pedantic nature, he had a whimsical heart. He was shacked up with a science fiction writer, after all.

A soft wavelet of depression rolled through Frank's thoughts. The happiness of his closest friend made him happy, of course. But it also highlighted a dearth of joy in his own life. Would it be too dramatic to say he hadn't truly been happy for thirty years?

Yes. Yes, it would, because he'd done amazing things and had met amazing people.

He'd led an amazing life—not only attaining his dream, but having been rewarded for it multiple times.

"Sell it a little harder, Frankie."

His voice was dry and his throat scratchy. He needed coffee, and not something punched out of a plastic cup into a mug that might not have seen a drop of dishwashing liquid in near on a decade. Nor threat of death from stained and cracked ceilings, and was the roof sagging as well?

Shaking his head, Frank slipped out of the musty sheets and reclaimed his clothes from the night before. The water pressure under the shower was abysmal and the towel smelled of bleach and mango, which was a truly baffling combination. He'd survived worse—in chasing authenticity, he'd just spent the better part of three weeks calling a moistened rag his bath. This was luxury.

By the time Frank had finished his ablutions, Ken's Auto Service had closed. Apparently Ken's work week did not extend past noon on a Saturday. The voice mail message did have a number for emergency towing, and Frank's conversation with the idiot at the towing service left him truly feeling as if he'd crossed an international border. Why had his sister insisted on doing all of this in person? Surely they could have met in Jersey City or even somewhere halfway between there and Cape May. Why trek out to the wilds in order to decide what to do with . . .

He glanced around room 206. The bedding was faded, the rugs threadbare, their designs indistinct. The floor beneath held the rustic charm of too many feet and not enough polish. All of the furniture squeaked. He dared not approach the curtains out of fear of disturbing the dust and mold spores no doubt nestling within their folds. And the paint. How did white paint fade? Well, he assumed the off-white/gray combination had started life as white. No one would pick this color on purpose, would they?

What were they going to do with this place?

Sighing, Frank tucked his phone into his pocket, slipped his feet into his loafers, and left the room. The air of neglect continued into the hallway. The place didn't quite feel postapocalyptic. More, it was empty. Soulless. There was no buzz of humanity waking to a weekend away. An unwilling smile pulled at his lips as the stairs creaked beneath his feet. That, at least, was familiar.

The odor of damp waned as Frank reached the first floor. He approached the desk and ran his hand along the surface, absently noting the lack of dust. Morning sunshine poked through the tessellated panes of the double doors, marking the rug in abstract patterns. Behind the desk, the old-fashioned cubbies held room keys. All were currently present except for 206.

His impromptu inspection tour led him back to the office behind the front desk. Tom wasn't there, but he'd left a note on the desk, folded on top of a large envelope, Frank's name scrawled in huge letters. Beneath the fold was a keyring. Tucking it into his pocket, Frank eyed the couch. The blanket was still draped over the arm. Was it odd that Tom had been sleeping here? That he slept here at all? Did they not have a night manager? Without guests, there probably wasn't much need.

Daylight spilled through the large windows overlooking the front porch, softening the red walls, but rendering the space otherwise . . . sad. Couldn't a writer come up with a better term? The entire lodge resided under a feeling of melancholy, as though it, too, missed its younger days. Families and couples and holidays and summer and all the hopes and dreams carried along by everyone who crossed the threshold.

Gravel crunched outside. Looking up from the sagging couch— which shouldn't be so fascinating—Frank brightened at the sight of his sister's car pulling into the circle. A moment later, she was up the front steps and banging through the front door.

"Yoo-hoo!"

Frank poked his head out of the office. "Anna."

"Frankie! You're here. I didn't think you'd be out until later today."

"Alas, I decided to drive through the storm last night."

"Come here."

She opened her arms, inviting him in, and Frank swept her into a close embrace. He saw his sister often enough not to feel longly-lost, but right now it felt as though she'd somehow rescued him from somewhere, something . . . some time.

"It's good to see you."

"You too. Was the storm terrible? Oh no, was that your car on Snow Hill Road?"

Frank let her go and took a step back. "Indeed it was. How did it—" He raised a hand and shook his head. "No, don't tell me. The past twelve hours have been depressing enough."

"Did you call a towing service?"

"Yes."

"Well, I can run you into town for a rental."

"Can we go now? I was contemplating using the Keurig thing again, and honestly, that might be more than I can handle and remain charitable."

"Sure." She smiled. "Where's Tommy?"

Frank pulled his phone from his pocket and checked the time. "Out. He said something about a job today, which I didn't really absorb as I was too stunned by the news he was managing Bossen Hill, or what's left of it."

"Probably a wedding."

"What?"

"The job. He's a photographer."

"I knew that." The admission of which brought instant heat to his cheeks. No big thing—he had simply followed the career of an old friend. Not too closely, of course, but, well. "He's, ah, quite good."

"Yes, he is."

"So why is he working here?"

"You haven't talked to him yet? I'm sure you two have a lot to catch up on. What's it been, a few years since you last saw him?"

"More like thirty."

Anna's eyes rounded. "I thought you got up here regularly? You've been in Pennsylvania three out of the last four times I've called you."

"Visiting Simon in Bethlehem."

Her expression softened. "Dear Simon. How is he? And Charlie, isn't it? And weren't they expecting a baby sometime soon?"

"Grandbaby. Sort of." Frank made a rolling gesture with one hand. "Charlie's daughter's progeny. What made you think I'd been up here?"

"I just thought you and Tommy—"

"Were childhood friends. Then I grew up."

Anna wrinkled her forehead.

Frank ushered her toward the doorway, reaching into his pocket for the keys Tom had left. "Town. Coffee. Rental car. Will any of these things be available after midday on a Saturday?"

"I think there's an Enterprise office in Stroudsburg, and there are a number of coffee shops. The whole ground floor of Wyckoff's is restaurants and cafés now. They seem to change hands all the time, but there's always something there. Main Street is actually quite lively. Stroudsburg hasn't become a ghost town like so many other places up here."

"I suppose the university keeps it alive."

"That, and tourism."

"Not according to the guest book."

By daylight, the grounds did not appear as unkempt as the night before. With the weather only just warming, the weeds hadn't had a chance to march across the drive yet. The hanging sign had been pulled down and currently rested against the hedge that poked over the top of the stone walls.

Evidence of the storm littered the road outside. The power pole had been pushed to the verge, and a work crew was restringing the cables. Thankfully, his car was gone. He couldn't have borne the sight of his precious in the daylight, and didn't want to see the damage until it was a distant memory, taken care of by a ludicrous insurance premium.

"Have you really not seen Tommy for thirty years? How is that possible?"

"I'd rather talk about what we're going to do with Bossen Hill."

"'We'? It's yours, Frank. I thought I explained that in my email." The one he'd finally been able to read at the airport just a couple of days ago. Well, skim. By the time he found a reliable charging station, his inbox had been rather full.

"How can it be mine? Didn't Dad want it?"

"He's perfectly content running the guesthouse in Cape May. Matty hasn't left the West Coast in years, and I prefer life in South Jersey. I'm only here today to see you. It's been ages. You should visit us more. You adore the Cape."

"I do." His parents owned and operated a charming Victorian B&B in the old part of town, walking distance to the beach and the shops. Annabelle lived close by with her husband, children, and single grandchild. All her family helped out at the inn during the season, and it was an established fact that she would take over when their parents retired or tottered off to the great guesthouse in the sky.

Frank had never resented her inheritance. He had no interest in running a bed and breakfast. He had no interest in running a dilapidated resort in the Poconos, either. What had his uncle been thinking?

"Did you read the will?" Annabelle asked.

"Hmm?"

She glanced over at him. "I'm sorry. I know you were away when it all happened. How was Puerto Rico?"

"I'd rather not talk about it."

"I heard things were bad down there."

"Like you wouldn't believe. I don't know what possessed me to accept the assignment."

"You were always after something new and shiny."

"Trust me, Anna, there is currently very little new and shiny in Puerto Rico." His visit had been too close on the heels of the latest disaster to catch sight of the projects he'd hoped to see, let alone for him to interview the people invested in rebuilding the country, literally from the ground up.

"Not a good trip, then."

"Let's talk about Robert. I honestly wish I could have been here for the funeral. Granted, I'd not seen him in a while. A few years." He'd been trying not to think about what it all meant—his uncle's passing, and the gift he'd left behind. Not the property, but the summers of thirty years ago. Everything Frank had run from because of a single kiss. "Is there a plot or something nearby? He's not buried behind the lodge is he?"

"No, his ashes are at Cape May."

Probably sitting in a dark corner next to the ashes of his wife. Frank's parents were not particularly sentimental people. "It was a heart attack?"

"Yeah. While he was asleep, apparently. He had a history of heart trouble."

Frank frowned at the passing scenery. "And was still running the lodge?"

"As it is."

"God, do I even want to examine the financials?"

"That's for you and Tommy to discuss."

"Tom."

"Hmm?"

"He always preferred to be called Tom."

"I didn't know that."

Frank glanced over at his sister. "Have you been in touch?"

"With Tommy—Tom?"

"Yes."

She paused at a light, and Frank looked back out of the window. They were in Stroudsburg now, and the town was both familiar and not. The outline hadn't changed, but the energy of the place had. It looked younger somehow. More vibrant than when he'd been a child.

"We email and call sometimes. He talks about you. That's why I thought you two were in touch."

"Talks about me how?"

Annabelle pulled into a lot behind a bank on Main Street. The building might be new—Frank couldn't tell. She stopped the car and turned to him, hands still resting on the wheel. "What happened between you two? You were so close. Weren't you going to go into business together or something? Travel the world? I honestly thought you'd be married with dogs or kids by now. Both!" Her smile seemed to recall distant memories with obvious fondness. "God, you were so cute. Tommy and Frankie. Frankie and Tommy. Never one without the other."

The seat belt suddenly felt too tight across Frank's chest. He fumbled with the catch and pushed open the car door. The air that blew in through the opening was that same combination of familiarity. Fresh after the storm, clean and bright with sunshine. Mountain air, country air. The scent of what had once been home.

Frank got out of the car.

Annabelle met his gaze over the roof.

"Coffee?" he asked, injecting a note of desperation into his tone.

"Coffee." Her smile was sad now, and all too reminiscent of the melancholy lingering in the dank hallways of Bossen Hill.

CHAPTER 5

The brides were beautiful and refused to allow a downed tree to ruin their wedding. Tom snapped several candid shots of both women helping friends and family relocate the chairs and arch to the smaller lawn on the not-so-picturesque side of the restaurant. They wouldn't have quite the same view, the one now bisected by a massive oak that had tipped sideways, pulling up roots and all from the sodden ground. And the side garden would be prettier in the late summer, when the vine crawling over the terrace thickened and greened. But they would have flowers and an arbor and a nice expanse of velvety green lawn—and from the unique perspective of his viewfinder, Tom could tell that these two would be happily joined in an alleyway behind the kitchen. They just wanted to be married.

Eh, he wasn't the only one who could tell that. All the guests could. It was clear that they were equally happy to be here, and why not? Two women marrying was still a new and wondrous thing.

As Tom snapped pictures of indulgent and philosophical smiles, he pictured the back lawn of Bossen Hill lodge bedecked with wedding finery. The vista wouldn't be quite as spectacular as the now-ruined view across the valley, but the surrounding forest and foreground of renovated patio—assuming the cottages were in good repair—would give any event a serene atmosphere, as though the party were enclosed in a bubble of green, tucked away from the world at large.

He'd entertained such thoughts before and had even discussed them with Robert when they put their heads together, trying to figure out a future for the lodge. The final and most important consideration had always been the same, however: where would they get the money? The resort carried no debt; Robert's investments had made sure of that. But the money he had saved for retirement hadn't been enough to improve Bossen Hill, merely maintain it. Sort of.

Stowing such thoughts away, Tom checked back through the candids he'd just taken and decided he had enough to fill an album the brides might not want. He made his way over to the larger back lawn to look at the tree. The light wasn't quite right for the compositions he wanted of roots and sky, but he was able to take some nice abstract texture shots along the trunk.

He was switching out his lens when a voice spoke up beside him.

"Pity about the view."

Tom turned around to find an older man. One of the fathers. No one was dressed too formally, including the brides, who were outfitted as woodland faeries in all shades of green and fawn.

"I don't think they'll let it ruin their day."

The older man glanced toward the side lawn, a bemused smile slipping across his mouth. "No, probably not." He looked back at Tom. "You get many requests like this?"

"To photograph faeries on their wedding day?"

The smile happened again. The man shrugged and reached up to worry the back of his neck as though embarrassed by the fact he might have to rephrase his question.

Tom decided to help him out. "They're obviously very happy."

"They are. My wife—" his eyebrows dipped down "—tried to talk Emily, she's the faery with wings, into wearing something more traditional. I think she thought that would somehow make sense of it, you know? Two women . . ." He gestured vaguely.

"You know what your daughter will remember ten years from now?"

"What's that?"

"It won't be the tree, or even her wings. Probably not the wings, anyway."

The older man chuckled and waited for Tom to continue.

"It will be that you're both here. That her family was with her on her wedding day.

Eyes shining with tears, Emily's father ducked his head. He nodded, his chin bobbing toward the ground. "Yes. You're right." Without making an attempt to wipe his eyes, he motioned toward the side garden. "I think we're getting ready to start."

Tom smiled. "After you."

Weddings often left him mildly depressed, but later, as he tucked his equipment away, Tom only felt unsettled. Not down, not up. Not somewhere in between, either. His emotions were in a state of flux. Uplifted by the energy of the wedding in a false sort-of high, perhaps elevated by the depth of his uncertainty regarding his own future, but tethered to a reality he'd rather not face, ever. if that face—light-brown eyes and strawberry-blond hair—had drifted through his thoughts all morning.

Tom heaved his bulky camera bags into the back seat of his Toyota and went to offer his final congratulations. He would likely never see the happy couple again. They'd view the proofs through his website and order prints and albums by clicking impersonal little buttons. That was the weirdest part of the job, the disconnect between the event and the product. But his website was definitely more attractive than the "office" he maintained in the basement of the lodge.

By the time he pulled up to the McDonald's drive through, it was after two and his stomach was eating itself. He couldn't remember when he'd eaten last, which was usually a good indication that he needed a meal. He ordered a couple of items from the dollar menu and waited with some trepidation to see if his debit card would be rejected. Letting out a sigh when it wasn't, Tom collected his order and poked French fries in the direction of his mouth as he followed Main Street through Stroudsburg. The road took him past the high school, where he deliberately blanked all memory, and on to the aged-care home where his mother resided. He usually visited on Sundays, but wasn't sure what he'd be doing tomorrow—except maybe hiding from Frank and everything he represented: dreams dashed and perhaps the most ill-calculated punch of his entire life.

Mountain Manor was the third assisted-living facility he'd moved his mother to since she'd lost the ability to care for herself—or, perhaps more accurately, to care about herself. Long-term alcohol abuse, among other things, had stripped her down to two basic functions: drink, sleep, and a constant desire for both.

The first facility had been a state-run home farther south. Between the distance and lack of personalized care, Tom had been quick to relocate her somewhere closer. Proximity cost more, though, as did the level of care she required. He shrank inwardly as he passed the Manor reception desk, against the fear he might be called to question over an unpaid bill. The woman at the desk smiled and waved, but Tom didn't relax and start breathing until he was two corridors away.

"Tom!" He glanced up to find Sandra Chen, his ex-girlfriend and favorite nurse, exiting his mother's room. "It's so great you're here! Wendy is with us today and feeling really good."

"I wasn't sure if I could make it tomorrow, so, um, here I am." Tom gave Sandra a peck on the cheek, and she kissed the air on the other side of his face.

She squeezed his arm. "I know Wendy doesn't always show her appreciation, but she knows you've been by. It's all we hear about for three days afterward. 'My Tommy came to see me' she says."

And not much more than that, probably. There were days when that was all he got out of her too, leaving him with the uncomfortable feeling he should look over his shoulder for his younger self. But Sandra was trying to be kind. She was adhering to the cheerful and optimistic attitude that had made Mountain Manor the best choice for his mother's accommodation and care. He'd be forever grateful Sandra had helped him place her here, even if his mother had been the straw that broke them.

"Do you think she'd like to go outside?" he asked.

"Oh, sure. She hasn't been out today. Why don't you take her for a walk on the lawn? Want any help getting her into the chair?"

He waved her off. "I'll be fine."

He knocked and pushed open the door without waiting for an invitation. Sandra wouldn't have left his mom "undone." Although there had been the odd occasion when he'd surprised his mother trying to undress herself. She'd gone through a period of being horrified by her clothes—sure they weren't hers. It'd been his fault. He'd bought her a handful of shirts in light, bright patterns, thinking she'd find them cheerful. Not so much.

Three years ago, she'd broken her neck and hadn't been the same since. Two weeks in a coma, then she'd had some sort of miracle recovery. That was his mom. She'd ruined all her internal organs with pills and booze. Had had so many pieces of her gut cut away, it was a wonder she managed to digest anything. She'd fallen through windows. Crashed cars. Taken enough sleeping tablets to kill an elephant. Had been caught drinking Windex for Christ's sake.

But something or someone watched over Wendy Benjamin. Cigarettes might burn to a scorching ember between her fingers, leaving her with scars, but they never dropped onto the bed. Even cancer hadn't managed to kill her. It was as though she'd spent so much time poisoning her body that the cells couldn't take a proper hold.

After she'd woken from her coma, a part of her had disappeared, though. She seemed diminished. More content to sit and do nothing, talk about nothing. On the days she didn't remember much about her life, she was little more than a faded copy of herself.

"Hey, Mom."

She glanced up with a smile that damn near broke his heart. "Tommy!"

"Saved this for you." He handed over the sundae he'd bought for her. It was close to being a strawberry milkshake, but she'd enjoy it either way.

"Sweet boy." She gave him a once-over and narrowed her eyes. "Have you been eating?"

"Now and then." He grinned.

Clucking her tongue, she held out a hand for a straw and set it into the top of the sundae with a delighted expression. While she sucked down the melting ice cream, Tom looked around her room. It was small, and beneath the slim veneer of "bedroom," it looked exactly as it was: a hospital room. The windows didn't open, but the view was nice. His mom's room faced the rear of the property, where a line of trees hid the highway.

If he allowed his vision to fall out of clear focus, he could almost imagine it was the same view they'd had out of the back of their trailer at Pocono Court. Except the lawn wasn't as scrubby, and the trees had hidden a creek instead of Interstate 80.

He turned back to his mom. "Want to head outside for a walk?"

"That'd be nice. Maybe we could go to the store while we're out. I need a few things. Milk, bread. What do you want for dinner?"

"I'm sure we've got something here," he answered. It was easier to go along with her plans and hope she forgot them than explain he wouldn't be here come dinnertime, or that if he did stay, they'd be eating in the dining room. "Walker or chair?"

She looked from her frame to the wheelchair. "Chair, I suppose. It's a long way to the store." She glanced up with a quizzical expression. "Isn't it?"

"We'll be fine," he assured her.

Helping his mother into her wheelchair always upset him a little. Though soft-cheeked, she weighed nothing and her frailty was frightening. If he dropped her, he might break her.

The late-May sunshine crowned his mother's silver hair as they made their way along one of the paths circling the home. For a while, she seemed to simply enjoy the outing. Then the questions started. She did better with questions than answers for some reason.

"How's work?"

"Good. Had a wedding today." He described the brides' costumes and all of the ceremony, hoping she'd have a good reaction. Her mood could swing abruptly from "isn't that lovely" to something less charitable in a nanosecond.

After listening, she nodded her head gently. "Maybe I should have tried that."

"What?"

"Being with a woman. Then you might have had two parents."

Tom leaned down to kiss her temple. "I had you." In an effort to direct their conversation away from potential pitfalls, he asked about the storm. "Did the power stay on here?"

"No idea. I was asleep. How did you do? Where are you living?"

"Still out at the lodge."

"What happened to your place?"

For a minute, Tom couldn't remember what he'd told her about his house. He tried to stay close to the truth so this sort of thing wouldn't happen, but the late night and long day were starting to catch up with him.

"Robert needed more help getting around after his second heart attack. I moved up there a while back."

"How is he doing?"

"Robert passed away two weeks ago." Sometimes her talkative days were more trying than her quiet ones.

His mom turned in her chair to look up at him. Reaching over her shoulder, she gripped his wrist. "Tommy, I'm so sorry. I know he was like a father to you."

With a lump blocking his throat, Tom could only nod.

She patted his hand before letting go. "I suppose that will mean Frankie might come back."

"What makes you say that?"

One shoulder shrugged. "Whatever happened to him, anyway?"

"He's a journalist." There was no point in reminding her that he'd told her this several hundred times. "He travels all over interviewing interesting people."

"That's right. He'd be good at that. He was always a talker, Frankie."

Tom smiled. "Yeah, he was."

"You were so sad after he left."

He answered with a shrug.

"You never found anyone else like him, did you? I liked Sandra, but she didn't understand you the way Frankie did. He knew you needed someone else to do the talking and the walking and just all the doing." She patted his hand again. "And that's okay. We're not all able to do it for ourselves. Look at me."

"You did okay, Mom. You always did okay."

She hadn't. His mother was too much like him. Not strong enough to cling to what was necessary and too closed off to admit it hurt when they were left behind. He didn't often contemplate the pattern of his life in her reflection, but when he did, Tom couldn't say he was surprised by the fact he owned nothing and lived nowhere. That he relied more on the kindness of strangers than his own talent for anything. But if he'd done one thing right, it had always been this. He hadn't always loved his mother, and she often frustrated him to the point of madness. But he hadn't left her behind. No. He'd always been there and he always would be.

CHAPTER 6

The lodge looked lonely and silent at the end of the drive, late-afternoon sunshine deepening the shadows behind loose shutters and warped guttering. It seemed to be waiting for something, and after staring up at his childhood for several long minutes, Frank decided it was waiting for sound. The drive was quiet, the windows dark. No chatter of hikers relaxing in rocking chairs on the wide front porch, a jug of lemonade between them. The rocking chairs were gone. No children whistled and yelled from the back patio. No splashing in the pool, which traditionally opened on Memorial Day weekend—though he and Tommy had always used it for up to a month before, usually under the cover of darkness. All he could hear now was the chitter of chipmunks and birds.

The front door was still locked. Frank searched his pocket for the keys and sorted through the compact ring until he found the right one. Or not. He tried another. No, no, and finally, yes.

Had the door creaked this morning? Last night?

It complained now, whining softly between halting groans. Perhaps if he pushed it open faster . . . Ugh, that smell. Mold and neglect assaulted his nostrils. Frank leaned back through the door to pick up his shopping bags, drawing in some fresh air as he did so. He abandoned any attempt to hold his breath halfway to the kitchen. He couldn't watch the ceiling for new and threatening cracks if he passed out.

"Hello?"

His call was another lonely echo, the lack of response depressing. Tom's absence felt distant yet distinct—as if the man who'd greeted him last night had been a ghost. Frank called out a few more times as he passed the guests' sitting room and dining room. The house answered with gentle creaks.

The kitchen was surprisingly clean and did not smell moldy. It didn't smell like cookies, either, and the jar his aunt had filled with treats baked just for family was missing from the end of the breakfast bar. Fading sunlight streamed through the west-facing windows, dusting across countertops, floors, and updated appliances. He couldn't swear the walls had been painted a pale yellow thirty years ago, but despite the small changes, the kitchen had much the same feel it always had—of a quietly beating heart. The center of what had once been a home.

Had he visited this room the last time he'd been up here? Frank couldn't remember. His three or four visits to the Poconos since finishing college had been brief and edged with trepidation.

The smallest of three fridges was humming, indicating it had power. Frank pulled open the door and found a block of cheese that had not been wrapped properly—the exposed part a dark, cracked yellow—a bag of slimy liquid advertising itself as celery, a jar of peanut butter, and nine cans of Mello Yello.

The kitchen reminded him of his aunt and uncle—his aunt in particular. She'd done a lot of the baking for the resort guests. The fridge screamed Tom. As a boy, he'd seemed to exist on peanut butter sandwiches and Mello Yello—though his battered old bottles had often been filled with homemade lemonade.

Frank unpacked his groceries, glad he'd had the foresight to buy a few things, and balled up the plastic bags. A muffled thump sounded behind him, from somewhere near the front of the lodge. After shoving the plastic bags into a drawer, Frank began to make his way back to the main hall. Just as he exited the kitchen, a shadow crossed the foyer. "Is that you, Tom?"

The shadow paused, obviously looking back at him, then darted toward the front door, which judging by the triangle of light across the floor, was open.

"Tom?" Frank started down the hall at a cautious pace.

By the time Frank reached the foyer, his heart pounded from more than the exertion of such a short run. The door remained open, but moving slightly, as though someone had just pushed past. A gentle whining groan rose from the hinges before it settled back into stillness.

A combination of mild terror and ridiculousness bubbled up behind Frank's breastbone as he sidled up to the door, took a deep breath, and poked his head out onto the porch. No one lurked to either side. There was no second car parked in the circle. No figure sprinting across the lawn or down the driveway.

He hadn't imagined the shadow in the hallway. Frank examined the door, not sure what he was looking for. Had he left it open?

"Something wrong with the door?"

Heart stopping mid-beat, Frank jerked backward, his body suddenly a loose collection of limbs wrapped in skin he no longer felt. He fell against the door, the back of his head catching the center-mounted knob on the way down, and landed in an untidy sprawl, half in and half out of the entryway.

Tom stood over him, all wide eyes and dark hair, mouth forming an O. He extended a hand and Frank batted it away.

"Where the fuck did you come from? And where were you?"

Tom tucked his hand into his jeans. "Are those two separate questions?"

Once his brain reestablished contact with his limbs, Frank pushed up to a sitting position and used the door handle to haul himself upright. "Did you come in and run out again?"

"What?"

"I saw someone in the hall. They ran when I called out."

"Just now?" Worry etched a few lines into Tom's forehead as he moved forward and peered through the doorway, poking his head out into the light. "Did you see which way they ran?"

"I didn't. It was like they disappeared."

"Probably a local kid on a dare. I've had to chase a few out of the barn before." Tom ducked back. They were separated by mere inches, closer than they'd been in thirty years, and the fading sunshine showed Tom in a way Frank hadn't seen in a long, long time. His hair was still longish and untamed. Not curly, more wavy and with a mind of its own. The dark brown was liberally streaked with gray, however; only the thickness and messiness of his cut hid the fact that he was older than he appeared. Frank resisted the urge to reach out and feel the dark strands, see if they had coarsened with age.

Tom looked up, his small, delicate features so achingly familiar. He'd always had a young face. Sweet and sharp, all dark eyes and light-brown skin. When they were boys, they'd often speculated on the identity of Tom's father—after learning he hadn't actually died in Vietnam. Hadn't been a soldier at all. For a while, Tom had decided he was a long-lost Inca. Or maybe an Aztec. Someone whose ancestors had been fierce warriors. The warrior part had been important. Frank remembered that.

Tom leaned away from him, widening the space between them by another handful of inches. By the width of the doorway. He said nothing, and seemed to be giving Frank equal scrutiny. Then one corner of Tom's mouth ticked upward. A half smile. "You really haven't changed. I think you're taller, but you're still . . ."

Frank felt one of his eyebrows arching upward. "Still?"

"You."

"Except older, grayer, and not quite as fat."

Tom's gaze swept back downward, taking in the trim of Frank's waist, his legs, and upward, across his chest and shoulders. Frank's skin tingled beneath his clothing. He swallowed.

"You were never fat," Tom murmured.

A scoff crawled out of Frank's throat before he could stop it. "Whatever." He pushed away from the doorway, his head throbbing slightly. He touched the spot where he'd connected with the knob and winced as his fingers grazed a warm egg.

Tom's brow wrinkled again, the concern gentler. "Did you hit your head? You went down pretty hard."

"Because you happened out of nowhere. Were you here the whole time? I was calling for you."

"No, I just got back. I used the side entrance and parked in the garage. We should move your car there. The sap from the trees over the front drive is hell on paint."

Though tempted to point out that his car was a rental, Frank only nodded. "Do you have any Tylenol in this mausoleum?"

Tom's smile returned, wider this time. "In the office. Where's Anna?"

"She left to drive back to the shore."

"Oh? Did she . . ." His expression shuttered a little and he turned away, leading Frank behind the desk again and into the office. He began pulling open desk drawers. "So, ah, I guess you guys talked about what you're going to do with this place?"

Frank frowned at Tom's back. His slim shoulders had drawn up and in beneath his dark-blue polo shirt. When he turned back around, bottle of painkillers in his hand, he was obviously trying for detached curiosity . . . and failing.

Frank took the pills. "We haven't." He glanced at the small white bottle with the red plastic cap. "And apparently it's all going to be up to me."

Tom said nothing.

"You don't look surprised."

Tom gave a shrug that was a touch too studied to be careless.

Frank shook his head. "I can't believe Robert left the place to me. All of it. And none of the rest of the family wants anything to do with it."

Tom's attitude of nonresponse was starting to grate.

"Have you had—" Frank checked his watch "—dinner? It's after six, we can call it dinner."

"I got something earlier."

Finally, an answer. "Well, I'm hungry. I bought a few things. Will you eat with me?"

Tom stared at him, making no response, until Frank feared he'd entered some sort of catatonic state. Then he blinked.

"What?" Frank asked.

Shaking his head slightly, Tom gestured toward the doorway.

In the kitchen Frank assembled a pair of hoagies, the act of layering in the meat and cheese, shredding the lettuce, stuffing tomato slices in between, and drizzling the wedge of fixings with salad oil taking him back to childhood, to sandwiches bought and shared with the boy—the man standing next to him. He sliced the long rolls in half across the middle, arranged them on the plates Tom had produced from somewhere, and gestured toward the items remaining on the counter. "Want a pickle? Some chips? Do you have anything other than Mello Yello to drink?"

"You bought all of this today?"

"Yes. There are supermarkets in Stroudsburg. Imagine that."

Tom looked up from one of the sandwiches. "They're like the hoagies we used to get from Vinnie's."

"That was the idea. I was feeling rather nostalgic this afternoon." And at a bit of a loose end, really. After Annabelle had dropped him at the rental agency, he'd found himself driving up and down random streets with his thoughts caught halfway between past and present. Then he'd seen a supermarket and become obsessed with the idea of making sandwiches. He had to eat, after all. Then he'd gotten lost on his way back to the lodge, but Tom didn't need to know all of that.

"There's still a bunch of wine down in the cellar," Tom said.

"Show me?"

The cellar held more memories, most packed away in boxes stacked floor to ceiling on wooden shelving. Another thing Frank's aching head didn't want to deal with. They passed a door with a small light mounted over the lintel.

"Do you still use your darkroom?" Frank asked.

Tom glanced over his shoulder. "Every now and then I get the urge to play around."

"I suppose it's all digital now."

"Mostly, yeah."

"Oh, how did your wedding go today?"

"How did you know I was shooting a wedding?"

"Annabelle told me."

"Huh." Tom's shoulders hitched up and down. "It was fine." His eyebrows crooked together.

"What?"

Again, he shook his head and continued on to the coolest part of the cellar, where row upon row of dusty bottles gleamed softly.

"Well now." Frank rubbed his hands.

After selecting two contestants, Frank followed Tom back up to the main floor and the almost familiar smell of mold.

"What is rotting?" he asked.

"I'm not sure. I can look into it tomorrow. One of the water tanks might be leaking."

"That doesn't sound good."

Tom answered with his eyebrows, raising them in an arc of *no kidding*.

Once back in the kitchen, Frank couldn't decide where to eat. The stools along the far counter, where kids and cookies usually took up residence, were still there, all tucked into a neat row. He glanced out of the windows instead, at the mess of woody vines covering the trellis separating the kitchen yard from the guest patio. "Want to eat outside? Are there tables on the patio?"

"One." Tom chewed on his lip. "I sit out there sometimes. It's . . . It's not pretty out there, Frankie."

The old nickname sent an odd thrill through Frank's middle. "Because of the storm?"

Tom shook his head. "No. Not this storm, anyway."

Frank located a corkscrew and a pair of glasses and nudged open the kitchen door. "Bring the sandwiches? And I suppose you'd better start filling me in on everything I've missed. All Anna kept saying was that it was all so sad. Economic downturn, hurricanes, no snow, and Robert being something of a sentimental old fool."

Tom grunted.

Waving a hand in apology, Frank walked around the trellis. "I fail to see how such a popular resort could have—"

"Not pretty" had been an understatement.

The patio extended about twenty feet from the back of the lodge, forming a terrace overlooking the pool area, and the setting sun was not kind to the bare expanse of flagstone. Long shadows showed where the pavement was uneven and stones were missing. The single table Tom had referred to sat alone and forlorn, rusting through flaking gray paint. The chairs rocked unsteadily.

Worse—and it got so much worse—were the bare planters. No bright profusion of green dotted with flower heads of all shapes and sizes lined the edges of the patio, screening diners from the pool. But the most devastating part of all was the line of cottages behind the empty pool. Two of them resembled malformed playhouses, the roofs sagging—one collapsed completely. Another two appeared relatively unscathed, but dark and unloved. The two closest were . . . missing?

Frank turned back to Tom. "There were two more cottages over there, right? Where those patches of grass are? Or did we always have a lawn tennis arrangement on that side of the pool?"

"Tennis used to be over by the stables."

An involuntary gasp parted his lips. "Do we still have stables? Tell me there are no horses." He couldn't stand the idea of horses living among all this neglect.

"Not for fifteen years. Robert got rid of the horses after Madge died."

Frank remembered his aunt's funeral. He'd come up for that, but hadn't stayed overnight. After driving straight to the church, he'd come back here for a short while afterward. He didn't remember seeing Tom, though. "Were you at her funeral?"

Tom shook his head. "Something came up."

"What happened here, Tommy?" Frank gestured with his wine bottle and glasses. "How did . . . How could you even have accommodated guests two months ago? Aren't there laws and licenses and . . . This place is a mess. This is more than storm damage." Anger pulsed through him, formless and aimless. "It's a tragedy. Our entire childhood smashed in and left to rot. How could you let this happen?"

"Me? Where were you? Where were you, Anna, and Matty? Robert had already had one heart attack before Madge died, and then it was like he was dead but still moving. He asked for help and no one came. It was me and the staff, and when the bookings dried up and he couldn't afford to keep anyone on, it was just me."

Tom paused for a ragged breath, his narrow chest heaving. Why was he so thin?

"We'd only just finished cleaning up the damage from the ice storm in '07 when the housing market collapsed, and no one took a vacation for like three years. Then we got hit with Irene. Then Sandy. Meanwhile, there was no snow and the big corps. out of Atlantic City and Vegas were building casinos with indoor water parks."

The plates clattered against the tabletop as Tom put them down.

"He got left behind, Frankie. By his family and by this town. He wasn't young enough to keep up. I tried. I advertised. I researched. I came up with ways to keep the place running, and when he was with me, when he was making sense, we'd make plans. Then he'd disappear into his own head again, and it was up to me to make sure the house didn't fall down around us."

Staggered by the brief and awful recounting of the resort's decline, Frank backed toward one of the rickety chairs and sat, not caring whether the thing gave way beneath him or not. He set the bottle of wine down and fished the corkscrew from his pocket. Once he had the wine open, he was tempted to drink it straight from the bottle. To guzzle it while liquid spilled across his chin and down his neck. He poured a glass and drained that instead. Poured another. Drank half of it. Placed the glass gently back onto the table.

"I would have come. If anyone had told me, I would have come."

Tom scoffed. "You've visited exactly three times over the past thirty years, Frank."

Not Frankie anymore. Frank.

Frank felt his mouth begin to form the words: *I was afraid.* He clamped his lips shut and shook his head, which did not improve the circular motion of his thoughts. "I'm sorry."

Another disgusted sound. "Bit late for that, don't you think?"

"It's not as if I killed my own uncle."

"No, you just left him to rot while you—"

"That's not fair! I was little more than a child when I left here, and last I checked, I was not the only Tern. I have two siblings and two quite capable parents. If anyone is to blame..." Well. "I suppose we all are, in part. But no one told me! Damn it."

Annabelle had mentioned the neglect, but she hadn't laid it out in quite this manner—a brokenhearted and sick old man watching his home crumble around him, only the boy Frank had befriended almost forty years before between him and utter dejection. How had this happened? Frank could feel his mouth moving again, trying to form more words. He shook them off, away. Drained his second glass of wine and reached for the bottle.

Why did it feel so much like his heart was breaking? And why was the sensation so achingly familiar? His hand trembled as he refilled his glass. As he lifted it, tipping the edge toward his lips.

"Frank?"

His hand jerked, spilling the wine over his wrist and down beneath the cuff of his shirt. He watched dumbly as the dark-red liquid spattered across his thighs, staining his trousers.

When Frank looked up, Tom's face seemed to waver as though viewed through rippled glass. Frank blinked. Warmth trickled down his cheeks. God, was this grief or shame?

Frank put down his glass and stood. Cleared his throat. "I think perhaps I'll head up. It's . . . been a long day."

Then he turned and fled. His departure was slow and dignified, marked by the sound of his even stride against uneven flagstones. But still he fled, just as he had thirty years before.

CHAPTER 7

July 4, 1980

The flimsy trailer door rattled beneath Frankie's knock, before opening to reveal Tommy, his face set to "grimace." With his big eyes and floppy hair, he more resembled a puppy with a chew toy than someone with a bone to pick. It was cute that he tried, though. Not that Frankie would ever say that to his face. Tommy had a thing about being small. And cute.

"Said I'd meet you at the creek," he growled.

"I got here early." Frankie scrutinized Tommy's jeans. "Don't you have any shorts? I want to go swimming."

Tommy seemed happy enough dipping his feet in the water, but he never wanted to swim. Said it was on account of not having any trunks.

Grumbling, Tommy said, "Wait there."

Ignoring the command, Frankie followed him inside the trailer. With all the shades drawn, it was like entering a smokehouse. Close and hot, the air thick with the scent of cigarettes and burned food. Despite working at a diner, Tommy's mom was a terrible cook. She waited tables well enough, or so his uncle said. He always left a big tip, anyway.

Tommy was shoving a sandwich into his old green backpack. He'd given up wearing camouflage about a year and a half ago, but he treated his army surplus rucksack as though it had mystical properties. It did hold a lot.

Frankie patted his own pack, which was stuffed full of snacks packed by his aunt. "I've got plenty of food. Come on! And don't forget your trunks."

"I told you, I don't have any."

Holding back a sigh, Frankie said, "We'll get you some at the lodge."

"Yours won't fit me."

"We have a bunch in the laundry. People leave them behind every year."

Tommy's shoulders hunched in and up in a sort-of shrug. He hated it when Frankie visited him at home—even more so when he came inside. Frankie didn't see how it was such a big deal, except for the fact Tommy's entire house would fit inside one of the garages at the lodge, with space left over, and the whole not having anything to wear but the same jeans he'd worn to school all year.

Personally, Frankie would hate having only one pair of jeans. He liked putting together different outfits at the start of every day. Matching colors and fabrics to the weather and season. His sister said he was vain, but Frankie saw his attitude as practical. Who wanted to sweat it out in the wrong material? And a bulky guy like him had to dress in a certain style if he wanted to look good.

Tommy didn't seem to hate being poor—he never complained about it. He just didn't like being reminded of it. He was a contradiction in every other way too. Small and dark where his mother had fair skin and blue eyes. Quiet, but full of words—he apparently wrote poetry in his head, or maybe that was something he said when Frankie complained about the quiet thing. Still but always looking as if he could just . . . go. Frankie fully expected to turn around one day and find Tommy had disappeared. Or had sprinted a mile distant without making a sound. Or shot off to the moon or something. He was packed energy personified.

And still fussing with his backpack.

Frankie wrenched it from his hands, fastened the last strap, and gestured for Tommy to turn. He slipped the pack over his friend's shoulders. "C'mon. You can adjust it later."

They had a lot to do today.

First up was checking the nesting boxes they'd nailed to trees at different points along the hiking trails. Since the summer they'd met, Frankie's uncle paid them both to maintain those trails. Pick up dead wood, or tell him where to go with the chainsaw, fill in holes, repaint the blazes, make sure the trespassing signs were posted all along the creek, and this year, they'd done the nesting boxes. They looked like little houses, and Frankie and Tommy had painted them all different colors before nailing them up at intervals along the trails. Today was the day they'd set aside to see if they'd enticed any birds to make a nest.

They still hid from the hikers now and again, making a game out of scurrying up a tree without getting caught. But since Tommy's mom had told him his father hadn't actually been a soldier, they hadn't played war. Instead they stalked. Played trapper or warrior. Frankie wasn't as into it as Tommy was, but he played along because Tommy was his best friend.

After jumping across one of the stepping stone bridges they'd laid across the creek, Frank led the way to the first group of nesting boxes, three miniature Tudor mansions nailed around a clearing. They were disappointingly empty.

"Maybe it's because too many hikers come through here," Tommy said while poking his finger inside one of the lower boxes. He had to lift up onto his toes to do so.

"Yeah, probably. Let's check on the ones we put down by the drop-off." Where the creek bank rose to an appreciable height. The trail looped close by, but not along the bank.

An hour later, they'd found no birds. Frankie was thoroughly depressed, but Tommy had his thoughtful face on. "I wonder if it's the paint. Or the varnish. Maybe we should have left the houses plain."

"But they look much nicer painted."

Tommy shrugged.

"C'mon, let's head back to the lodge," Frankie said. "My aunt was baking this morning."

"Don't you have enough food in your pack? I can hear it rattling around in there."

"No such thing as too much food when it comes to cookies."

Tommy allowed a smile for that.

Sure enough, Aunt Madge was baking, but pies not cookies. And they weren't allowed to touch any of them. *And* she had the same comment about Frankie's full backpack. "Why don't you go swimming?"

"We were going to head along the west trail and look for fossils," Tommy said. He'd argued for that before returning to the house too, but Frank wanted to swim before they took another hike.

"Aunt Madge, where's the lost-and-found box?"

"In the laundry where it always is. Why?"

"Tommy doesn't have any trunks."

Tommy was studying the floor with great interest, but even though he'd already caught a good amount of sun this year, Frankie could see the blush spreading across his cheeks.

His aunt studied Tommy for a moment, her softly wrinkled brow creasing just a little more deeply, and then she started wiping her hands on her apron. "Wait here a minute and do not touch my pies. Eldon?" One of the other cooks glanced over his shoulder. "Make sure they don't touch the pies?"

"Yes, ma'am," Eldon answered with a grin.

As soon as she left the room, Tommy sidled over to the counter lined with cooling pies. He held out a finger, waved it through the air, and slowly lowered it toward one of the dishes.

"Don't make me break that finger off," Eldon warned.

Chuckling, Tommy continued his pantomime, dancing around the counter and pretending to touch every pie. He even leaned in to lick the air over one, murmuring something about it being his favorite. Eldon cautioned him about health code violations.

"What if this one fell on the floor? We could say a cat did it."

"Tommy, you are just a bundle of mischief and all sorts of bad influence on Frankie here."

Tommy rolled his eyes.

"Aunt Madge always makes an extra pie or two for family," Frankie said. "Which one is it?"

"Never you mind."

His aunt returned with a bundle of familiar fabric in her hands: a pair of trunks his mom had bought for Frankie last summer. The waistband had been too tight, though, and he'd only worn them once, afraid he'd drown when the lower half of his body went numb from lack of blood.

"Here," she said, handing them to Tommy. "Try these on."

Tommy eyed the trunks with suspicion, rubbing the dark-green fabric between his fingers and studying the seams. "Are these new?"

"Just about." Auntie Madge was inspecting the pies, and Frankie got the feeling that she knew the less attention she paid to Tommy right now, the more likely he was to accept the gift. Tommy would steal a pie—for fun. But despite the fact he often didn't seem to get enough to eat, he never stole something he actually needed. He had a weird set of boundaries.

"Can we swim now?" Frankie asked.

"I guess."

Frankie led the way to the bathhouse, where they exchanged clothes and backpacks for trunks and towels. By the time he stepped out across the patio, Tommy looked like a man condemned. He had his arms wrapped around his middle and stood with his legs pressed close together. The trunks fit, and exposed more of Tommy's dusky skin than Frank had seen before. His legs were longer than Frank had supposed. Arms too. His chest and hips were narrow, but he was pretty well defined for a kid. Probably because he was so skinny. His lean muscles didn't have to compete with the comfortable layer of flesh Frank carried on his own person.

The pool was close to packed. The resort was busy all summer, but especially around the holidays. After finding a free spot in the deep end, Frankie ran and jumped, tucking his knees up high and wrapping his arms around them. One of the best things about being on the bigger side was the ability to displace great quantities of water when he cannonballed. He hit the water hard, the slap of it stinging the back of his thighs and hips, before he plunged deep, the burn of chlorine already racing through his sinuses. Bubbles tickled his face and ears, and his hair waved around his face. Frankie blasted back up out of the water, buoyed by a bounce off the floor, and reached to push his bangs out of his eyes. The surface of the pool sloshed around him, and from the expressions of the swimmers close by, he might have managed to displace a child or two along with half the pool.

The reaction he cared about most, however, was the one he got from Tommy, who was bent in half and holding his stomach. Laughing.

Frank splashed over to the side of the pool and rested his arms across the warm flagstones around the edge. "C'mon in!"

Tommy crept forward slowly, glancing every which way, and sat at the edge of the pool, allowing his legs to dangle in the water. His eyebrows shot up in surprise. "It's cold."

"Yep."

"Weren't you worried about your heart stopping? Just jumping in like that?"

"Nope. They do it in Sweden all the time."

"Cannonballs?"

"No, jumping in cold water. They warm up in a sauna and then jump in ice pools or something."

"Wow."

"Right? We should try it when we get there."

Tommy patted his pocket, or where his pocket would be if he were still wearing his jeans. "Don't have my notebook with me."

"That's okay, we'll remember. I'm pretty sure Scandinavia was already on our list anyway."

"Probably. We're up to thirty-three pages."

Frankie grinned. "By the time we're done with school, we'll have three notebooks. No, ten!"

"We'll never live long enough to visit all those places. We should do the important ones first."

"Maybe we need a new book already. One where we list what order we'll do everything."

Tommy shook his head. "We'll be following stories. And whatever order we decide, life will take us somewhere else. That's what happens."

"You could be right." Frankie splashed some water up over Tommy's legs. "So are you coming in or what?"

"I'll just watch you swim."

"What? No! You're always telling me you won't swim because you don't have any shorts. Now you've got some. It's time to pay up."

Tommy's eyebrows pulled down, and his eyes darkened from chocolate to moonless night. "I don't owe you anything."

"Yeah, you do. Trunks mean swimming."

Tommy lifted a leg out of the water, and Frankie caught him around the ankle. "Where are you going?"

"Nowhere."

"What is it? Can't you swim or something?"

Fear pinched Tommy's brow, briefly, and then he put on his angry face. "So what if I can't?"

Not all that surprising, but the fact he'd wound Frankie along for nearly two years without saying so stung about as bad as cold water across the back of his thighs. Not sure how to respond without sounding like a spoiled brat, Frankie let go of Tommy's ankle. Tommy stopped trying to stand up, but he was doing his closed-off thing. Being still.

All friendships experienced bumps. They'd smooth this one before the day was done—Frankie just had to figure out how. He glanced at the shallow end of the pool, currently crowded with splashing toddlers and little kids. If he didn't know how to swim, he sure wouldn't want a lesson right then. Not with everyone looking on.

Then he got an idea. "Wait here."

Tommy nodded at his hands.

Frankie wrestled his way out of the pool and shook, sending water flying in all directions. Tommy raised his hands to shield himself. A hint of a smile played around the sides of his mouth. By the time Frankie returned with his idea, Tommy had relaxed from stillness into something less stiff.

He narrowed his eyes at the bright-pink inflatable ring Frankie was carrying. "No."

"Yes." Frankie produced rope. "I'm taking you for a ride. Slide on into this ring and I'll tow you from one end of the pool to the other." He could see the interest in Tommy's eyes warring with everything else that made him stubborn as a mule, and held up the ring again. "Chariot." He slapped the rope against his chest. "Horse. Pretend you're Ben-Hur."

"Really? Ben-Hur in the pool?"

Frankie shrugged. He had nothing better.

Tommy smiled. "Okay. Pass it over. But you don't have to take me for a ride."

He did, though. Once Tommy got into the water, he showed no fear—only delight. He even started saying pink was his new favorite color as he splashed in circles, making the plastic ring spin. When

Frankie tied on the rope, Tommy didn't discourage him. Instead, he whooped as Frankie swam the length of the pool, dragging his best friend behind him.

Later, Frankie snoozed by the side of the pool, getting too much sun. He'd have a million freckles by next week, but he didn't care. Having Tom spread out beside him, humming as he drew patterns in the water spreading across the patio pretty much canceled out most worries.

Dinner for family was at a long table set up between the kitchen garden and the guest patio. Frankie sat next to Tommy and looked around his friend at the empty seat next along, the one they were saving for Tommy's mom.

Tommy elbowed him back into place, his face set into a determined "she'll be here" expression.

Sure enough, a minute later, Robert waved from the top of the table and called out, "Wendy! Glad you could make it."

Wendy returned a shy wave and bent down to hug her son from behind. "Hey, little man." She kissed the top of Tommy's head and though Tommy didn't go all gooey, he did smile the sort of smile that made other people feel bright, just from being nearby.

Wendy pulled out the chair next to Tommy and sat down before putting a small newspaper-wrapped bundle on Tommy's plate. "Got this for you." They were weird like that, the Benjamins. Giving gifts on days that weren't birthdays. Frankie always thought it'd be fun to get something unexpected, though.

Tommy tore at the paper and grinned as he held up a Rubik's Cube. It wasn't packaged up like a new one, but looked pretty clean. "Awesome! Thanks, Mom."

"I bet you can solve it by the time we finish dinner," Wendy said, giving him a proud smile.

Tommy immediately set to trying and only put the thing aside for pie.

After dinner, the adults sat around talking, Wendy moving up the table to sit with Robert and Madge. Frankie and Tommy joined the other kids, sitting by the pool, waiting for dark. Frankie had nearly fallen asleep listening to the *creak* and *click* of the Rubik's Cube when a warm hand touched his shoulder.

He glanced up to find his uncle looming over them. "You boys want to help out with the fireworks tonight?" Robert always did fireworks for the Fourth of July. He got a permit and had a sheriff out there supervising and everything.

Frankie didn't think he'd ever stood up so fast. Tom was quick to follow, his new toy making a bulky shape in the pocket of his shorts. Robert held a finger to his lips. "Shh." He pointed to the dark side of the garage. "Meet you over there in—"

"Robert Tern, where are you taking those boys?"

Robert straightened and turned to face Aunt Madge. "Just going to—"

"They're too young."

It seemed to Frankie that his uncle's shoulders dropped about as much as his and Tommy's did. His aunt shook her head. Then Frankie's mom was there, and Wendy, and they were all agreeing the boys were too young to help out. Even his dad was no use. He kept nodding and making "hmm" sounds, despite Frankie's plea that Matty had been doing it since he was twelve, which, yeah, was still a year away.

Robert squeezed Frankie's and Tommy's shoulders. "Next year, boys. And we'll make it special. Your dad and I'll take you shopping beforehand so you can help us choose the best display." Then he leaned in to whisper in Frankie's ear. "Best view is from the roof, but don't tell your mom I said so."

Technically, the roof was off-limits, but Frankie knew how to get up there. He helped Tommy climb through the window at the far end of the lodge, and together they crabbed over the slate tiles until they got to the flatter space over the second-floor balcony.

It was a little while until the fireworks started, but for once Frankie didn't feel compelled to fill the quiet. He watched the guests assembling on the lawn and then peered into the dim distance to see if Uncle Robert and his dad were getting ready to set off the show. Beside him, Tommy worked his Cube, and it was comfortable, just being there and saying nothing.

Then Tommy spoke, his voice little more than a murmur over the buzz from below. "Benjamin and Franklin."

"Huh?"

Tommy turned to him, his face mostly shadow, except for his eyes, which always seemed bright and lively. "Our names, sort of. My last name, your first name. That's what we should call ourselves when we start traveling. You can write about our adventures, and I'll draw pictures or maybe take pictures." Tommy had recently developed an interest in photography, one encouraged by Uncle Robert. "And whatever we put together can have those names. Sounds better than Frank and Tom."

"Frankie and Tommy."

"*Tom*."

Frankie snorted. Then he tried out Tommy's idea. "Benjamin and Franklin."

A soft chime sounded somewhere inside him, announcing the rightness of the name, of the link between them, and the idea they'd always be together. Living, growing, exploring. He nodded. Said it again. "Benjamin and Franklin. I like it."

Frankie slung his arm around Tommy's shoulders and drew him into a sideways hug. For once, Tommy didn't get all stiff or spiky. Instead he relaxed against Frankie's side and even let his head drop onto Frankie's shoulder. Man, it was nice. That warmth at his side. It was almost as though they shared a body for a minute, or a space where two people could be one.

For longer than a minute.

For the whole fireworks show.

And it didn't matter that Tommy fell asleep before the end—though how anyone could sleep through all that banging and whistling was a mystery of the ages—because he should be that comfortable.

This was Tommy's place. Right at his side.

CHAPTER 8

Present Day

The rain started up again in the night, the sound of it beating against the porch roof moving through Tom's dreams in different ways. Memory and fear twisted, the steady patter of rain becoming the ticking of a clock. Shadows darted out from corners, lingering only long enough for him to step close. The scent of rot wrapped everything, and a sense of urgency underscored all of it. By the time he cracked his eyes open to a gray and miserable dawn, Tom felt as though he'd spent the night running in circles.

Also, his mouth tasted like a skunk had laid a turd inside it. Drinking the rest of the bottle of wine had been a mistake. Frank's departure from the patio had left him feeling oddly bereft, though.

Well, maybe not *oddly* ...

Fuck.

Scrubbing his eyes, Tom rolled away from the window and contemplated pushing his face into the darker side of the sofa. Overhead, the floor creaked. He listened to Frank cross his room, the bathroom door squeak open and close, and what sounded like a fire hose draining into the toilet. Ignoring the press of his own bladder, Tom stared up at the ceiling and wondered, in a vague way, why they were both awake so early on a rainy Sunday. Surely if any day deserved a late start, it was today.

Maybe Frank would go back to bed.

The shower started.

Tom pushed the blanket back and got up.

By the time Frank arrived in the lobby, he was alarmingly put together in another pair of pants, another button-down shirt, both casual, but obviously expensive. The kind of clothes Tom would mistake for business wear until he arrived in a boardroom and realized he was actually dressed for Saturday lunch in the Hamptons or some such crap. Frank didn't have a suitcase with him, but Tom expected him to announce he was leaving.

Instead, he regarded Tom with surprise. "You're up."

And washed, and dressed, and still looking like the discount version of Frank. "Yeah. I can make breakfast if you want."

Frank's eyebrows rose. He gave a short nod. "I could eat."

Given he'd skipped dinner last night, he must be starving. Frank had trimmed down since boyhood, but he wasn't a small man. He wasn't stocky, but neither was he willowy. He was tall and strong and solid. Tom liked the look of him. Then again, he always had, even when Frankie had had round cheeks and shocking hair. Frankie . . . Frank had always been Frank.

And Frank had always liked food.

Tom gestured toward the guest dining room. "Do you—"

"The kitchen is fine. If that's all right."

"It's fine."

Frank took a step toward him, and Tom forgot to step back. His heart beat wildly in his throat as he struggled with the concept of moving his feet independently to his thoughts, and found he was still standing there a moment later. Hopefully it had only been a moment. A couple of breaths? Frank wouldn't be in front of him, eyebrows raised, if he'd been standing still for too long, would he?

Then again, Frank had always had incredible patience when it came to his moods—the understandable and the just plain weird.

"I'm sorry about last night. Yesterday afternoon," Tom said.

Frank answered with a grunt.

"I feel like . . ." Tom licked his lips. "When I found out you were coming up, I thought about leaving, you know? Just leaving all the paperwork on the desk and locking up. I figured that would be the best thing all 'round. But . . ." *I wanted to see you.* "I also kind of figured I might be able to help, and that maybe it would be altogether too sad to let you do this alone."

Frank's eyebrows had been slowly settling. Now his entire expression changed. Sadness happened first, pinching his brow. Glancing away, he rubbed at his forehead and took a step back, thankfully, widening the space between them. When he looked up again, his expression had saddened further. His smile, what might have been a smile, had turned into a grimace.

"I appreciate all you did for Robert. Don't for a minute think I don't. And I know—" he squeezed his eyes shut. Opened them "—I should have come back more often. It's too late to tell him I'm sorry, but I am. I'm sorry, Tom. And I'm sorry if I made you feel as though you weren't welcome here. This place has always been your home."

Shaking his head, Tom swallowed over lumps of emotion until his feet finally decided to move. Unsteadily. He backed up a step, then another. Shook his head again and tried to say something, but his voice had ceased cooperating, which was for the best. What could he say that Frank could possibly understand?

"Let's have breakfast and then maybe we can sit down and go through the paperwork," Frank said. "Figure out what we're going to do with this place."

We're. The intimation that they might work together sent a sharp pain through Tom's chest . . . and he nearly said it. Nearly blurted out the other apology, the one he'd been holding in for so long, it might not meant anything anymore.

Swallowing again, he led the way into the kitchen.

After filling Frank with pancakes and coffee not made by the "nasty little machine," they returned to the office where Tom indicated the thick envelope on the desk. "That's for you. Guest logs are over here." He pointed toward file drawers. "Older logbooks are in the basement. We did start transferring everything to computer, but only the last ten years or so, which isn't a lot? I just didn't have time to go back further, and Robert wasn't interested in using a booking system. The website we have is pretty out-of-date, but honestly, there hasn't been much point in updating it."

"Unless you're trying to sell the authentic experience of yesteryear, not updated since then."

"Which reminds me, I need to head up to the attic and find the source of that smell. It's only gotten bad over the past couple of days, so hopefully it's nothing major."

"Okay. You do that and I'll start going through all of this."

Tom paused by the doorway until Frank looked back at him. "There's no debt. The biggest reason the place is in such bad shape is that Robert didn't want to spend money on it. He paid his taxes and his bills and . . . I dunno. I don't think he minded so much that we were all but closed. He would have retired when Madge died if the place wasn't doing as well as it was, even then."

Frank nodded. "Good to know. About the debt."

Still, Tom lingered, but he couldn't ask the question he most wanted the answer to—probably because he already knew what Frank would do. What any sane person would do: sell up and walk away.

Another minute passed, Frank waiting patiently for him to say his piece. Tom ended the weird quiet by offering a nod and departing. He visited the laundry to grab a flashlight, a couple of towels, a bucket, and a roll of silicone tape, hoping the problem would be as basic as his supplies.

It wasn't. It never would be. The water heaters were all fine. The water was coming in through the roof, and it obviously wasn't a new hole because the insulation beneath it was dark with mold. He suspected it had been a small leak and a small problem until the recent storm.

Tom put down his bucket of useless supplies, pushed up his sleeves, and prepared to roll the insulation back to see what sort of mess lay underneath it.

"Let it not be bad," he whispered. "Please let it not be bad."

CHAPTER 9

Frank suspected Tom's hand in the organization of the logbooks and receipts. His uncle had been a fun-loving and easygoing man. Robert had been the one who greeted guests, socialized with them, and made sure everyone was having a good time. Madge had done the books and behind-the-scenes stuff. Tom—according to the fifteen years of logs stored in the cabinets upstairs—had done just about everything else, and more of it, since Madge had died. He'd been added to the books as a manager seven years ago, but his paystubs probably extended back to their childhood when Robert Tern had paid both of them for the upkeep of the hiking trails and other small gardening chores. Money Tom had needed and Frank hadn't.

Until 2010, the decline was only visible in the log books. They'd been busy, but not as busy. Fewer family groups for summer vacation. Some couples and honeymooners. A rash of retreat groups and a conference. Then a serious dry spell.

Frank leaned back in the chair and let his gaze rest on the window overlooking the front porch. Was such decline endemic to the area, or to the family-resort industry in general? Was it really all about indoor water parks now?

He flipped open the laptop on the desk and looked up a map of the area, enlarging it to show the route he'd taken back from Stroudsburg the previous afternoon. The route he should have taken. There was another resort down on 447, wasn't there? Right after the turn off. And another one on . . . Creek Road? He found the first and switched to the satellite view. Even with crappy resolution, it was clear the tennis courts were cracked and overgrown and that half the buildings were in a state of collapse. There was no website. The one on Creek Road looked about the same.

But there was a new casino just six miles farther along the highway and ski slopes dotted all around. Shawnee was still in business—of course, they had the river and a championship golf course. Two of the other golf courses he remembered were gone, though. One completely unrecognizable, the other turned into a nature preserve.

A story started to tickle his brain, one that matched the missing pieces inside of him. He'd come home only to find home wasn't here anymore. It wasn't just that his parents had moved away some twenty years ago, or even that he no longer knew which road went where. It was as though the place he'd left had rotted behind him.

And Tom was still here.

Frank did a quick search for Bossen Hill Family Resort. A link popped right up and he clicked it, holding his breath as the website loaded—and letting it out again as a photograph of the lodge unfolded across the screen. It was a gorgeous photo. The gray stone and sloping slate roof of the lodge were framed by trees with leaves of every color. Purple, red, and orange leaves also patterned the lawns, but more toward the edges, as though obligingly keeping off the grass. They formed another frame, Frank realized, and so did the angle of the driveway, which curved beneath before opening into the circle.

Looking at the picture, Frank could feel the warmth of the sun over the chill of a fall afternoon. He could smell the leaf mulch and cinnamon and the weird, bitter scent of mums. He could imagine the fire burning in the hearth of the guest lounge and the plates of cookies spread around on the tables. The big bowl of apples that always occupied a table in the foyer, inviting guests to help themselves as they headed out or returned.

His skin prickled as he thought about the planning that must have been involved in getting just this picture—from raking the leaves back from the lawn, lining up the pots of chrysanthemums along the porch and steps, to making sure the sun was at the right angle to light up the entire front of the building. Waiting for that exact minute when the trees still held most of their leaves.

Only Tom could have done this.

Frank wondered if anyone else understood the subtle brilliance of the composition. He also wondered why anyone landing on this page, with the photo and a discreet invitation to explore, wouldn't immediately book a room.

Of course, the reality would be a shock.

Beneath the front page, the website was fairly basic and included a message indicating that the resort was currently closed for renovation.

Renovation?

Frank leaned away from the desk again and scanned the office. He had to admit that on a gray and rainy morning, the red walls did lend a cozy atmosphere to the space. And it wasn't a garish red, more a warm rust. If sunlight were to poke through, the room would glow. He instantly recognized Tom's photos hanging in the misaligned frames, and then found the picture he was looking for. A concept sketch. The lodge at the bottom, much as it stood today, but the lawn at the back was very different. No cottages. The stable and barn were there, the pencil lines rendering them in better repair than the wreckage at the bottom of the slope. The path leading from the patio to the barn had been widened and the lawn leveled. A proposed trellis between the lawn and the pool and gardens behind.

There were small circled numbers dotted around the plan, but no accompanying notes. Were these the plans Tom had mentioned yesterday afternoon? Where had they expected to get the money from? There might not be any debt—thank the Lord—but there wasn't any money for repairs let alone renovation.

Frank glanced toward the ceiling. Where was Tom?

Crunching gravel grabbed his attention. Frank leaned back over the desk to peer out of the window and saw a silver Town Car pulling to stop at the top of the circle. Someone needing directions, no doubt, but even as he pushed to his feet, Frank found himself wondering if they could possibly offer accommodation.

No, of course not. Why would he think that?

The faint scent of mold still lingered in the lobby, effectively shutting off the part of his brain that had gone back fifteen years to when the resort had been alive. Grunting softly, Frank opened the door and waited for the figure emerging from the car to duck through the mist and up the steps. It was a woman, dressed in a sharp business suit, and she seemed as out of place on the porch of the resort as Frank felt standing in the doorway.

"Is this Bossen Hill?" she asked.

"Were you looking for Bossen Hill?"

She produced a business card. "Patricia Nolan. I'm with the Tinden Group."

Frank took the card and studied it. He learned nothing more than what he already knew. The back side was blank. "Did you have an appointment?"

Surely she didn't have an actual booking.

"No. I'm sorry. I was in the area visiting another property and heard Bossen Hill was for sale."

"What?"

"This is Bossen Hill Family Resort? There's nothing out front, but I followed the signs up from the road."

"This is Bossen Hill, yes. But what makes you think the place is up for sale?"

One perfectly manicured eyebrow arched. "You're obviously not in business, or renovating. Mr. Tern, is it?"

Frank took a step back. "Listen—"

"Who's this?"

Tom stood in the foyer, looking as though he'd tunneled through insulation to get there. Also, he reeked of mold. Trying not to let his nose wrinkle, Frank held out the card. "Tinden Group? Ms. Nolan here seems to think the resort is for sale."

Tom didn't take the card. Instead, he pushed past Frank and stood directly in front of Patricia Nolan. "You're trespassing. You have one minute to return to your car and leave the property before I call the police."

She rocked back, but made no move to leave the porch. "As I understand it, you are not the owner on record, Mr. Benjamin, therefore I am not trespassing on your property. Regardless, I am simply following a lead."

"Well, you can follow it right back to the highway."

Ms. Nolan's eyebrows peaked in the middle of her forehead. She turned to Frank. "Might I—"

"Now isn't a good time." Frank pocketed the card and gestured toward the Town Car. "Perhaps you might consider calling ahead and making an appointment."

She looked from one to the other for a moment. Then, shaking her head, she backed off the porch and down the stairs. Once inside the car she didn't leave, however. She made a phone call, glancing through the window as she spoke.

"Who do you think she's talking to?" Frank asked.

"Might be Tinden Jr. He was out here last week, two months ago, a year ago, three years ago, and..." Tom's forehead wrinkled. "Six years ago? Right after Hurricane Sandy."

"That might explain how she knew who I was. She specifically asked if this was Bossen Hill, though, and she definitely knew who you were."

"Yeah, that was freaky." Tom was eyeing the Town Car with consternation. "Before Sandy we had a couple of visits from Tinden Sr. too."

"And Robert didn't want to sell?"

"Nope."

"But why? You said he seemed happy to be retired." Or as retired as he could manage while sitting on top of a dilapidated resort. "And according to the website, the resort is closed."

"About that—"

"Let me guess. You didn't want to give me all the bad news in one night."

Tom shifted uncomfortably. "Something like that."

"So why not sell?"

"Two reasons. One, he would never sell to Tinden. No way, no how. They're not in the resort business, they're in the housing business. They have a development across the creek, where the trailer park used to be. If they got planning permission for a bridge, the neighborhoods combined would extend between two major roads."

But... "They'd have to cut away half the forest for that." Frank glanced over his shoulder. The forest was mostly hidden by the bulk of the lodge, but he could picture it from the other side. The wide sweep of lawn surrounded by a deep, dark mystery of trees. He couldn't imagine the forest just being gone. It would be like peeling all the pictures out of his childhood album.

"That, and Robert didn't like the idea of his lodge being bulldozed, either."

Frank focused on the dilapidated building again and sighed. "Much better to wait for the place to collapse around him."

Snorting softly, Tom continued, "Second reason is . . ." He bit his lower lip.

"What?"

"He was waiting for you to come back."

Nolan finally ended her call and left, the Town Car pulling quietly down the drive. Frank frowned in Tom's direction. "What?"

"He always meant for you to have this place, and if he'd sold it, then you wouldn't have it."

"What did he think I was going to do with a rotten resort in the Poconos!"

"Didn't you read the letter?"

"What letter?" The conversation was starting to make Frank dizzy. Also, the wind was blowing cold droplets of mist in through the front door. Frank stepped inside the house, beckoning Tom to follow. He shut the wet morning out. "What letter?"

"In the envelope on the desk."

"Oh. I started with the records."

"And?"

"Not that I doubted your account of things, but they pretty much backed up everything you said last night. What I'm really wondering right now, though, is why he didn't sell."

"It was his *home*, Frank. And he wanted it to be yours too."

"Why me?"

Tom let out a sharp and exasperated sigh. "Read the letter."

"You know what it says, don't you?"

"He said you'd get tired of traveling, and when you did, you'd come home."

"To this." Frank extended his arms to indicate the gloomy foyer. "To a big old house that smells like mold, and a yard full of collapsed sheds."

"A big old house with a hole in the roof."

"What?" He was getting tired of that word.

"The smell. The roof's been leaking. It's not a disaster, but I'm pretty sure an estimate for the repair is going to include replacing most of the slate up there. And a good portion of the insulation. And the ceiling over room 209."

"Can't you do it? Fix the hole?"

"No, because it's probably not just one hole, Frank. The roof is O-L-D old. I could push my fingers through one of the beams."

"Shit."

"Honestly, you might be better off selling, but not to Tinden. I know a house is just a house, but Tinden estates are soulless, Frank. If you really want to be done with this place, maybe we could find a local developer." Tom looked depressed by the thought, but it was something Frank supposed he should consider.

He paced the length of the foyer, to the bottom of the staircase and back to the desk. As he passed the table where the apple bowl used to sit, he noted a ring in the polish. Not a bad one, simply a mark of something no longer in residence. For an instant, he felt like the apple bowl, missing and perhaps forgotten. Then he decided he was more like the ring—the faint reminder of what used to have been.

He glanced over at Tom. "What would you do?"

"Me?"

"If this place was yours, would you sell it?"

Tom's answer was instant. "No."

"But isn't this why you're still here? You wanted to travel the world, Tommy. Why didn't you ever leave?"

Sadness crept over his face, the expression becoming eerily familiar, even after just two days. "I went away to college."

"And came back, obviously."

Tom shrugged, and Frank remembered that was what he did when he didn't want to elaborate, answer, or finish a conversation. Yet Frank pressed. "Why are you still here?"

"Because this is where my life is. Not all of us . . ." Tom let out another sigh, this one longer and softer. "Not all of us are meant for something glamorous, Frank."

"What is it you're not telling me?"

Tom's eyes darkened. "We're not kids anymore. We're not even friends. You don't have the right to pry into my personal business."

That hurt. Frank took a step back, caught his hip on the apple table, and put his hand down to steady himself. His palm fit perfectly inside the faint ring. He drew in a slow breath, letting the act of filling his lungs ease his thoughts—nudge them back from old pain. When he looked up, Tom was watching him, his own face a mask of tragedy.

"You're right," Frank said. "I forgot. We're not friends." Friends punched friends all the time. But they invited a return strike, or offered an apology. Tom had done neither. He'd simply broken Frank's nose and never spoken to him again. "What I don't understand is why? Why didn't we ever talk about what happened?"

"Because it was a mistake."

"You made that abundantly clear."

"No, the punch. I . . ." Tom closed his eyes and swayed in place as though a tide of emotion passed through him. When he opened his eyes, they shone brightly. "It was my mistake. It was my fault. All of it."

The same tide caught Frank, making the world swim around him. "You couldn't have said this thirty years ago?"

Tom shook his head. "No."

"Why?"

"I can't tell you that."

CHAPTER 10

Tom wished he could attribute the burn behind his eyes to the odor rolling off his clothes and hands, but the hurt on Frank's face would shift the heaviest heart. And it was Tom's fault. He'd put that expression there and had never stepped up to wipe it away. He didn't even know if it was possible.

And he didn't know if he could explain his actions anymore. Time and life had smoothed some edges and sharpened others. He couldn't rely on his memory of certain events, because he viewed history through the lens of a broken heart. Worse, he'd done the breaking himself.

How did you go about fixing that?

The stillness of the gray, Sunday morning finally intruded, pressing between them until Frank cleared his throat. "Well, then. I need more coffee."

"I need a shower."

"Yes, you do. Afterward, can I take you out to lunch? We don't have to talk about that night." Frank held out his hands, fingers spread. "But I do want to talk. If you don't want to share what you've been up to over the past thirty years, we can talk about Robert. And the drawing on the wall in there." He pointed toward the office. "And talk over what we might do with this place."

"'We'?"

"You're still here." While Frank seemed intent on pointing that out, this time his tone was different. Softer, gentler. "And you're probably the only reason the lodge is still standing, current roofing issues aside. So, yes. We. I want your opinion on what to do with this mess. And I want to know how any decision I make will affect you."

Tom shook his head. "You don't have to do that."

"Go take a shower, Tom. You stink."

Tom turned to do just that before remembering that someone who only stayed at the lodge occasionally wouldn't have a full wardrobe stashed away somewhere. Say, in one of the two guesthouses with roofs and locking doors. He hesitated, half-turned, aware Frank had likely noticed the pause. Now would be the perfect time to tell him. To admit to Frank he was sort of living at the lodge and had been for months now. That he'd slept on the couch in the office so often he knew where the lumps were. That he'd been using Robert's bathroom for two weeks and had been "testing" each shower upstairs before then.

That his future hung on whatever choice Frank might make.

He'd tried to tell him last night, in the kitchen, and had been glad afterward that he'd kept his secret to himself. Studying Frank now, seeing the restful patience in his expression, Tom opened his mouth . . . and lied. "I'll just, ah, get my car keys. I've got a clean change of clothes in the trunk."

"Sure. Take your time. I can always do a little work."

"Work?"

"I have a story to piece together, some notes to make for another idea I have, and I need a list of reasons why I don't want to go to Texas."

"What's in Texas?"

"A career direction I don't really want."

Tom left him to it. Whatever kept Frank busy kept him from prying too far into Tom's business. Present and past. He retrieved his clothes from the guesthouse and ducked into Robert's bathroom. After showering, he inspected his reflection and decided he should shave. Lunch with Frank probably meant somewhere other than McDonald's.

When he arrived back in the office, Frank gave his appearance a quick but obvious examination and a smile.

"I'm glad you approve," Tom said.

It'd taken him a while to find a shirt that wasn't frayed, discolored, or emblazoned with the faded logo of some local business. He had his Bossen Hill polos, but preferred to keep those for work—such as it was. Finally, he'd found a short-sleeve shirt (with a collar and buttons!) at the back of the wardrobe. Paired with his cleanest jeans, it was the best he could do.

"Red suits you," Frank said.

Grunting, Tom checked his pockets for phone and wallet. "You want to drive or should I?"

"Why don't you? I ended up in Scotrun yesterday trying to find Cherry Lane Road."

"Cherry Lane Road? Do you mean Shine Hill Road?"

"That would have made sense, wouldn't it?"

Chuckling, Tom checked the front door, locked it, and led the way through the laundry to the side garage. He rolled open the door and turned back to find Frank staring at his neat and tidy Toyota with disappointment.

"Where's Bojangles?"

Tom laughed. "Jeez, how do you remember that?"

"Bojangles was the stuff of legends."

"And you thought I'd still be driving it?" His 1970 Mercury Cougar had been well used in 1985, and had died three years into his commute to Marywood University in Scranton.

"I can't even remember why we named your car that," Frank mused.

"You were obsessed with that tap dancer, Bill . . . Roberts?"

Frank's confusion cleared. "Robinson. Bill 'Bojangles' Robinson. Man could *move*."

The grin pulling at Tom's cheeks felt unfamiliar but welcome. Same with the warm little dot spreading out from the center of his chest. "So I guess I should introduce you to Delany." He gestured toward his car.

"Delany?"

"He's a writer."

Frank's eyebrows shot up. "You mean Samuel Delany."

Tom shrugged. "His books are pretty weird, but I like 'em."

Frank considered the car for a few seconds before nodding. "Nice to meet you, Delany."

"Do you still read romance?" Tom asked. Frank used to filch historical romance novels from his mother's nightstand. He'd first tried to say he wanted to laugh over the lurid covers, but Tom had caught him reading them too many times to believe that.

Frank smiled. "Yes, I do. Sometimes. They write gay romance now, you know. With happy endings."

"Seriously?"

"Mmm."

"How 'bout that."

The drive started out quietly, Frank either reminiscing about teenage jaunts in Bojangles or love in historical times. He spoke up just as the hot dog stand on 447 came into view. "Oh my God, Spanky's is still open?"

Frank seemed so surprised, Tom had to laugh. "Yep."

"It looks exactly the same. How are they still in business?"

Tom glanced at the shack nestled inside a stand of tall pine trees. The exterior had faded—red paint now a shade of salmon and the chrome facing not quite polished, but still silver against the shade. A few tables dotted the clearing, one with a mostly useless umbrella advertising the iconic name. Being Sunday, a line had formed in front of the window and cars bunched in the small lot.

"Want to stop?" Tom asked.

Frank shook his head. "Not sure I have enough Mylanta in my suitcase to deal with a Spankin'."

"I'd forgotten we called it that. How did we not permanently damage our digestive tracts back then?"

"Who says we didn't? We used to ride our bikes down here at least once a week. More often in the summer."

"It was probably the ride back that saved us. All up hill. Now the thought makes me weep."

Frank side-eyed him. "You look pretty fit."

Ignoring the blush working its way down from his hairline, Tom focused on the road ahead. "I was always a skinny bugger. You seem pretty fit yourself."

"I actually enjoyed being skinny as you call it for about a year in college, until I fainted—not prettily or delicately—outside my neighbor's door. Turns out it was a great way to meet an attractive man, even if it did make me look the fool. Anyway, Simon, that was his name, picked me up, fed me, and took me to the gym. Aside from becoming a good friend, he also taught me a lot about nutrition and exercise."

Sunshine had begun to burn away the mist, turning the morning into one of those rare pockets of beauty—wide swathes of light cutting through the densely packed trees, each carrying a dizzying array of dust motes as they slashed across the road. The same light played over Frank's face in an on/off pattern, highlighting his smiles and deepening his frowns. Bringing his story to life in a series of half-second glimpses of expression.

It was nice to hear him just talk the way he used to. With no hint of self-consciousness and plenty of self-depreciation.

"Though, if you want a true specimen of male fitness, Simon's partner Brian would make a lovely example. Bastard."

Tom felt his eyebrows rise up. If Frank and Simon had ever been a thing, it was obviously long past. Was Frank with anyone now? A glance at Frank's left hand showed no evidence of a ring—though that wasn't always proof of singledom.

"In love with his own reflection?" Tom asked.

Frank offered a faint smile. "Oh, yes. And everyone else who admired it."

"How long have they been together?"

"Oh, they're not anymore."

"Huh."

Frank waved a hand. "Anyway, I soon discovered that I'm just not built to be willowy. Under Simon's tutelage, I figured out what I could eat and what I couldn't. How to exercise properly. I will say that turning forty changed a lot of that, though. I still watch what I eat and I still workout when I can, but I've found I care less." There was something wistful in his tone. "And the closer I get to fifty, the more I let go."

"So by sixty you'll be doing your best John Candy impression?"

"No. But I'm not going to lie in my coffin wishing I'd eaten more cured meats. Or regretting a serious lack of cannoli. Life is too short to forgo cannoli, Tom."

"You do know that by the time you land in a coffin, you won't be thinking."

"Says you."

Tom signaled to turn onto North Fifth and guided the car around the gentle curve and over the bridge crossing Brodhead Creek. "Do you always drift into philosophy while traveling?"

"Hardly, though it does feel as if we're taking a journey. Maybe we should have stopped for a Spankin'." Frank leaned toward his window to glance over the side of the bridge at the rail tracks and creek, both far below. "It's a pity they never delivered on the promise of commuter trains out this far."

Tom shrugged. "It's still supposed to happen. Soon as they figure out who's going to pay for it. By then, of course, the developers will be carving up farmland all the way to Harrisburg and we'll just be another stop on the commuter lifestyle."

Frank leaned back into his seat. "It really hasn't changed, you know. This area. Town looks busier and there are houses where there used to be woods. Too many cars on the roads, everyone going everywhere. But Spanky's is still here. And that little coffee caravan is still on the far side of the mall."

"It's like everything else, Frank. Bits fall off, get replaced by other bits, but underneath it endures."

"That's . . ."

"As deep into philosophy as I get."

Scoffing, Frank turned his attention back to the passenger-side window.

CHAPTER 11

It was nice, this driving and chatting. This quiet passing of time without pause for recrimination and regret. If he were honest with himself, Frank would admit that this was what he hoped for. That he and Tom could sidestep the past and connect on a new level: as men approaching their fifties rather than men who'd somehow hurt one another and then refused to discuss it.

He had decided almost twenty years ago that he might never understand what he had done wrong, aside from kissing his best friend. He had also decided to let it go.

Obviously he hadn't.

Frank did draw some comfort from the notion that Tom had yet to let go either. But they were moving past it now, and he was enjoying this. Being a passenger on a journey through the streets of memory. He'd hardly taken note of his surroundings yesterday. He'd been too tired in the morning and too lost in the afternoon. Now, he let the roller skating rink and tiny public elementary school press the small buttons recessed into the corners of his mind, each accessing a memory he could term as *fond*. By the time Tom found them a parking spot along Sarah Street, two blocks from Main Street, a happy bubble of contentment encompassed most of Frank's thoughts.

"So, where should we eat?" he asked over the roof of the car while Tom checked his pockets again for phone and wallet. Seemed to be a habit of his. "Annabelle took me to a fairly bland café yesterday for coffee. Her boycott of Starbucks is still in effect."

"I can't even remember why she stopped drinking it."

"Neither can I. Do you need money for the meter?"

"Not on a Sunday."

Tom cocked his head and Frank listened for the sound that had caught his attention. A voice amplified by a megaphone. And was that music? Frank glanced around at the cars lining the road and the handfuls of pedestrians all making their way toward the County Courthouse.

"I think there's a festival going," Tom said. "Want to see what's on offer?"

"As long as it's not a hot dog. Spanky's was closer to home and emergency resources."

"They'll have paramedics stationed somewhere along Main Street." Tom grinned.

Frank fell into step beside him, leaning in closer as they avoided a couple walking the other way. Their shoulders touched, and Tom didn't flinch away. When Frank remained close, their arms and hands almost brushing, Tom didn't widen the gap and . . . it was strange. Personal space had always been his thing. Many of Frank's most cherished memories of their shared childhood were the moments when Tom had relented, allowing Frank's affection. By the time they'd been teenagers, it had happened more often.

Had he been wrong to assume Tom might have reverted to his old self in Frank's absence? Or would it be wrong to assume he was responsible for Tom's relaxed attitude now?

"I can smell the fire, you know," Tom said.

"Oh? What are they burning?"

Chuckling, Tom reached up and pushed the side of Frank's head. "Inside your head, Frankie. You're thinking up a forest fire in there."

Frank quelled the urge to grab Tom's hand on the way down, lace their fingers together. He did smile.

They turned a corner and the street fair was upon them, banners slung across 7th Street announcing the celebration as the Pocono Raceway Festival. There were people everywhere. Adults and children. So many children. Frank tried not to flinch as he sidestepped small humans. He didn't have a particular aversion to kids; he was more worried by the idea he might trip over one. Or step on one of the very little ones. Also, children made a lot of noise—nonmusical noise.

A band was set up on the pavement in front of the courthouse. Pavilions lined the streets to either side, forming a rough circle around the war memorial. Striped and plain awnings continued down 7th toward Main Street. Frank couldn't see farther than that. Once past the band, or far enough past they could hear themselves think, Tom paused in front of a climbing wall covered with dangling children and pointed out a few likely food vendors. "Jock N' Jill's do a good burger, so does Siamsa. Marita's do burgers too. And good burritos."

"I'm sensing you like burgers."

Tom shrugged. "Hard to fuck up a burger."

"We'll have to agree to disagree on that one."

"What are your thoughts on wings?"

"As in the hot variety?" Probably as much a risk as a hot dog, but surely more fun on the eating end of things, particularly if they were good wings.

"Sarah Street Grill has the best wings. Let's get some of those."

Though Frank preferred linen-tablecloth dining, there was something fun about being in the midst of a festival. Nearly every face bore a smile and the band was lively. He wasn't vain enough to imagine the festivities were for him, but seeing his old hometown bedecked and celebratory was a much nicer welcome than the storm he'd driven through on Friday night. The tension was practically rolling off his shoulders as he wove his way after Tom, heading toward the spicy unknown.

The stand Tom had picked had quite a line, which spoke to the quality of the wings. While they waited, Frank noted the activities placed around the center park, his thoughts already straying toward how best to describe each if he were to write up the event. Except for the rock wall, everything was raceway themed—shirts, hats, posters, pinwheels—with a bright orange car as the center attraction. Dressed in a jumpsuit bearing as many sponsorship logos as his vehicle, the driver posed for pictures and gave out autographs, never losing his smile.

Set a small way back from the actual car was a cutaway that kids could climb all over. Another photographic opportunity, and parents were taking full advantage, calling out instructions for this one and that to hold the wheel and stop climbing over their sister. And to smile. Always smile.

Frank turned to comment and saw Tom had his cell phone out and was taking pictures of everything. He wore a faint version of the same smile decorating every face.

When he lowered his phone, he blushed. "Sorry. The kids look so damn cute. And the light is great."

"It is a lovely morning," Frank acknowledged. "And I don't see why you should apologize, unless you're planning to abduct one of the children."

The person in line ahead of them turned around, frowning.

Tom's face reddened further. "What would I do with a kid?" A wistful expression caught him. "It's nice to see them having fun. I do the school photos for Stroud Township and getting those kids to smile is pretty much half the day. Here, they don't even have to try."

"What do you do with photos like the ones you just took?"

Tom shrugged. "Not much. If there's a good one of the car and driver, or the festival in general, I might sell it to the paper or one of the local magazines."

"The photo on the website, for the lodge. That's one of yours, isn't it?"

"Oh, man, that one is old, from maybe nine years ago? Took me forever to set it up and the clouds kept threatening all day. I had maybe five minutes of late-afternoon sunshine to work with. I think I got about a hundred shots off in those five minutes and only a handful I could use. That one was the best. Everything just about perfect."

"It's a beautiful photograph." Frank shut his mouth before he asked why Tom hadn't put it on his other website, the one Frank visited from time to time. The website Frank had ordered several prints from. He'd have bought the one of the lodge without a moment's hesitation. Or . . . he thought he would have. Today he would.

Tom shrugged again and stepped forward. It was their turn to place an order.

"Tom!" A hand shot out from beneath the pavilion to grip Tom's, and one of those complicated shakes ensued. Up, down, fist bump, back of the hands together, and done. "How's your mom?"

"Doing good. I visited her yesterday. How's Evelyn?"

"Still in the kitchen. She's got a stand somewhere down 7th. All cakes and stuff."

"We'll make a point of visiting, then. Gerry, this is Frank. Robert's nephew."

The hand extended again, and Frank could now see the man beneath the pavilion. Everything about him was round—his bald head, his cheeks, his shoulders, and most notably, the belly pushing his striped apron out. "Frank . . ." he said thoughtfully. His narrow-eyed gaze had a slightly possessive edge to it, as though he was sizing up competition for . . . Tom? Frank glanced at Tom only to find him obliviously perusing the menu. "You're Marty's little brother!" Gerry finally said. His eyes had un-narrowed.

"That would be me," Frank said, accepting a handshake. No fist bump for him.

"Is he still out west somewhere?"

"Seattle."

"Where the real mountains are." Gerry laughed. "So what can I get for you guys?"

They walked away with an order of everything, compliments of the tent. Gerry had spent the entire five minutes it had taken him to load up two cardboard trays reminiscing with Tom. The possessive vibe had surfaced now and again, but Frank hadn't been able to tell if it had been because Gerry had been around when Frank had not, or if Gerry was secretly pining after a completely unaware Tom. What he did find out was that Gerry's parents used to own the diner where Tom's mom had worked, which meant Gerry probably knew about as much as he did about Tom's mother.

Wendy Benjamin had baffled him as a kid. She'd never acted the way Frank had supposed a mom should, smoking, drinking, and drifting into increasingly harder habits the older Tom had gotten. Tom seemed to have spent most of his childhood on his own recognizance.

"I neglected to ask after your mother," Frank said now. "We got started on the wrong foot. I don't know why things have been so awkward, except . . ."

"I'm the one who made it awkward. I always did. And not answering any of your letters . . ." Tom gave one of his characteristic shrugs.

"It was a long time ago."

"Yeah, it was."

"Can we start again? Should we? Can you be friends with someone you haven't seen for thirty years?"

Tom smiled and the earnestness of it—the way he ducked his chin a little—took Frank back through the decades to the time when he'd played for that smile. When he'd clowned and joked and would have done just about anything to make Tom happy.

Holding up his platter of wings, Tom said, "You might regret it in the morning."

Frank laughed. "If only."

The wings were good, both the sweet and the spicy. The hot ones weren't so intense he forgot he was eating something, let alone the fact that he had taste buds. They remained in place, not screaming as he savored the hints of smoked pepper and honey. The sweet wings had a sharp, plummy flavor, which went well with the sticky, chewy texture of the skin. And the chicken beneath wasn't dry and leathery.

Frank was sucking the tips of his fingers, quite unconcerned with the display he made, when Tom returned from a neighboring stand with two plastic cups of liquid the color of urine.

"That's not Mello Yello is it?"

Tom just grinned and held his cup up. "Chill. It's lemonade. No one sells Mello Yello outside of a can, and I can't get it in the stores around here. I have to order it from Amazon."

Frank struggled with the concept of ordering soda from an online retailer for a moment before confirming the facts. "You order it."

"I have a subscription."

"I don't even know what that means."

Tom pressed his cup into Frank's, making a slightly squishy toast. "Drink up, I enrolled us in the zucchini derby. We've got half an hour to carve our squash before our race begins."

Obviously the wings had been hotter than Frank anticipated. He was in the grip of a chili fever. Or they'd been laced with an illegal substance. "Carve our squash?"

"Finish sucking your fingers and c'mon."

Frank followed, a bright ball of something forming behind his breastbone. He'd just sucked down sauce that would sear an unapologetic path through his gut and would likely follow it with an afternoon of bad carbs. And now he was off to carve squash.

They weren't the only adults lining up for oversized zucchini, plastic knives, and a small container of toothpicks. Seated at a table, Frank examined his squash, end to end. "I've never seen one so large."

Next to him, Tom started giggling. "That's what he said."

Frank glanced over in time to see familiar mischief lighting Tom's dark eyes. Without thinking too hard on it, he circled his thumb and forefinger around the zucchini and stroked downward. He got caught halfway, the sheer girth of the vegetable separating his fingers. "Oh my."

Tom opened his mouth into an O and poked his tongue around.

The woman seated across from him snort-giggled and Frank laughed. "Dare you do put it in your mouth," he whispered.

Tom glanced left and right, then put the end of his zucchini between his lips. He seemed to be working on a more lascivious expression than surprise when his eyes widened and he pulled the vegetable back out.

Frank nearly groaned. "Tease."

"I'm getting odd looks from the other end of the table."

From another pair of men, both dressed in Pocono plaid—summer version. They were eyeing Frank and Tom with open suspicion. Frank gave the cuter one—as if he could ever find a man dressed in deer stalking camouflage in anyway attractive—a suggestive eyebrow raise.

Tom elbowed him in the ribs. "Stop, they've probably got a shotgun between the seats of their pickup."

"Of course they do." How Tom had managed not to end up a statistical smear on the sidewalk sometime over the past thirty years wasn't exactly a mystery. He didn't wear his otherness quite the same way as Frank did. Still . . .

Frank turned back to his zucchini. "Okay, tell me what to do."

There was little point in attempting to make their zucchini any more aerodynamic than nature intended. Instead, they spent their time making wheels—out of zucchini—and attaching them with toothpicks. Tom fashioned a complicated axle arrangement while Frank carved numbers in the side of their dark-green vehicle. When they were done, Frank eyed their zucchini with a mixture of pride and embarrassment. How could he explain this to anyone outside of Pennsylvania? Would he even want to?

Tom took a few pictures, and they assembled by the top of the truncated skateboard ramp that formed the raceway. They would be competing against the deer stalkers. Not optimal, but preferable to having their asses kicked by the little girl whose father had actually tried to shave some sleekness into their vehicle.

Frank had the job of racer as Tom wanted to photograph the event. He posed with the zucchini, gesturing like Vanna White as he demonstrated the features of their vegetable: "Wheels. Toothpicks. A motivating motif of mesmerizing lines."

"Nice alliteration."

"It will be the secret to our success," Frank replied.

"Racers ready!"

Frank placed his zucchini behind the starting line, aiming it toward the bottom of the ramp while trying to take into consideration the possible drag of their not-quite-even wheels.

"And go!"

He let go.

Their racer made it halfway down the ramp before losing a wheel, causing it to careen sideways, narrowly missing their opponent's vehicle, which moved out of range on rotating disks of greased lightning. Frank watched sadly as their zucchini tottered toward the edge and fell into oblivion.

He turned to face Tom, forming a mask of dejection for the camera.

Tom was waving him toward the ramp. "Pick it up, pick it up!"

That was allowed?

Frank picked up their racer, stuck the wheel back on and launched it from the derailing point. It wobbled down the ramp after the other zucchini, finally crossing the finish line and landing end to end with its mate, delivering a vigorous bump.

"Oh look, they're making friends."

Thankfully, the deer stalkers didn't hear him.

Because there were no losers in the zucchini derby, each of them was handed a plastic medal announcing their second-place win. Frank held his hand up for a high five, and Tom slapped their palms together. Then, as he would have done when they were kids, Tom cuffed the side of Frank's head, squeezed the bottom of his ear, and circled his neck with an elbow, dragging his head in close.

Tom seemed as surprised as Frank as their foreheads met, the faces coming together so much older than the ones that used to share such happy and exuberant grins. His grin only widened, though, and he gave Frank's neck and shoulders another squeeze before letting go.

And Frank stood there, clutching his big zucchini and dinky little medal, wondering when he'd last felt so light and bright.

CHAPTER 12

B y Friday afternoon, Tom had found and patched seventeen separate sections of the roof. The worst breach was over room 209, and his repair job consisted of two folded trash bags stapled to the rafters. Professional, not. But until Frank came to a decision regarding the future of the lodge, it made little sense to call in someone who actually knew what they were doing.

Tom tossed a lot of the insulation, stacking it by the side of the garage, and went from room to room upstairs, cracking the windows at the top for ventilation. The lodge already smelled less musty, even if the stink of his sweat followed him from window to window. He really needed a shower.

Tom paused just inside the door to Room 206, hesitant to enter the room though Frank had been gone all week. He'd taken off Monday morning, muttering his way out to the rental he'd parked beside Delany in the garage. That Frank seemed more reluctant to leave his baby in the care of local mechanics than to leave Tom and the lodge, was understandable. If another storm blew through before he returned, taking off the roof—perhaps made buoyant by seventeen separate trash bag balloons—all the better. It might be easier to sell half a house, something so beyond repair that a potential investor was interested in the land value only, than a sad old lodge that still resembled a home.

Room 206 smelled like Frank. The scent was faint, but recognizable. The woodsy cologne Frank wore along with the smooth vanilla notes of . . . something. Of Frank? Or maybe his soap.

Tom's feet pulled him across the room until he stood in front of the bed. Because he needed to check the sheets for mold, right? Sure.

He picked up a pillow and sniffed it, catching that delicate thread of forest that drifted through the mist on a cool, autumn morning. The perfume of bark and mulching leaves after a heavy rain. And vanilla, definitely vanilla, as though Frank kept cookies under his pillow.

Frank kept his pajama pants under his pillow. Tom smiled at the soft and silky pile of fabric, amused that Frank thought to tuck his pj bottoms away for the day, and that he'd left them behind when packing. For several long moments he indulged a quick fantasy of Frank wandering around his Jersey City apartment in nothing but a silky pajama top, half unbuttoned, delicately heavy folds of material creasing gently over the bulge of his exposed penis. Would he be soft or . . .

A groan worked through Tom's chest, sensation shooting up and down his torso. His arms tingled in that peculiar way they did when he was turned on. It wasn't hard to imagine Frank standing in front of him, one hand on his cock, stroking until the shaft thickened and lengthened. The ruddy head parting the soft material just under that last button, silk falling away from glistening flesh.

Clutching the pillow to his chest with one hand, Tom reached down to palm the bulge behind his zip. The wrongness of standing over Frank's bed, rubbing one out to a pair of pajama bottoms only sent a keen edge of longing through his veins. His blood thrummed in response, leaving his brain locked on the image of Frank, half-dressed, to flow southward, filling his cock.

Tom unzipped his jeans and felt inside, the fumbling shake of his hand more perfect than he could have planned. It was Frank's hand—Frank's fingers poking at the warm cotton beneath, slipping between the fly to take his cock out. Then it was his hand, stroking the length of an unfamiliar erection, fingers rolling over the head, squeezing, feeling, learning. Frank's thumb flicking across the slit to gather the pearl of pre-come rallying there. Fisting downward, pulling back up.

Moaning, Tom buried his face in the pillow. The vanilla forest parted to reveal a deeper scent. Male sweat and the essence of Frank. The man who'd slept here, who'd left a trace of himself behind. Tom pictured Frank's sleeping face—an image patched together from memory and the glimpses of the weekend: hair darkened almost to orange again, shining hazel eyes. That small, upturned mouth with lips always pursed as though waiting for a kiss.

Tom kissed the pillow. Pressed it against his mouth and let his moan deepen. He stroked down and up, feeling the skin of his cock slip between his fingers, wrapping his fingers more tightly. Pumping. Jerking his hips until he thrust into his hand.

It was over quickly. Embarrassingly so, if he wanted to get technical, which he didn't. Instead, he stood, legs shaking, ears ringing, yell muffled by vanilla and cotton. The sound behind his ears vibrated and sang before settling into a crunchy hum. Like tires on gravel.

Oh shit.

Dropping the pillow, Tom crossed to the window and peered out, only remembering he had one hand cradled protectively around his dick when the late-afternoon sun cast a warm glow over his exposed skin. He ducked back, tucking his junk away while wiping his hand ineffectively against his boxers, and leaned toward the window from the side.

A silver Town Car idled in the circle.

Fury didn't mix well with the aftermath of an orgasm he'd been waiting too many years for. Blood pumped through his body with an intense burn, all but flaming across his face. He rocked back again, legs still unsteady, and stood just out of view, panting, nearly spitting. He got why the Tinden Group wanted this property so badly. In their position, he'd want it too. The housing boom might be over, but this was still a really nice piece of land. Large and mostly untouched. What he didn't get was their persistence. Robert had threatened these people with legal action if they didn't desist in their attempts to buy Bossen Hill. Tom had all but kicked Patricia Nolan off the porch the previous weekend.

There were other defunct resorts. Other fallow farms. Plenty of undeveloped property in the Poconos, most of it cheap. Of course, most of it didn't have the access to main roads afforded Bossen Hill.

Curling his fingers in against his palms, Tom breathed in and out until his pulse stopped tickling the side of his throat. Until his skin stopped burning. Rushing downstairs with his head full of vitriol wouldn't help anyone. He needed to remain calm. Not do anything that would jeopardize his position as manager of . . . a pile of moldy stone.

A knock sounded against the door downstairs. Tom leaned toward the window again. The light outside would shine brightly enough off the panes to hide him, or so he hoped. After waiting through another knock, he watched as Patricia Nolan stepped off the porch, cell phone clutched to the side of her head. She was talking, but not clearly enough for him to make out the words. When she got back into the car, a shadow moved in the front passenger seat. Someone was sitting there. A Tinden? Patricia gestured toward her passenger, then the house. Then she put both hands on the wheel and guided the car around the circle.

Tom watched until they turned from the distant gate. Then he shivered. Reached up to rub his cheeks and caught the whiff of sex.

Fuck.

Reality felt less real for a moment, as he thought over the possibility Frank might sell the lodge and the fact he'd shot all over Frank's bed. Jesus Christ. Exhaling enough air to drop his shoulders three inches, Tom sloped toward the bed, cheeks burning. This was an inn. He was supposed to change the sheets and refresh the rooms for guests, not whack off over their beds.

His palm drifted over the abandoned pillow until his fingertips landed on a corner of silk.

Fuck.

After detailing the bedroom and bathroom, including fresh linens and towels—nothing to see here, just cleaning up for a returning guest, and he needed a shower anyway—Tom grabbed a can of soda from the fridge and returned to the second floor of the lodge. He climbed the ladder to the attic and crawled through a window.

Even now, after a hundred times over the sill, Tom always felt a small thrill as he scrambled out onto the roof. He'd been up here to inspect the slate; he'd been up here simply to lie back on the flat part over the back balcony. The memory of his first visit was pinned to each subsequent visit. He and Frank giggling in the darkness, trying to shush each other. The brave feeling that always settled in the center of Tom's chest as he crawled over the sill and out into summer twilight.

So high up. The sky, fading into darkness. The stars. The fireworks. Frank next to him, warm and solid.

Always so warm and so solid. His . . . Not his rock. His mountain. The person he'd loved most in the world.

Tom settled down on the shallow incline of the balcony roof. He set his soda can beside him and lay back, folding his hands beneath his head. The day hadn't relinquished its hold yet. Overhead, the sky glowed that early-evening blue: purple mellowing into cerulean, that weird shade of blue/yellow. The brilliant fire of impending sunset.

To say this was his favorite time of day would be seriously understating its importance. In this moment before the sun ducked around to the other side of the planet, it seemed like time slowed, giving space for occasion. For deeper thought, for action and reaction. For a lonely man to look back at his life and wonder what he'd been doing for almost fifty years.

To wonder why it had taken Frank this long to come home.

To not hope he'd stay.

To—

A flock of birds rose from the edge of the forest bordering the lawn. Tom sat up and squinted into the distance, wondering if he'd catch a rare glimpse of a coyote. He heard them sometimes, howling in the distance. They didn't often wander out of the cover of the trees, though, and he didn't know if any of them lived in this forest, or occasionally roamed down from the game lands.

A shadow shifted against the gathering gloom, no more distinct than one dark shape among the diffuse shadows of the long tree trunks in the evening. Then a figure stepped out, head swiveling left to right, and started across the lawn.

Tom swallowed a yell. If he called out from up here, he'd frighten the intruder off. Sure, that was probably the go-to solution, but he was still on edge from Ms. Nolan's earlier visit. From here, the intruder didn't appear large or threatening. Something about the way they moved suggested they might be young or maybe female. Could this be whoever it was Frank had seen last weekend?

On his hands and knees, Tom crawled to the edge of the roof. He could swing down to the balcony if he needed to. Drop to the trellis separating the kitchen yard from the patio from there if he had to give chase. He watched the figure dart across the lawn toward the four remaining guesthouses and disappear. Nothing else happened for a while, and he began to wonder if he'd imagined all of it when a head poked out from between the last two cottages, looking left and right again.

The combination of evening and a hoodie pulled up tight obscured their features, but the intruder was definitely small. Probably even more slight than Tom. A teenager, then. Tom was about to call down when a familiar chime broke the quiet. His cell phone. He scrambled for his pocket, turning away from the guesthouses just long enough to reach his fingers into his jeans. When he glanced up again, the figure was streaking back across the lawn toward the tree line.

Tom thought about shouting. Calling out for them to wait.

He answered his phone.

"Tom here."

"Tom, it's Sandra."

Something told him this wasn't a social call. Panic hammered up from his gut, grappling for his heart. He felt curiously spent, but his voice still managed to shake. "What's up?"

"Nothing to worry about."

The calls always started that way. *"Nothing to worry about, but Wendy found some pills." "Nothing to worry about, but your mom took a little spill today." "Nothing to worry about, but we had to move Wendy to another room. She and her neighbor weren't getting along."* Meaning that his mom had been helping herself to things that weren't hers.

The worst had been: *"Nothing to worry about, but your mom fell and broke her neck."*

Tom hadn't had a phone call like this for a couple of years, and never one from Mountain Manor.

". . . a little chest infection," Sandra was saying. "She hasn't been as active lately, so some fluid settled in her lungs. This is common—"

"Is she there?"

"We've moved her to the clinic on-site, yes. I just wanted to make sure you were—"

"I can be there in about fifteen minutes."

"She's going to be fine."

"I'll be there soon."

No point in explaining the dark thoughts crawling through his mind. Detailing the fear that he might miss her if he didn't come now, whether the doctors thought she'd be fine or not. Besides, Sandra wouldn't call over nothing. She knew Wendy Benjamin's story. Yeah, she used the phrase "nothing to worry about"—they must teach that in nursing school or whatever—but she also understood that Tom and Wendy had no one else but Wendy and Tom. They were a unit. A weird one, an unbalanced one, but a tight one. She was his mom. He was her son. They were *it*.

The drive took seven minutes less than it should have, but he arrived without incident and carried a few tics into Mountain Manor with him. The palm of his left hand constantly shifted from pocket to pocket as he checked for his wallet and phone. His car keys jingled from his right hand, moving up and down as he rolled the beads of his keychain between thumb and forefinger.

He started breathing again when he heard the reassuring beep of machinery next to his mother's bed. Giving little regard to the oxygen tube, IV, and leads running this way and that, Tom leaned in to kiss his mom's forehead. He found her hand and squeezed it. Rested his temple to hers.

"I'm here, Mom."

She didn't stir, but that was okay. She'd know he was here. That she wasn't alone. That her son would never leave her as his father had—alone and heavily pregnant. Her Tommy would never abandon her. Even if this was her last night, she'd go off into the next life with someone at her side.

CHAPTER 13

Frank slowed as he passed the modernized ranch Simon used to live in. For a second, it seemed appropriate that he'd almost pulled into the wrong house with the wrong car. The rental wasn't crappy, but neither did it inspire joy. He hadn't earned this car. How those thoughts applied to the knotty feeling in his gut as he turned into the house next door was anybody's guess. What he did know was he needed a moment to fortify himself against the chaos of Charlie's place.

He started by parading back through his week, mentally checking boxes for everything he'd managed to accomplish. He'd pulled together his last essay on what he'd found in Puerto Rico: not the story he'd gone for, but a city full of dislocated people and more reality than he'd been prepared to deal with. The piece was good, definitely better than the one he'd already posted, but he knew he couldn't continue to write in the same vein. He was better at interviewing people, singular, than dwelling on the fate of so many. He was all about entertainment, insight, finding out what made someone interesting, not . . .

God, was he really that shallow?

Article written, check. Self-examination, in progress. Twitter . . . He was still letting his PA take care of it. When had he stopped caring about Twitter?

Personal finances, examined. Letter from his uncle, read. It had been short and to the point and could be summed up in five words: *This is where you belong.*

Humph.

Brooding, accomplished.

Dinner with Simon was the last item on his list, well, except for the matter he'd not so successfully tried to ignore all week: Tom.

What to do about Tom? Any plans Frank might have for Bossen Hill felt secondary to that.

After a last fortifying breath, Frank collected his bag of yumminess from the deli he'd discovered off Main Street in Bethlehem, and approached the newly painted porch. He knocked on the door—when was someone going to fix that bell?—and gaped as Charlie's teenaged daughter Olivia opened it past a belly so round, she appeared ready to pop.

"Well, aren't you looking . . . radiant." That was the right thing to say to a pregnant woman, yes?

Olivia returned her usual greeting—an eye roll and a smirk—before calling over her shoulder. "Simon, Frank's here."

And then she left him standing on the threshold. Because that was what teenagers did. Another teenager passed by while he was waiting there. A girl with dark-brown skin and the most stunningly beautiful face Frank had ever seen. Olivia's friend, Rosie. She lifted a hand in greeting, but did not invite him in. As a third person approached the door, Frank invited himself inside and came face-to-face with the father of Olivia's child.

Were Charlie and Simon running a flophouse now?

"Hey," said the boy. Jason? Justin? He did the calling thing too. "Simon, your friend is here."

The dog appeared next, followed by Charlie, who seemed to move in much the same manner as his canine. Buoyant steps, mouth open in a wide grin. His tongue didn't loll about, but he did whuff slightly before saying, "Hey!"

"Is Simon here?"

Frank's palms had started to sweat a little. He wasn't necessarily a shy man. One couldn't be, in his line of work. But he didn't care for large crowds of people he was supposed to know—and didn't. Charlie, being the man he was, immediately put his hands on Frank, dragging him away from the door, pulling him into a complicated hug arrangement, and guiding him down the hallway. All at once.

"Great to see you. Simon's out back cleaning the grill. Apparently we're not allowed to put meat on it until every part is shiny and disinfected." Charlie shrugged. "I've tried explaining we're only going to mess it up again, but you know Simon."

Frank chuckled. Oh, yes. As he progressed through the house, he could see traces of his best friend elsewhere too. It was subtle, but noticeable to someone who knew of Simon's need for order. Windows had been cleaned, curtains pinned back, walls repainted. Furniture rearranged and replaced.

"The house looks . . ."

"Clean," Charlie finished for him.

"I was going to say very nice."

"Did you know he can't go to bed without doing the dishes?"

"I did know that, yes."

Charlie rolled his eyes in a good imitation of his daughter. Or perhaps she'd learned the skill from him. Frank and Charlie had made it through to the kitchen at this point, the back half of which was missing, the gaping hole covered with gently flapping plastic sheeting. Through the plastic, Frank could see Simon out on the patio, bent over the aforementioned grill. He wore an apron, gloves that covered him to the elbow . . . and a face mask.

"Oh my."

"Right?" Charlie grinned. "He's one of a kind."

And Charlie obviously adored him for that reason. In fact, Charlie fairly exuded the sort of emotions that usually had Frank cringing: love, contentment, happiness.

They stepped outside, Charlie calling out. "Simon!"

Simon glanced up and quickly pulled his face mask aside. "Frank." He gestured at his gloved and aproned self. "I'd say hello properly, but I'm a little grimy."

"Detailing the grill, apparently."

"It hadn't been cleaned properly in three years."

"Perish the thought."

Charlie was examining the grill plates stacked against the leg of the patio table. "Wow. These came out of there?"

"Mm-hmm." And there it was, the same sappy expression painted all over Simon's face: love, contentment, and happiness.

Frank's stomach curled tight. Vital organs in his chest wanted to do the same. A deep sense of unwelcome rolled through him, pushing him back a step. He didn't belong here. He wasn't a part of this family.

He wasn't a part of—

Simon cut short Frank's roll into the pity pool by clanking something against the grill. "Just need to finish this last piece and I'll come in." Simon glanced at the bag and wine Frank still held. "You want to drop those off in the kitchen?"

"I'll take them," Charlie said. "Let you two catch up!" He smiled his brilliant smile at Frank, and though he still felt uncomfortable, Charlie's pleasure in having him here was clearly evident.

Frank returned a smaller smile. "Thank you." He passed off his goods and waited until Charlie had ducked inside the house before turning back to Simon. And couldn't think of anything to say, which was absurd. This was his closest, dearest friend. Dressed in an apron and wearing a surgical mask.

"You look ridiculous."

Simon chuckled softly, the mask puffing out a little. "I know. Makes Charlie happy, though."

"Surely you don't—"

"It's not like that. I'd have worn one of those suits the CDC takes into disaster areas if I thought I could get away with it. This grill is a biological hazard. But knowing how much enjoyment he gets out of my odd quirks only makes them seem . . ." He shrugged. "I find I don't care as much as I used to. Either that, or he simply makes me feel better about being me."

"I've been here five minutes and already I want to throw up."

"So that's why you're studying me like I'm something you found washed up on the beach."

"I'll have you know, I've discovered treasure on the sand at Cape May." Everyone had a jar of milky glass and pretty shells tucked away somewhere, didn't they?

"Oh?"

Frank appraised him in all his Simon-ness and smiled. "I can't fit you in my souvenir jar, but I'll keep you nonetheless."

Simon started laughing.

Frank preened. Charlie wasn't the only person who could amuse Simon Lynley. He'd been here way before and would be here . . .

Simon was gazing over his head toward the flapping plastic. Through the plastic at the shadow moving about in the kitchen. And he wore that expression again.

Sigh.

"Olivia looks ready to burst," Frank said.

Simon returned his attention to the grill. "Yes! She was due yesterday, actually, but apparently first babies can take their time. We're all on high alert. Bags packed and whatnot. I finished decorating the nursery only last week. Do you want to see it?"

"Maybe later." Frank tipped his head toward the plastic wall. "And this?"

"We're going to extend the kitchen out here—" a gesture encompassed the patio "—and build a new patio from the side around. We'll have two casual eating areas, then. Indoor and outdoor. Glass doors opening outward so we can combine the space when entertaining. We'll use the same siding as the rest of the house. Well, the same color. And I'm thinking of building a fieldstone chimney out here to house a proper grill. As a surprise for Charlie."

Up until that last, Simon had sounded almost normal.

"Nice."

"Mmm." Simon finished picking grime off the last part of the grill and started cleaning up. "So, how are you?"

"Oh, you know. Overworked, bitchy, in need of a fuck."

Simon arched a single eyebrow. "Perhaps a stop at the casino on your way . . . Are you heading home or up to Stroudsburg? How is everything going up there?"

Charlie returned to the patio, drinks in hand. He had wineglasses for Frank and Simon and a beer for himself. If there was one thing Frank admired about Charlie, it would be his honesty. He didn't care for wine and so he didn't pretend to drink it. Charlie lifted his bottle in a sort of toast. "Thanks for coming, Frank."

Simon had stripped off his gloves and mask. He took his glass, Frank took his, and raised they toasted Charlie in return. The stupidly nice, quite handsome if you were into the "boy next door" look, and just all around charming Charlie.

Frank had spent too many hours examining his feelings about Charlie, and he didn't like what he'd found. He was jealous of this man. Not because he'd taken Simon away. Simon deserved this. Needed it. More it was that—

Well, now wasn't the time.

"Thanks for having me." Frank sampled his wine.

Charlie smiled. "Anytime. So, Simon. Can I destroy the grill again yet?"

Simon cast a forlorn look over his gleaming grill parts. "I don't suppose you'd agree to covering—"

"Nope. But think of it this way. Cleaning the grill can be one of your summer things. You, a surgical mask, and quiet evenings out on the patio."

Frank laughed. He couldn't help it. Charlie had Simon pinned.

Simon pushed the side of Charlie's head and then curled his arm around his lover's shoulders and pulled him into a sideways hug. "Goof."

"I thought you were going to cook, Simon?"

"I was until I saw the state of everything. That will be a challenge for another day, I think."

Frank smiled. "So, what's on the menu, then?"

The evening passed rather pleasantly from there, Frank's hors d'oeuvres rounding out a full menu of kebabs, grilled vegetables, couscous, salad, and dessert. By the time he and Simon had effectively killed Frank's bottle of wine, Frank had drifted into a state of fuzzy fullness.

"Want to walk the dog with me?" Simon asked.

"Really?"

"We didn't get a chance to finish our chat earlier."

Frank grumbled quietly, but inside he was pleased at the prospect of spending a little more time just with Simon. Unless Charlie intended to accompany them. This would usually be their thing, hmm? Walking the dog together after dinner. But Charlie excused himself to start on the dishes—after unabashedly wrapping his arms around Simon's shoulder and kissing him on the corner of the mouth. "Might even get you to bed early tonight if I get all of this done."

Ugh. So disgustingly cute. Men their age shouldn't be cute in any way, shape, or form. Of course, Frank's thoughts immediately drifted toward Tom. His large, dark eyes and elfin features. He might have to revise his opinion. Maybe.

"Ready?"

"As I ever will be to walk a dog through a suburban neighborhood on a summer evening."

Simon waited until they were past his old house before bringing up his mood. "You've been very quiet. I'd say not as bitchy as usual, but for the feeling the bitchiness is all mental. And I know you."

"Too well."

"What's up?"

Where to start. His jealousy—or was it envy? His dissatisfaction with his career. His loneliness. The rotting resort he'd inherited. The notion he didn't deserve it, even if it was something of an albatross. Tom.

"Frank?" Simon had stopped walking. The dog, Herbert, didn't seem to mind. He was sniffing around a mailbox pole, probably preparing to deliver a message of his own.

Frank glanced up at Simon. "I have a lot on my mind, that's all."

"Want to talk about it?"

They were approaching fifty and quite gay and therefore able to talk about feelings and thoughts without fearing the impact on their masculinity. Yet they rarely unloaded all at once, or in depth, whether out of long-held habit or simply because men weren't programmed that way. Frank started with the easiest issue: the resort. Without mentioning Tom, he described the state of decay, the visit from Patricia Nolan, and his lack of certainty going forward. The question of what he was going to do with the place.

"I've heard of the Tinden Group," Simon said. "They'll subdivide and build crappy little houses. I can refer you to other developers if you do want to sell. If you're interested in what happens to the land after you sell it."

"I'm not sure that's what I want to do. Sell it. But I don't know why." As the words rolled out, Frank realized they were true. All week, while putting together his piece on Puerto Rico, he'd constantly found himself researching the history of resorts in the Poconos and the current state of the industry. He didn't know why, but recognized the urge well enough. Whether it was a story or just an idea, he'd have to keep picking away at it until it unraveled. Until he found a person who *represented* the story. And then he'd write, or act. Do something to break this mental congestion.

"Why would you keep it?" Simon asked. "Sounds like the place is about to fall down. I mean, if it's not too bad, you could think about restoration, but it'd probably be a huge job."

"Meaning expensive. Would you come up and take a look? Tell me what you think?"

"I'd love to, but—" Herbert decided to move on, yanking Simon sideways. He managed to walk on without tripping over, and around the shrubbery lining the sidewalk. When Frank caught up to him, he continued, "Brian would have a better idea of what's involved than I would. He knows land values and development potential."

"Brian. As in ex-douchebag Brian."

"It's his area of expertise. He sees a far bigger picture than I do."

Frank frowned. "Are you two friends now?"

Simon shrugged. "The sort of friends who don't really know how to be friends, but can't be anything else."

"Are you still working together?"

"On and off. The Burnside project is all but finished, but we've been talking about some other ideas."

"That's . . . Is that good? How is it working with him?"

Pulling Herbert to another halt, Simon regarded Frank carefully for a moment. Then his face relaxed. "It's sometimes odd. I forget we're not together. But I don't have to catch myself out. I mean . . . How to put this. There's no desire there. No spark. I'd have thought we'd lost that years ago, but maybe we hadn't. I don't know. But now that I'm with Charlie, everything has changed in ways I would never have expected. I can look at Brian and just see Brian. A man I have a lot of respect for, professionally, and even like quite well." He shrugged again. "I'm happy, and so I find I'm not as broken up about everything as I was last year."

Frank found it difficult to hold Simon's gaze while he talked about being happy. He turned away, pretending to study the neighborhood, which was mostly quiet and mostly dark. Summer proper was still a couple of weeks off.

"Frank . . ."

"I'm happy you're happy," Frank said to the ground.

"It doesn't feel that way."

Frank shook his head. "It's not about you." He glanced up. "I'll admit that last year I thought . . . I wondered . . ." Simon's eyebrows drew together. "But we're friends. Good friends."

"Then what's got you so tied up?"

"Did I ever tell you about Tommy? I mean Tom. Thomas Benjamin."

Simon's eyebrows bunched together again. "Name sounds familiar."

"Boy I grew up with."

"Yes! You kissed him and he punched you. Didn't you write him letters all freshman year?"

"So pathetic."

Simon chuckled. "Why are we talking about Thomas Benjamin?"

"He's there, Simon. At the resort."

"What do you mean?"

"He never left." Frank lifted his hands to gesture, but didn't really know what to do with them, so he tucked them behind his back. "And for the past ten years or something, probably longer, he's been managing the place."

"Oh."

"Yeah."

"Do you still . . ."

Frank closed his eyes. Opened them. Prepared to shake his head and stopped. Swallowed. Checked in with the twisted thing in his chest, the organ that was supposed to beat happily when he met The One; the place where he was supposed to store all his most cherished memories. And it was beating. Slowly, steadily. A light drumming that pulsed beneath his skin and echoed lightly in his thoughts.

Tom. Tom. Tom.

He nodded. Thought about lying, changing the subject. Sighed. "I don't think I ever stopped."

"Oh, Frank."

CHAPTER 14

T he bride and groom sweated their way through a thankfully short ceremony. Tom sweated his way around the periphery, already calculating how he would tone down the glow in the bride's cheeks as he edited photos of the kiss, the smile, and the oh-wow-we-actually-did-it moment. There was always one photograph that made his day, and he captured it seconds after that: the flash of pride on the groom's face as he congratulated himself for making the best decision of his life. The June sunshine agreed.

While he packed his gear, Tom's heart and mind were already in the forest around the lodge, maybe on the south trail where the trees gave way to a small, rocky beach. By the time he stopped to check on his mom, the sun would have passed around the bend in the creek and he'd have ample shade to sit while cooling his heels in a very real sense.

Fatigue checked his enthusiasm a little, as well as concern over his mother's health. The doctor had listed her condition as stable, but if there was one thing Wendy Benjamin didn't know how to do, it was "stable."

The receptionist called for his attention as soon as Tom ducked into the air-conditioned lobby of Mountain Manor. He strolled up to the front desk and stood sweating as two hours under the sun evaporated beneath a cool swirl of air. The receptionist tapped a few keys on the keyboard in front of her and an old, familiar tension slid down Tom's spine. He wasn't completely unaware of the state of his account with Mountain Manor, but he'd had a lot of practice in ignoring the obvious until it became painful.

Experience had taught him that being the last to say something often bought time.

Without looking away from her monitor, the receptionist spoke in a confidential tone that wouldn't have been quiet enough to exclude anyone else hanging around the front desk. "I'm showing your account is two months in arrears, Mr. Benjamin." It was always Mr. Benjamin when they wanted to talk about money. She glanced up, showing him a practiced smile. "How much can you pay today?"

"My checkbook is in the car." Tom gestured in the opposite direction. Toward the clinic. "I can grab it as soon as I've checked in with my mom."

If anyone else had been at the desk, watching this exchange, they might not have noticed the subtle expression change—unless they were also the deadbeat son of a mentally *unstable* woman with a long history of substance abuse. Another receptionist might prefer he got his checkbook now. Would prefer he paid something instead of the fat nothing he obviously planned. But this one was too polite to say so, even in front of an imaginary audience.

Next month she wouldn't be so polite.

Taking her silence as his cue, Tom dipped his head in a little nod, patted the top of the front desk—*my check will be here, soon*—and went to visit with his mom, where he stayed for an hour, holding her limp hand, then left after being assured she was responding to treatment. He remembered his checkbook as he left the parking lot and almost paused, gripped by a combination of guilt and the need to defy expectation. Then he turned onto West Main in the direction of home, because however he felt, he couldn't afford the overdraft fee.

Frank's rental was in the circle in front of the lodge. Tom pulled around the side and parked in the garage. He considered hiding in there, but it was hot in the car and hot in the garage and just too damn hot for June. Could he sneak into the guesthouse and grab a pair of trunks before Frank spotted him? The creek beckoned ever more insistently.

Frank met him at the kitchen door. "There you are." His easy and relaxed smile held a similar quality to the receptionist's. Not so easy, not quite relaxed. For a moment, Tom actually wondered if he owed Frank money too. "Here, let me help you with that." Frank took one of the camera bags and held the door open as Tom hauled the rest of his equipment inside. "Where does all this go?"

"Downstairs."

"In the cellar?"

"I've got an, um, office down there."

"In the cellar."

"Next to the darkroom."

"Why didn't you say so last week?"

Tom felt his forehead crease. "What do you mean? I thought I pointed it out."

"No, we walked past the darkroom, which you said you only used sometimes, and then we went on to where the wine was."

"Oh."

Frank stood still, as though waiting for something, and Tom's mood slipped further south.

"So, I have an office down there." Oh, was this a . . . "Robert offered me the space. I can clear it out in a day, though. If you give me two days, I can clear out the darkroom too. And my tools. I'll need to borrow a truck." Did Gerry still drive a pickup? Fuck, where would he go? Would Gerry offer him a corner of his garage as well?

"Christ, Tom. I didn't mean for you to pack your things, I was just surprised you'd work in the cellar, is all. Isn't there a workroom next to the laundry? Or there's the office up here."

Hot, tired, and pulled this way and that by emotions he didn't have names for, Tom stared at Frank until Frank took a step back.

"What?"

Tom shook his head. "Sorry, it's been a long day. And too hot."

"Another wedding?"

"Yeah."

"You do a lot of weddings?"

"This time of year, yeah."

"Well, show me where this office of yours is and then maybe we can have something cool to drink. You look as though you've spent all morning on the roof."

"That was all week, actually."

Frank's chin lifted as he glanced upward.

"I patched all the holes I could find, but the roof needs proper attention."

"I'll add it to my list."

With a grunt, Tom led the way to the cellar stairs, down, and into the office he kept next to his darkroom. Robert had made both of the same offers Frank just had: use of the workroom next to the laundry and the main office. Tom liked his basement cave, though. It was cool, dry (thanks to a dehumidifier), and private. He could lock the door and leave knowing that the most valuable possessions he had were safe, and he enjoyed being down here when he worked. Hidden from distraction.

Tom set his bag on the counter running the length of the narrow space and began pulling out his cameras and lenses. "I want everything to cool down before I clean it up and put it away," he explained. "Condensation is bad."

Frank studied his computer setup and light table before turning to take in the prints on the walls. Tom let him do his thing while Tom did his. He unpacked, jotted a few notes to himself—reminders of which photos he wanted to do something special with—and put his bags away. By the time he was done, Frank had migrated to the cubby-style shelves at the end of the counter and had a magazine in his hands.

He'd made a small stack on the empty shelf beside him.

Oh shit.

Frank looked up. "These are mine."

"Um, technically, they're mine. I paid for them."

"No, I mean"—he closed the issue of *GQ* in his hands and held it up for Tom to see—"I have a column in this one." He put the magazine aside and picked up an issue of *Traveler*. "I have the cover of this one." He picked up another two magazines. "An article in this one and an essay in this one. All of these magazines"—he gestured at the stack he'd made—"have my work in them."

What to do but shrug and pretend to organize his cameras again. "Tom?"

"Are you about done? I want to lock the door and go upstairs." Even though it was cooler down here.

"Tom." Tom turned around. Frank held up the magazines. "Can I ask why you have these?"

"Probably for the same reason you have twelve of my prints."

Frank's mouth dropped open. It would have been funny if it wasn't so weird. "How did you know it was me?"

"I didn't until the third order. Same account. I wanted to know who liked my work enough to buy three separate prints, so I reverse googled your address."

Frank looked down at the magazines in his hands. Shuffled them like oversized, floppy cards. Then he began stacking them back on the shelf he'd pulled them from. Something slipped from beneath the stack and fluttered toward the floor. Recognizing the cover, Tom jumped forward. But Frank had already bent to pick up the very old, very creased notebook. The last one. The one they'd called the list of lists. The final itinerary for Benjamin and Franklin.

Watching Frank flip through the pages, Tom decided he was imagining the shaking of Frank's hands and the reverent way he handled the notebook. Frank got to the end, closed the book, and squeezed it between his hands a moment before tucking it back into the shelf beside the magazines. His voice was quiet, his words facing away. "I don't understand us."

Neither do I.

Frank seemed somewhat more composed when he turned back around, but his hazel eyes held questions.

"Want to come swimming?" Tom asked.

"What?"

"Swimming. You know, getting wet. And hopefully cool."

"I don't have any swim trunks with me." Frank frowned. "And there is no water in the pool."

"We haven't run the pool since 2015. Too expensive. I meant the creek." Tom felt the grin before it broke over his face. "Pretty sure I have a box of forgotten trunks in the laundry, though."

He half expected Frank to scoff at the idea of wearing something from the lost and found. The guy wore slacks on a Saturday, for Christ's sake. But Frank gestured for him to lead the way back upstairs and seemed content to sort through the box while Tom held it, both of them connected by cardboard, castoffs, and memories.

Frank pulled out a pair of Sponge Bob trunks. "If only these were my size."

Tom snickered.

Next was a ladies black one-piece. Frank pressed it to his chest with one hand, and molded his empty, sagging "breasts" with the other. "This doing anything for you?"

Tom's lips twitched. "No."

After digging deep, Frank came out with a bright-red pair of trunks about his size. "They're so red."

"More red than your hair." They looked up at the same time. "Well, than your hair used to be. Do you dye it now?"

Frank's smile narrowed. "Something like that."

"Seriously?"

"You really think this strawberry blond is the natural product of age?"

"I dunno, man. Orange hair could go one way or the other, right? Though, if I remember correctly, Anne with an E suffered under the curse of the carrot for most of her life."

Chuckling, Frank said, "If there's anything more ridiculous than carrot-colored hair, it's carrot-colored hair highlighted with white. Not gray, not silver, but white."

"Because gray would be too mundane for Franklin Tern."

"I'd already been lightening my hair for years, to tone down the orange, so I simply went a little lighter. The plan is to one day go gracefully white. When I'm tired of this reddish sort of blond." He shrugged. "Or when my vanity finally gives in to the fact I'm nearly fifty."

"It looks good."

Frank smiled, the compliment obviously touching something other than a peripheral need for reassurance. "And you look about the same."

"Except with gray I'm not . . ." No, he wasn't going to say that. Frank didn't need an excuse to color his hair.

Frank finished the sentence anyway. "Vain enough to color?"

"No." Tom shrugged. Frowned. "I just don't care, I guess."

"You never did."

"Sure I did or I wouldn't've been pissed when you wanted me to wear trunks out of this box all those years ago. I hated the idea of wearing hand-me-downs."

"That's not what I meant. Okay, so you've got some gray going on. The fact you're not trying to hide it is what makes you so you. You were never one to apologize for who you were, Tommy. I always envied that. Your confidence."

"I don't know what you're talking about. I followed you around like a bad smell. I wanted so badly to be in your life. To have your life."

"And I wanted yours."

"A drunk mother and a shabby trailer? Your father was a doctor, Frank. You lived in the nicest house in town and spent afternoons and weekends at your uncle's resort playing with all the kids who could afford to get away for a few days. You had everything."

Frank was shaking his head. "No, I didn't. Not until . . ."

"Until what?"

"Not until you."

CHAPTER 15

Frank thought Tom might drop the box. He went rigid and took a step back. Then he turned to set the box onto the counter beside the row of washers and driers that served as the lodge's on-site laundry. Frank knew for a fact that they used to send the majority of the laundry out: sheets, towels, tablecloths. The washers and driers were for incidentals. Guest laundry. Now they stood silent sentry over a conversation that had veered badly from an attempt at humor to what felt like the revelation of an awful secret.

He had to say something. "I'm sorry."

"For what?" Tom didn't turn.

"For making this awkward."

Tom's shoulders rose and fell. The gesture was so familiar, Frank's heart ached. He wanted so badly to lay his fingers atop one of those shoulders. To pull Tom back against him, wrap his arms tight around Tom's chest, and whisper against his ear. Ask what had made him so sad, so tense, so dark. Why he looked so worried. Frank also wanted to ask the smaller questions. How Tom had spent his week—aside from patching the roof. About the wedding. If he'd eaten anything other than peanut butter sandwiches. Ordered some Mello Yello. But for all his capacity for putting words on the page, they failed him now.

After another interminable moment, he tried, "So, where did you want to swim?"

Tom finally turned around. He kept his face slightly averted so it seemed he peeked at Frank when he spoke. "I was thinking by the south trail."

"Let's go, then."

He thought Tom might beg off. Instead, Tom gestured toward the door. "I think I've got some trunks in my car."

"Meet you back in the lobby in a few, then."

Frank had packed a more sensible bag this time, and had been more than pleased to be reunited with his favorite pajama pants, washed and pressed and tucked back under his pillow. He wasn't sure how long he'd be staying, but he'd come prepared for a week or two. With an article and several columns filed and nothing immediate pending, he had time to sort out a few messes. Taking a swim with Tom seemed a fine way to start on the most important one.

Dressed in the sordidly red trunks, sandals, and a moisture-wicking workout shirt, Frank arrived back in the lobby to find Tom's taste in swimwear was about as eclectic as it had ever been. He wore board shorts in pale blue and pink, the pink part being a bright pattern of seashells. They fit well, cutting off at mid-thigh to show toned legs beneath a light covering of dark hair. The view above the waistband was as lovely. He was still too thin, and gray sprinkled his chest hair—when had Tom grown more than three separate hairs?—but obviously fit and so obviously Tom, the Tom he remembered from all those years ago. Wiry and capable and always dressed in something slightly odd. In comparison, Frank felt just . . . old. And not as fit, despite the fact he'd hit the gym every morning that week.

Frank looked up to find Tom giving him a sardonic smile.

"What?" Frank asked.

"Do I pass? Am I me?"

"So *very*. Where did you get those shorts?"

"Wildwood. Day trip and another *friend* who insisted I had to swim. These were the least objectionable pair I could find on the boardwalk."

"They suit you."

Tom laughed, and it was as though the awkward moment in the laundry hadn't happened. Almost. "C'mon." He had a couple of beach towels over one arm. He passed one across and they left the lodge, Tom leading the way across the patio, around the sad and empty pool and collapsing cottages, over the back lawn, and into the quiet embrace of the forest.

Happy memories surfaced when they found a path and Frank felt the cares of the week dropping away as one foot fell in front of the other. With summer only just starting, the canopy had yet to blot out the sky and the sun broke through, dappling the ground with color. Roots snaked across the path now and again, and flattened rock cairns marked the turns. It wasn't until they'd nearly reached the creek that Frank became aware of just how well maintained the path was.

"You did this," he said to Tom's back.

Tom glanced over his shoulder. "What?"

"The paths. You're still maintaining them?"

He shrugged. "It's mostly habit now, but I use them often enough that it's not much effort. It's only really a pain when a storm or age takes a tree down and I have to clear it away."

Evidence of such work lay around them. A long tree sliced in half by a saw and pushed to either side of the path. Another cut and stacked like firewood a little farther on. "Robert always enjoyed the trails."

Tom turned again. Smiled. "Yeah, he did. He hadn't used them in a couple of years, but he asked after them. Sometimes I felt like I was walking them for him. Keeping them up for him. But I'm not that altruistic. I was doing it for me too."

"Mm-hmm." Frank smiled. "Whatever gets you through the day."

Chuckling, Tom faced forward again, and soon they were veering south and down to the narrow beach in front of the creek. Tom's hand was evident here too. The bushy weeds that grew along the shore had been trimmed back, exposing long, flat rocks for sunbathers and swimmers. A stone path crossed the creek a short way along, and more rocks had been arranged to form a pool. The shallow, natural falls were clear of debris. Under the sparkling sun, the scene was idyllic and inviting, the burble of water and occasional bird call all the chatter Frank wanted to hear. Peaceful, but welcome.

He stepped over the small ridge shoring up the side of the trail and stopped. Glanced up at Tom, who stood still, watching him. From his expression, he was reliving the same memory.

"This is where I fell," Frank said. "The day we met. Broke my ankle."

Tom nodded.

"And you almost carried me back to the path."

He nodded again.

Frank looked around, grasping for other memories—summers after then when they'd swum and played and talked and rested together, sure every summer would be the same. "Did I ever thank you for that?"

"About a thousand times."

Frank gazed across the creek at the line of trees beyond and frowned. The neighborhood replacing Pocono Court was tidy, but bland. Soulless, as Tom had suggested, with one model of house represented in varying shades of brown and gray. Perhaps the saddest part was the removal of all the trees that used to shade the trailers. In the midst of summer, the trees would have been the most pleasant part of the rundown park. "Do you get a lot of trespassers from the new neighborhood?"

"About the same as always. Mostly kids. Had someone run across the lawn at the back of the lodge a couple of days ago, actually."

"Yeah?"

"I wondered if it might have been a kid inside the lodge last weekend."

"Maybe. Either that, or one of Patricia Nolan's spies." Frank offered a wry smile.

Tom snorted.

Frank spread his towel on a warm rock, kicked off his sandals, and dipped a toe in the water. "Shit! That's not water, it's liquid nitrogen."

Tom stepped out of his flip-flops and stepped into the pool until the water lapped at the bottom of his shorts. "I seem to remember someone once telling me you had to jump in all at once. Like they did in Sweden."

Frank met his gaze. He hadn't expected Tom to talk about the notebook. "I never got to Scandinavia," he said by way of continuing the conversation.

Tom's mouth crooked up on one side. "You've got time."

Nodding absently, Frank picked his way carefully over the arrangement of stones until he finally stood face-to-face with Tom in the shockingly chilly water. "It's still cold."

"You'll go numb soon."

"I might never find my balls."

A flicker of something passed over Tom's face, then he smiled a certain smile. By the time Frank had figured it out—what that smile meant—Tom had ducked down into the water and warm hands were tugging at Frank ankles. It was too late to steady himself. Set a stance. Find a rock big enough to hold on to. Too late to do anything but fall backward until he splashed down into freezing hell, creek water sloshing up his nostrils and over his head. Frank swallowed a yelp and more water. He splashed and flailed. When he surfaced, his sinuses burned and his mouth tasted like old tea. And Tom was sitting across from him, hair plastered in a wet tangle across his forehead, laughing.

Slicking his hair back with one hand, Tom lunged forward with the other, catching a wave and pushing it toward Frank's face. Frank's block came too late. After swallowing another bellyful of creek, he gathered water on both sides, creating a wave on two fronts that Tom couldn't escape. Except he did, the bastard. He ducked underneath the swell and splash, and his hands, cooler now, tangled with Frank's ankles again. Frank kicked backward only to find he'd reached the rocks stacked around the edge of the creek. Tom pulled him under.

Frank opened his eyes under the water and sought out Tom's sleek shape, catching a leg before Tom managed to swim away. He yanked him backward and pushed him down. Bubbles rose up. He let Tom surface briefly before dragging him down and rolling over him so they tumbled through the shallow pool, each fighting to be the one on top. Frank forgot about air and breathing until he tried to suck in a mouthful of water. He tapped Tom's side, a gesture from thirty years or more gone by, and Tom immediately let him up.

And then they went at it again, remembering how to play. How to tease each other with the thought of drowning, how to sneak in a small pool of water. How to shout and laugh and splash too many times, but not once more because enough was enough.

Frank could feel bruises developing on his elbows and knees. His hip ached and by the time he dragged himself out of the water to lie on his back on a wet, slick rock, chest heaving toward the sky, he existed in a place he hadn't visited in forever. A space without conscious thought.

Tom landed beside him with a wet squelch, and panted breath joined his chorus.

Sunshine dappled through the trees, warming him in patches. Birds chittered and chipmunks scurried about behind them. Twigs cracked and the wind whispered. Forest sounds. Frank closed his eyes and let the resonance of summer fill his senses. The smell of the water, the tiny movements next to him something he'd always taken for granted. Tom's breath, a soft hum, him blowing his nose, the rasp of a wet fabric against stone.

Frank rolled his head to the side, opening his eyes. Tom was stretched out on his back, his head inclined toward Frank. Watching him. They locked stares, brown eyes to brown. Whether it was being here by the creek, or recent familiarity, Tom seemed more real than he had a week ago—whatever that meant. And his older face, still narrow, still delicate, was unbearably beautiful. Or maybe that was just Frank's heart taunting him.

He lowered his gaze to Tom's mouth, to lips that remained red despite the chill of the creek. Or perhaps because of it. The tip of Tom's tongue appeared. Disappeared.

Breath stuttering in his throat, Frank rolled onto his side, facing Tom. The movement was a not-so-subtle invitation, one that could easily be ignored. If Tom wasn't feeling it—and Frank sometimes wondered if he ever had—then he could continue to lie where he was, and they could talk. Maybe that's what they should do. Kissing Tom now wouldn't change the past.

Tom rolled onto his side, facing Frank. His gaze had been pretty steady, focused mainly on Frank's, but now it dipped slightly. Frank stopped breathing. The forest fell silent, every creature as still as his heart. Even the creek seemed not to burble, caught in this delirious pause. Fingers of unreason pushed at Frank's shoulders, urging him to just do it. To lean forward, to press his lips to Tom's. He was old enough to laugh it off if Tom rejected him. He could say he'd been playing. Teasing. That sort of behavior had become second nature. His motto was easy come, easy go.

But this was Tom. Not so easy. Already gone beyond his reach?

Frank found a breath, sucked it in.

Then Tom was there, closing the distance. And it was his breath at Frank's lips. His mouth. A kiss, as light and crisp as a fallen leaf. Another breath, a second kiss, this one firmer, a lingering touch, a question begging for an answer.

There was no time to debate the merit of it, and Frank wouldn't have anyway. Not with Tom. Never with Tom. With a soft groan, the simple sound hiding every complication, he gave in to the invitation. He kissed Tom back. Not a peck to the lips, not a return brush. He fastened his mouth to Tom's and *kissed* him.

And flinched . . . sure history would rewind and play forward, bringing a fist out of nowhere to land sharply against his nose.

Instead, Tom curled a hand behind Frank's neck and pulled him closer. Kissed him harder. Then moved, tasting Frank's lips in small touches out to the corners of his mouth and back again. A looser kiss, openmouthed. The curious graze of tongue. Another invitation.

Frank caught Tom's shoulder and opened for him. Tom didn't dive in right away. Instead he seemed to look for Frank's rhythm, for that pattern of kissing lovers found when their mouths fit in a certain way, and then their tongues were touching, tasting, sliding. The distance between them evaporated. Tom's thighs were against his, warm and cold at the same time. Water trickled from their trunks, slicking the skin of their stomachs as they came together, arms wrapping around each other's shoulders.

The kiss deepened, became something other than a *hi* and *hello*. Became *I want more*. A need to get farther inside the skin of the other. *I want to roll you over and fuck you.*

Frank traced his hand down Tom's back until he reached the slight dip before his hips. Stroked there a moment, reveling in the smooth tightness of skin before grasping the wet cotton over the curve of his ass. Tom jerked against him, rocking forward, something hot and firm poking Frank's thigh. Not something. His cock, and it was hard. Frank was hard too, and getting harder, blood rushing gleefully southward in a surge he hadn't felt in years. He didn't thrust against Tom's erection, though. He retained enough sense to know that might be the moment they flew apart—when it all became too much. Too real.

Tom's ass, though. Tom was apparently fine with having his ass manhandled. Frank skimmed his palm up and down, molding wet fabric to warm flesh, and then he groped. Because this *was* an ass and it was Tom's and, oh God, was it possible to come from a kiss?

The fact Tom wasn't clutching him quite as manically became clear when Tom rolled away, the sudden break weirdly loud, though they'd probably been embarrassing the forest with the sound of wet sucking and moaning. Leaving Frank bereft and confused, Tom flopped onto his back and stared up at the sky. Frank remained where he'd been left, on his side, the nape of his neck cold without the warmth of Tom's fingers. His hand lonely. His mouth bruised. Then Tom was pushing up. Sitting. He looked as though he wanted to glance sideways, but didn't. Instead, he slid off the rock and back into the pool, dipping under the water until he disappeared. Staying under while Frank counted his breaths. Staying under . . . Just staying under.

Jesus.

Frank crawled to the edge and swept his hand down under the water, hooked it under Tom's shoulder, and hauled him upward.

"What the fuck?" His yell was almost lost to the splash and heave of breath as Tom surfaced and inhaled. Restraining the urge to shake him, Frank let go. "What the hell was that?"

Still sitting, Tom turned in the water and looked up. He was below Frank, right at the edge of the pool. He lifted a dripping hand out of the creek and touched cool fingers to Frank's mouth. Frank didn't know whether to kiss the fingers or grab on, hold them there incase Tom decided to sink below the water again.

Who tried to drown themselves in two feet of water?

"I wasn't trying to drown myself," Tom said.

"How do you do that?"

"What?"

"How did you know what I was thinking?"

"All over your face, man." Tom pulled his fingers away.

Frank let them go. "What was that, then?"

"I . . ." Tom's throat moved. "I don't know."

"Fuck."

Frank pushed back from the edge and started gathering up his towel. He reached for his shirt and sandals. The fact Tom remained in the pool, watching him, only made him angrier. Just, what the fuck? What had happened? Had Tom meant to make a fool out of him? Once with the kiss; again with the weird underwater thing. Confused and hurt, Frank got to his feet and toed into his sandals.

He heard Tom leaving the pool behind him. A wet hand landed on his shoulder. "Frank, wait."

Shrugging him off, Frank started up the steep bank.

"My thoughts were going every which way, and I needed to cool off before I tried to suck you off in the middle of the forest."

Frank stopped and turned. "I don't get you."

Tom was shaking his head. "I know. No one does."

"Why now?" Frank spread his arms, his wet towel sweeping through the dirt. "And who was going to stumble across us here? What really stopped you?"

Tom bent to collect his towel, shoved his feet into his flip-flops, and started up the hill behind Frank. He drew abreast and took another step so his chin was actually level with Frank's. He met Frank's gaze, his expression unabashed. Then his face seemed to crumple inward and he looked away, down at their feet. Tom shuffled his. Frank tried not to shift his. They were nearly fifty, for fuck's sake. Why was this so awkward?

"I don't know how to do this," Tom said.

"That makes two of us."

"And I know we shouldn't."

"Why?"

Tom's chin jerked up. "Why? Because I'm me and you're you."

"That's the part I never understood, Tom. That's the part that was supposed to be easy. You and me. Benjamin and Franklin. We were going to take on the world. Be us, forever. What happened to that? Why did you . . ." *Push me away*? No, Tom had thrown him away. Tossed him out the door and kicked it shut behind him. "Why did you let me go?"

Tom shook his head. Looked down again.

"Why didn't you answer my letters?"

Another head shake.

"What was so wrong with us?" God, he'd wanted to ask these questions for years. "Why didn't you want me?" Why did it still hurt, after all this time? "And why, for the love of everything, did you kiss me just now? So not fair, Tom. You can't do that and then roll away and try to pretend it didn't happen."

"I'm sorry."

"No, you're not."

Tom's jaw hardened. "I am."

"Well that's not good enough! Sorry doesn't cut it—"

"Frank—"

"I'm not done. How could you do this? How could you give me the thing I've been waiting for, for thirty goddamned years, and then take it away again and think a word like 'sorry' covers it?"

Tom's head snapped up. "Seriously? It's not like you've been sitting in a cell on a hillside, chastely waiting for the boy you never forgot. God. Why do you always have to be so dramatic?"

"Fuck you."

"Is that the best you've got?"

"What do you want from me?" Frank's chest hurt. Every breath rasped against his throat and the sides of his head pounded in an uneven rhythm. His skin was hot and his fingers tingled the way they only did when he was really, really angry. Yet, absurdly, tears burned behind his eyes. The afternoon had been perfect and now it wasn't. And he didn't know what had happened. Couldn't grasp the why.

Tom took a step back and covered his face with his towel. He scrubbed as though merely drying off after a swim, but Frank recognized the gesture. Tom was hiding. Frank's tingling fingers now itched with the need to yank the towel away and make Tom face whatever this was, but he stood still and seethed. Then he took another breath and . . . the fire of his indignation faded a little. Birdsong cut through the angry pulse of his blood. The air moved. He took another breath. Tom lifted his face from the towel. His wet face.

Goddamn it.

One moment Frank stood there wondering why Tom was crying. The next he had Tom in his arms, pulled close, his hand pushing Tom's head toward his shoulder, to the nest he'd made there forever ago. His fingers drifted through wet hair as he attempted to calm another storm. It was so natural to do it, to settle Tom against his skin, to be there for him, to help him, that Frank had to suck back his own tears—and the urge to say sorry. Which he definitely wasn't. Fuck that. But he'd hold Tom until the crisis passed. Because, goddamn it, this was Tom.

And because it was Tom, he nestled in, his skinny arms immediately circling Frank's ribs. He held Frank just as tightly, as though he were the last man on Earth. Then he said the words that finished cracking Frank's sore heart into those two final pieces.

"I missed you, Frankie. God, how I missed you."

CHAPTER 16

Mountain Manor had called while they'd been out. Tom almost couldn't hear the voice mail over the panicked thrum of his blood—which rose to a quiet roar as he listened to the almost polite message regarding the state of his account. He called Sandra's cell and left a message asking after his mom, then hid his phone under a wet towel and stepped into the shower.

He took his time, standing under the hot spray until his thoughts ceased firing in random patterns like hopped-up fireflies. Then he just stood there. When tepid water stung his shoulders, he lingered a little longer, not knowing what to do next. But he couldn't live in the shower, or even hide in Robert's bathroom. Eventually, Frank would come to find him, like he always had.

The mirror had unfogged by the time Tom finished drying and dressing. Continuing his mission to avoid thinking, Tom ignored his reflection as he combed out his hair and considered a shave. He didn't realize he'd been staring at nothing—through his own face into God only knew what—until faint strains of music drifted over the nothingness. Frank was showered, most likely dressed to impress, and apparently determined to be lively.

Why couldn't Frank spend the evening in his room? Or, better yet, pack his bags and head back to Jersey City? Not that Tom wanted him to go, but it would be easier if he did. For about a minute, Tom contemplated sneaking out himself. He wasn't sure he could stay the night, anyway. He wasn't being paid to manage the lodge anymore. His employment had ended with Robert's death. Telling Frank he had nowhere else to go was too much on top of the events of the afternoon, however.

Also, Frank was cooking, and whatever it was smelled amazing.
He'd stay long enough to eat.

The music was coming from the kitchen. Tom paused outside the door to listen as Frank's voice rose above the radio. He was singing along with Sam Smith and doing a credible job. Leaning against the wall, Tom smiled and waited until the song was done before ducking into the kitchen. Frank stood facing the range, his back to the doorway. He flipped something in one pan and leaned over to stir whatever he had in another.

Idly, Tom wondered how much food Frank had stuffed the fridge with this time.

Frank turned and broke into a smile. "Hey."

"Hey." Tom propped his hip against the counter opposite the range. "What's cooking?"

"Balsamic chicken, wilted greens, a caprese salad—do you eat cheese? Wait, what am I asking. You eat pretty much everything, don't you?"

"Given the opportunity."

"What about onions and garlic?"

"Onions not so much." The cheese, the garlic . . . not if he and Frank were . . . Frank obviously wasn't planning to jump him after dinner. That was good, right? Then again, why would Frank want to pursue something Tom had effectively killed that afternoon?

"I had to give them up when I turned forty-five. But I shall cling to garlic until I am old and gray," Frank said.

Tom wrestled his thoughts back to the present moment. "You already are gray. Or is it white?" He plucked a slice of tomato from the fan on the salad plate. "So, when did you come up?"

"Hmm?"

"To the lodge. Last night, this morning . . .?"

"Last night. You weren't here."

"I stayed at my place." His place being the back seat of his Toyota. Moving on. "Do you enjoy cooking?"

"Are you kidding?" Frank patted his abdomen. "Of course I enjoy cooking. A little too much sometimes."

Tom smiled. "Can I do anything?"

"Set the table. A table? Where do you want to eat?"

Tom glanced around the outsized kitchen, checking the long counter by the window, thinking about the dark and dusty guest dining room and the lonely table out on the decrepit patio. "I can clear off a corner of the desk in the office."

"That works. Feel like some wine?"

"Sure, I'll grab a bottle from the cellar."

Dinner passed in a blur of nonconversation. The weather, the wine, how well tomatoes did not grow in the Poconos. Memories of apple picking with Robert, Madge, and Frank's parents. How winter had seemed like fun when they were kids. The weather again. Throughout, Tom picked at his food until he'd cleaned his plate. He drank two glasses of wine. It was more than he'd had to eat or drink since—well, since the week before.

"You don't eat enough."

He glanced up. "And you think I'm the only one who can read minds."

"It's our connection." Frank's smile started out warm, cooling slightly as his expression became thoughtful. "Are you ready to talk about what happened this afternoon?"

Tom wished he had more food. He leaned back in his chair, away from his corner of the desk, and ran over possible dessert options in his mind. Maybe he could—

"I'll start, if you like."

Breathing out, Tom nodded. "Sure."

"What's going on with you? We can talk about what happened when we were kids if you want, but I'd rather talk about what's happening now. You're like a ghost, Tom. You were always quiet, but now . . . Something's up. I know I've been gone forever and, well, I could have come home sooner. I'm not going to make excuses."

Tom made a noise in his throat. A scoff, if Frank's raised eyebrows could be taken as a reliable measure. The sound wasn't a direct response to Frank, though, or even derisive. Tom was dismissing himself.

He didn't want to tell Frank what was up.

"But if you were going to make an excuse . . ." he prompted instead.

"I stayed away because everything between us was so awkward." Frank lifted his glass and inspected the contents for a moment before taking a sip. He swallowed the way a man did when he'd taken the time to taste what was in his mouth and set his glass down again.

"The letters made it more awkward," Tom said.

"Only because you didn't answer them."

Heat not generated by a good meal and a couple of glasses of wine flushed Tom's cheeks. "So you're saying it's my fault you haven't been back."

"Isn't it?"

"You didn't even know I was working here."

Frank looked confused for a moment, as though he'd forgotten what they were talking about, and Tom realized they'd switched tracks. They were supposed to be discussing his freak-out at the creek. Frank apparently wanted to talk about the much earlier freak-out, and Tom wanted to talk about why Frank had never visited Robert. Except he didn't. Not really. Because there was a point where those three tracks crossed and he wasn't sure if he was ready for the resulting derailment.

"Talk to me, Tom," Frank said, his voice quiet.

Tom considered his empty glass, then picked it up. Held it out toward Frank. "This is me."

Frank looked at the glass. "Is this a half-empty, half-full thing?"

"It's a completely-empty-and-has-been-for-a-while thing."

"Tommy."

"You asked."

Frank dipped his chin.

"Don't feel sorry for me," Tom continued. "You could have come back, sure, and I could have left. But I didn't. I chose to stay here because of my mom."

"The same woman who nearly let you die from pneumonia."

"It wasn't that bad."

"You're not the one who had to watch you pass out from coughing. Your lips were blue, Tom. And there was no damn phone in that trailer. None of your neighbors would answer their doors, and I had to pay the super to use his phone to call my dad. I've never been so scared in all my life."

"She kept clean, or as clean as she could, for years after that." Tom kept his voice even. "You know she did."

"But . . ."

Tom let out a sharp sigh. "But about six months after graduation, her boyfriend up and left town." Another man leaving her behind. "She fell sideways and everything started again. She never got any better after that. I spent most of my time at college running back and forth between here and Scranton."

"Then you came home to look after her."

"I did and that was my choice."

No, his mom hadn't been the best provider, but Tom had never had to question the fact that she loved him. He might not have seen her for five or six days, between shifts and drinking binges, but then she'd be in the trailer one afternoon, singing, smoking, burning dinner on the hotplate. There'd be a gift for him. A book, a cassette tape, a pair of sneakers. Always something he'd really wanted, though he could never figure out how she knew. For that single night, he'd be able to pretend that's how it always was, and he had, even when he'd been old enough to understand the idiocy behind the pretense.

She'd never apologized for not being around. Hadn't told him she'd been busy, or that she was working. She'd just been *there, then*, and he'd learned quickly to cherish those evenings, when she'd listen to his stories and encourage him in his hopes and dreams. When she had been a mom and she'd looked at him with bright mom eyes.

"She was never good at taking care of herself," he explained to Frank. "But she managed the rent most of the time, and she let me dream." Was that a stupid thing to say? "So when she slid too far, started getting sick, it felt like it was my turn. She was a crap mom, but she loves me, Frank, and I'm all she has."

Frank acknowledged this with a sober nod.

Tom took a deep breath. "And I couldn't have done any of it without Robert. Madge too, but mostly Robert. So if you want to know why I look like a ghost, well, it's because I just lost a man who was my friend."

His childhood might be a cliché, but Tom hadn't had it that bad. So long as he had a camera in his hand and the ability to use it, life would always be interesting at the very least.

Robert had been the one to put a camera there in the first place.

Tom had been dealing with his mom his whole life. With Robert, he'd never had to deal. Robert had been father, uncle, mentor, and friend all in one, and the hole he'd left in Tom's life couldn't be measured. Not by the current deficit in his checking account. The panic when he considered the immediate future. Definitely not by a single empty glass.

Leaning forward, Frank spoke quietly. "He loved you, Tommy. You were the son he never had."

"Don't—"

"No, it's true. I might not have been around, but Annabelle was and she knew how he felt. Hell, he should have left this place to you."

"Like your dad would have been pleased about that."

"My dad left. He and Mom moved away and they've been up here, what? Maybe twice as often as I have in the past five years?"

"So . . . twice nothing is . . . double nothing?" It was a poor stab, but the wine and full belly were working against him now. Any anger he'd hoped to feel had abandoned him, leaving him spent.

"Something like that," Frank muttered. "They probably figured the same as we all did. Robert had you. And Dad was never interested in this place. He liked having the use of it when we were all young, but he was just as happy to move down to the shore when he retired. Get his little B&B up and running."

Tom tried to shrug, but his shoulders were heavy.

"If this place *was* yours, what would you do with it?" Frank asked.

"Don't ask me that."

"Why not? You're the reason the roof hasn't caved in entirely." Frank frowned thoughtfully. "We need to work out what we're going to do."

"What's to figure? You should sell the lodge and be done with it."

"Is that what you'd do?"

Tom shook his head. "I . . . I don't know, Frank. Today I feel like saying 'Yeah, sure,' because I'm so fucking tired. And if my mom . . .'" He tightened his grip on the glass, feeling as though he had more in common with the stem than the bowl.

"What about your mom?"

"She's . . . I stayed in town last night because she's on oxygen. Another lung infection."

"Jesus fucking Christ, Tom! Why didn't you tell me?"

"I'm telling you now."

Frank stood up and paced the office—which didn't take long. He looked as though he might kick the wall for being so close, then he turned and paced back. Stopped in front of Tom and vibrated in place. "Tell me you have some friends up here. People you can tell all this shit to."

Tom shrugged. "My ex, Sandra. She's one of the nurses at the home."

"Ex...?"

"Girlfriend."

Something complicated passed over Frank's face. Carefully, he sat back on the couch. "Tell me about your mom."

"Can't we be done for tonight? You've got your facts."

"You haven't changed a bit."

"Whatever."

"Please?"

Tom pushed out a sigh, more to show his discomfort than any need to refresh his lungs. "Mom's going to be fine. Probably. She's had lung infections before. It's from not moving around enough. And all the smoking, I guess. Honestly, it's a wonder she's not dead already. I used to daydream about that, you know. About what I'd do after she died. Where I'd go." Briefly, he thought of their notebook and winced. "Made me feel like such a fucking heel." Why was he telling Frank this?

"If you think you're the only person to ever have entertained such fantasies, then I'm sorry to disappoint you. You're a good man, Tom. A good son. You always have been."

Tom ducked his head.

"Play a game with me," Frank said quietly. "If money were no object, what would you do with the lodge? It's yours, free and clear, and someone is willing to invest."

Tom was too tired for this, but Frank's question was just so damn familiar. He did this. He always had. Whenever Tom decided he'd had enough, Frank would challenge him. Ask for more.

Tom looked at the plan on the wall, the rough sketch he'd made three or so years ago, and recalled the discussions he'd had with

Robert—when he'd been able to get Robert to care about what was happening. He thought about the faerie wedding of a couple weeks back, the one relegated to the side of a restaurant. About the ceremony he'd been to that morning and the rigid formality of it. The church, the bland reception center.

Taking a breath, he held it, then decided to share his dream. The true one. What the hell? Maybe Frank would laugh or scoff or finally just give up. "I'd turn it into a wedding venue."

With one pointed finger, Tom indicated the framed sketch. "The barn and stables? I'd turn them into a three-season sort of hall. Where the stalls are, put in an outdoor kitchen and catering area. Turn the barn into a reception hall. See that path leading away from the patio? That'd be where the bride and groom or bride and bride or whoever and whoever would do their thing. There's enough lawn for chairs on either side, and they could get married with a view of the forest, a redone patio area, all trellises and vines, or the restored barn if they wanted something rustic."

If the weather wasn't cooperating, they could put up a tent. Or they could do the ceremony inside. The dining room would make a nice venue, cleaned up and cleared out.

Tom got up, crossed to the sketch, and tapped the guesthouses. "And we could rebuild a couple of these. Maybe three? Make them really nice. Honeymoon suites. Family suites." He drew a circle around the garage. "If we moved that back, we'd have room for them. And the room upstairs? The one with the balcony? That'd be a suite too. 203 is tiny, anyway. Just knock out the wall.

"Then clean up the pool and patio, maybe put a pergola over here. A summer house arrangement behind the new guesthouses, but leave the lawn as it is. The forest as it is. No tennis courts, no horse-back riding. Just weddings and receptions. And in the off-season, wine tastings, dinner and libation series, book clubs, theme weekends. We could think about theming the whole resort to cater to LGBT couples. There's another place up here doing that, and they're way overbooked."

Tom turned to look at Frank, who was being uncharacteristically quiet. "I know. It's a dumb idea. Even Robert knew that. He listened, he humored me, but he also knew no one was coming out to the Poconos just to get married anymore."

"But they are." Frank stood up. "I did a little research this week, and people are coming out here to get married. It's close to New York, it's cheap, but it's still two states away. This area holds the same allure it always did. It's just not the only forest on Manhattan's doorstep anymore."

"So how do we get people to come here instead of wherever else they're going?"

"By offering something unique, but not weird."

"And that would be . . ."

Frank tapped the picture on the wall. "This."

"What?"

"I could see it before you described it to me. The layout, the atmosphere, the focus on happy beginnings. Small events. Instead of catering to the family vacation, we'd do honeymoons, or intimate gatherings. I think you could narrow the focus even more. Skip the B&B customers and weekenders and do all weddings and anniversaries."

"That's not particularly unique."

"Perhaps not, but by limiting the type of function, you not only specialize, but you offer something few other places can—a complete focus. A complete experience. A beautiful setting where everyone feels welcome."

"Would you make it all same sex, maybe? Cater to only that market?"

"I don't know. I mean, is that an issue anymore? Maybe it would be better to be all inclusive, but not . . . I can't believe I'm saying this, too gay."

"How do you mean?"

"For a long time when I pictured my own wedding, I'd always imagine myself thumbing my nose at tradition by getting married in some loud and obnoxious manner. Something overwhelmingly pink and purple and not . . . solemn. Not a groom and groom dressed in tuxes exchanging vows, but a party where people could wear whatever they wanted and where we could truly celebrate the fact that no one cared what gender anyone was."

"That sounds very you." Tom didn't allow his thoughts to wander too far toward the guy Frank would be marrying, but the rest of it? Yeah.

"I've been to that wedding and it was fun. I've been to that wedding half a dozen times. I've also been to the boring, traditional bride-and-groom-wear-white wedding and it was beautiful. I've come to realize that a wedding is what you make of it and . . . I don't even know what I'm trying to say anymore. Maybe we should have some more wine."

"Frank?"

"Mmm?"

They were standing close. As close as two men could without getting either uncomfortable or very comfortable indeed. Tom could smell Frank's cologne and a slight whiff of wine and garlic. He wanted to kiss him again. Take him upstairs and undress him.

"What are we doing here?"

Frank tilted his head. "What do you mean?"

"This." Tom tapped the framed sketch. "Why are we talking about this as though we might actually do it?"

"If I could get it financed, would you be interested?"

"Are you serious?"

"I won't know until I try, but . . . yes. I think I am. I mean, there's a lot to work out and a lot of it depends on you. On whether we could do this together. But I'm ready for something different. I'm not inspired by my work anymore. I want to write something else and I want to do something else. And I have money put aside."

"You . . . You *are* serious about this."

Frank nodded.

Breathing out slowly, Tom took a couple of steps back. He needed some space. Some air not scented with Frank. A gap wide enough to ask the big question. "What if we find we can't work together?"

"I don't think that's the question you want to ask."

Tom tried again. "What if we can't resolve whatever this thing is between us?"

Now that he'd acknowledged it, Tom was consumed by the fear Frank would refute the fact that anything remained of what had once been. That he would leave.

Frank smiled a gentle smile. "You were my best friend, Tommy."

"We barely know each other now."

"That's not true. You can say it, but it's not true."

"Frank—"

"Just hear me out."

"You don't know what you're saying."

Frank held up a hand. "I don't think it will come as a surprise I want more. That I want us to figure out what this . . . this *thing* as you've so eloquently put it . . . is between us. But if we can't, then we'll simply have to be friends."

"How?"

"You're already in here." Frank pressed his palm to his chest. "You always were."

Tom's heart took a long, painful pause. He knew, even before he could spare a thought toward rearranging his face, that his expression had given him away. That Frank knew he felt the same.

The bastard smiled. "We've got some ground to cover, sure. But we'll always have that."

CHAPTER 17

October 1985

With the bell echoing in his ears, Frank pushed himself into the clog of students who were trying to pass through the single open door. A teacher's efforts to wrestle a second door open were impeded by the flow of book bags and elbows. The second door came free, and Frank followed the swell outside, making his way down the line of buses until he reached his.

He hated the bus, especially after having had two older siblings with cars. In a few months, he'd be sixteen and have wheels of his own, God willing.

Climbing the steps, he scanned heads for the familiar dark mop, and stopped when he saw that Tommy wasn't alone. Grace Carleton had wedged herself into the seat next to him. Well, not *wedged*. Though there was more of Grace than most girls. She seemed thrust into the seat next to Tommy in the way a cork stoppered a bottle. Sealed tight and not leaving without a lot of twisting and prying.

And Tommy didn't seem to mind. His head bobbed up and down and his hands flew up over the back of the seat in front of him. He was telling a story. To Grace. A story Frank really wanted to hear, even if he'd already heard it a thousand times. Which he probably had? Unless something had happened today.

"Find a seat already," came a grumble from behind.

Frank moved down the aisle and paused next to Grace. Cleared his throat. She didn't notice him. He threw a silent and desperate plea toward Tommy, but he didn't look up either. Face burning with embarrassment, Frank continued on toward the back of the bus and the only empty seat—the one next to Neil Crook. Neil was weird. He wore big googly glasses and smelled like mothballs. Thankfully, he didn't try to make conversation. Frank might have had to smother him if he did. Anything that distracted him from the back of Tommy the Traitor's head was forbidden.

Why was Tommy sitting with Grace?

On some level, Frank had known this would happen one day; that his infatuation with his best friend was a one-headed beast with only one known direction. Okay . . . so maybe that metaphor didn't quite work. Frank dug into the side pocket of his backpack and pulled out a bag of Twizzlers. He peeled one from the warm and sticky clump and folded it into his mouth. Now wasn't the time to eat it bite by bite, seeing if he could find the hollow space in the center. He simply needed something to chew and swallow and chew again.

His angry chomping finally distracted Neil from the book he was reading: a tattered paperback with a spaceship on the cover. Neil peered at the packet of Twizzlers and licked his lips. Narrowing his eyes, Frank got ready to tell him to piss off when he noticed that Neil's leg was pressed against his, and that Neil's hand was creeping across the back of his book.

He glanced at Neil's face again, right when Neil looked up and sideways. Behind the thick lenses of his glasses, his eyes had an indistinct appearance. Or maybe it only seemed that way because Frank was staring. Frank blinked and Neil's face came into focus. Huh. He'd changed since third grade, which, okay, most people did. His glasses were just as nerdy, but his face had new and interesting angles to it. And he didn't seem to suffer the same rash of acne that infected half the high school.

Frank nudged the Twizzlers packet toward Neil and watched, fascinated, as Neil stretched long fingers toward the licorice. Did long fingers really mean a long dick? Frank had measured his but didn't have anything to compare it to. He *had* spent a lot of time thinking about the length of Tommy's fingers—among other things.

Neil peeled off a Twizzler and lifted it toward his mouth. Frank couldn't stop staring. Neil's lips parted and his tongue poked out again, touching the tip of the red strip. Then his lips closed over only that part and his cheeks hollowed slightly. He was . . . sucking it. People sucked Twizzlers? Apparently Neil Crook did.

Why was he sucking it? Was this a clue? A cue? A hint?

Blood left Frank's brain in a dizzying rush, flowing directly southward. His dick twitched. Frank thought in metaphors until it seemed he had the errant appendage under control. Neil shattered all such illusion by opening his mouth and licking the Twizzler, wrapping his tongue around the end, nibbling, and sucking. A keen built in Frank's chest. A whimper. Maybe a moan? Swallowing, he scrunched the bag of Twizzlers closed and shoved it in the pocket of his backpack, which would remain right where it was in his lap, thank you very much.

The crinkle of plastic drew the attention of the guy across the aisle, who looked over just in time to see Neil thrusting the licorice in and out of his mouth with alarming focus.

"That has got to be the most disturbing thing I have ever seen," he said.

"You and me both," Frank muttered.

Neil's antics were weirdly arousing, but also plain weird. As soon as the bus turned the corner into his neighborhood, Frank got up out of his seat, ignoring the bus driver's instruction to wait until the damn bus had stopped. The urge to growl as he pushed past Tommy and Grace was strong and strange. Walking with a semi-chub was also strange. The bus pulled to a halt and Frank practically leaped down the stairs. He turned toward the end of the street, desperate to get home and to his room where he could think about a few things. Like why his dick was sort of hard and what Neil's tongue might feel—

"Wait up." Tommy fell into step behind him. "Jeez, where's the fire?"

"Probably in Grace's panties."

"What?"

Snorting, Frank lengthened his stride. If he got far enough ahead, Tommy might just wander off. But Tommy caught up and kept pace, panting slightly as he talked. "What's your malfunction? Was it Ms. Hines? Did you get your essay back?"

Frank clamped his mouth shut and walked faster until his heart knocked wildly behind his ribs. An athlete he was not. At least his dick was under control now.

Tommy grabbed his arm. "Frank, stop. Is this about Grace sitting next to me? It was just a bus ride. What's wrong?"

"Neil is a freak is what's wrong."

"You had to sit next to Crooked Neil? Sorry, wow. Okay, I'm going to make it up to you. What do you want?"

"Not Twizzlers."

"But those are your favorite."

Frank stopped, chest heaving. "I may never eat them again."

"Why?"

Unable to explain all the thoughts zipping around his brain, Frank shook his head and pushed through the front gate of his house. Tommy followed. Frank turned a couple of times to tell him to just go home, but the words wouldn't come, and when he reached his second-floor bedroom, he was hot, sweaty, tired, frustrated, horny, and kinda mad.

"Do you like her?" he asked Tommy.

"Who, Grace?"

"No, the other girl squashed into the seat with you."

Tommy narrowed his eyes. "Are you going to make fat jokes? Because if you are, I'm heading out."

"She's not fat." Frank should know. He'd been wearing husky sizes since he was six. "I just . . ." She was a girl. Female. And not Frank. Obviously. And how did you tell your friend you wanted to suck his dick like a Twizzler and—

Whoa, where had that thought come from? The candy bag in his head, obviously.

Frank flopped backward onto his bed, letting his book bag thump to the ground, and stared up at the ceiling until the white no longer looked just white.

"What happened with Neil?"

"I gave him a Twizzler and he sucked on it like it was . . ." Frank gestured toward his crotch.

"Wow."

Frank pushed up to his elbows. Tommy had his desk chair turned sideways so he could sit with his heels up on the desk, ankles crossed. "Are you and Grace going to go out?" Frank asked.

Tommy shrugged. "I dunno. I think she wants to, but . . ." He chewed on his bottom lip. "I don't know if I like her like that."

"Who do you like?"

Letting his head drop back, Tommy groaned. "What, are we twelve? I don't like anyone. Or I like everyone. I don't know. Why are we having this conversation?" His head jerked up and swiveled toward the bed. "Wait, do you like someone?"

Frank shook his head.

"Liar. I can see it all over your face. Your cheeks are red."

"That's because I ran home."

"Nuh-uh. You like someone. Who is it?"

"You're right, this is a stupid conversation. We should do our homework." Or something.

"Is it Neeeiiil?"

Frank felt his mouth drop open. He tried to push some words out, but his tongue got all tangled up. Did Tommy know? No one was supposed to know. Not about Neil, because there was no Neil Crook in any of Frank's fantasies. Before he'd licked the Twizzler, there might have been a little spark of interest. Neil's thigh had felt pretty good pressed against his. But now? No way, Jose. Not happening. Ever.

"Not sure if you're noticed, but Neil's a guy," Frank finally managed, his argument solid, his tone feeble.

"So?"

"Guys aren't supposed to be with guys." According to nearly everything he'd read on the subject—which hadn't been a lot. The local library didn't have any books helpfully titled *Advice for Kids Who Think They Might Be Gay*. Frank tried not to fidget, but couldn't control the reflexive movement of his fingers as he gripped and squeezed the quilt. "It's not normal," he said, spilling the most often repeated fact. "And, you know, there's AIDs."

Tommy's forehead wrinkled. "Two separate issues."

"What makes you say that?"

Tommy touched the tip of his pointer finger. "One, AIDS isn't confined to gay men. It doesn't help that some guys don't want to use condoms or that people hate the idea of gay sex so much they're not willing to help educate people on how to do it safely."

Frank's mouth was edging open again.

Tommy touched his middle finger, "Men have been having sex with men since the dawn of time and the planet hasn't managed to fall out of orbit yet. Even dolphins are doing it."

Dolphins?

Next finger: "People are always scared of what they don't understand."

"That's three issues."

"Not really."

"How do you know about all this stuff?"

"I read." He'd obviously discovered books Frank hadn't.

Tommy dug in his book bag until he found a magazine. It was the August issue of *Time* magazine, the one with the scary cover picture of a magnified AIDs virus destroying healthy cells. Frank had read it when it came out—his dad had a subscription—and he remembered feeling sick for about a week afterward, and wondering whether he could catch the disease just by thinking about having sex with ... Not Tommy. Surely what he felt for Tommy was too pure and lovely to be threatened by such awfulness.

"Why would you read about a gay disease? And why is that in your backpack?"

"I was doing a report on it for biology." Tommy was studying the front of the magazine. He glanced up, his expression unreadable. "And because I wanted to know about it."

But why?

Even unvoiced, the question hung between them—as did a strange and uncomfortable silence. They'd been able to do the quiet thing together for years. Sit side by side, each reading or doodling or daydreaming while the other did whatever. An hour might pass, or only ten minutes, then one of them would say something and it was as though they'd never stopped talking.

Frank looked away first, down at his backpack. The corner of the Twizzler packet poked out of the side pocket, and just the thought of the sweet, strawberry licorice made his stomach flip and fold. Was Tommy reading that magazine because he knew where Frank's interests lay? He would do that. Research and study and prepare. Or was he reading it because he had the same thoughts?

Tommy got up and came over to sit on the bed. He didn't lean in close like he sometimes did and the distance felt all wrong. Frank could hear him swallowing and moving his tongue around as though he was searching for words. Then he spoke, quietly, a tremor in his voice. "I think about guys sometimes. So I wanted to know."

Head snapping up, Frank studied Tommy's profile—at the way his dark shaggy hair brushed over his cheekbone. The shape of his mouth. The line of his neck as his chin dipped forward. Frank's fingers itched with the urge to touch those three points. To see if his skin was warm or cool.

Before he could make such a move, Tommy turned his head slightly, peeking up at him. "I figured you'd be the first to say it, but you never did. So I'm saying it."

"Saying what?"

"I might be gay."

Frank waved his hands in the air. "But what about Grace?"

"What about her? She's nice, Frank. I'd ask her out if I thought she'd say yes."

"Do you actually know what 'gay' means?"

"Homosexual."

"Right and 'homo' is 'same.' Not sure if you noticed, but Grace is a girl."

Tommy rolled his eyes. "So maybe I don't feel gay all the time. Maybe it's just a phase."

Frank sucked in a careful breath. "Do you ever think about me?"

Tommy stiffened. He went to shake his head and stopped. Dipped his chin once. Then faced him with a fierce expression. "Don't even pretend to be surprised, Franklin Tern, because I know you think about me."

Gaping was getting to be a new habit, one Frank did not particularly enjoy. "What, no, I . . . How did you know?" And did this mean they could kiss?

"Because of the way looking at guys makes me feel. I see it in your eyes when you're looking at me sometimes. So I got to wondering."

Frank thought he might choke. On nothing, which would be embarrassing. Boy found dead. Choked on air. "I, ah." This was Tommy and hadn't he been trying to find a way to say this? No, not really, but maybe? "So, I guess I might be gay too." But a different sort of gay to Tommy, because the idea of kissing Grace only made him feel uncomfortable. And a little ill. "So does that mean you want to—"

"No!"

Frank leaned back, hurt by the quick rebuff. "Um . . ."

"I've thought about it."

"Then why can't we? If ever two guys were going to keep a secret, it would be us."

"That's just it, Frankie. Everyone already thinks we're queer for each other."

"They do?"

"You're not in my gym class, so you don't hear the same shit, I guess."

And because of his size, people rarely messed with Frank. He'd used that to protect both of them in junior high, but hadn't realized Tommy was still having a hard time. "Who's saying this? Tell me their names."

"So you can punch them out? No way."

"I'm confused. I mean, okay, if we both think about guys, why can't we try it out? Because if it's true"—if? *Oh, please*—"then we might have a hard time meeting other guys who feel the same we do, or who don't want to tenderize us with their fists first."

Tommy was shaking his head. "It can't be me and you."

Frank might just die. Surely such a statement was designed to kill. "Why not?" Fuck embarrassment. This might be his only chance to know how Tommy's lips would feel against his own. Kissing his hand while he jerked off just wasn't going to cut it after this.

"Because you're my best friend and I already love you. I don't think we should mess with that."

"But if you—"

Tommy put his hand over Frank's mouth. "Don't, Frankie. Please? You're all I have. You know that, right? You're it. My every day and every night. My sun and stars. No one gets me like you do, or loves me like you do. But we have our whole lives ahead of us. We're too young to decide here and now that this is it. Might be the best decision we ever made, but it could also be the end of us, of everything, and I don't want to risk that."

Frank peeled Tommy's hand away but didn't let it go. He threaded their fingers together and was mildly surprised that Tommy let him do it. "If we're already throwing the l-word around, maybe we're past the hard part."

Tommy shook his head. "It's a different love. We're . . . soul mates or whatever. Sex doesn't work like that." His expression darkened. "It's another love and it fades."

Frank rarely mulled over the fact Tommy didn't have a father, but as he sat there, fingers entwined with those of the only person he thought he could ever love for the entirety of his life—a person who said they couldn't possibly be what he wanted them to be—he felt a surge of anger. The camo shirt and rucksack he understood. The Aztec-warrior thing. The secret billionaire who was waiting until Tommy turned twenty-one to introduce him to his empire. The rock singer who'd forgotten he'd stopped by Pennsylvania on the way to somewhere, anywhere. The astronaut who'd had higher ambitions. The professor, the chef, the movie star. He'd been through every iteration with Tommy until it had become a sort of game. But this . . . Right now, he hated Tommy's father, whoever he was.

It hurt to pull his fingers from Tommy's. To disentangle two hands that should be forever joined. But whatever Tommy's thoughts on love, Frank had his own ideas. He wrapped his arm around his best friend's narrow shoulders and tugged him close. Tommy unbent slowly until they inclined together in a comfortable, familiar slump.

Words revolved around Frank's head. A few even teased his tongue. But in the end, he swallowed them. He didn't want to mess this up . . . and besides, this was where it was at. Just this. And if this was all he could get, then it would have to be good enough.

CHAPTER 18

Present Day

T he crunch of gravel distracted Frank from a stream of mindless crap. How had he ever been invested in Twitter? Why did he even have an account? At some point, it had no doubt seemed important, but lately—since his return from Puerto Rico, his reunion with Tom—social media felt utterly frivolous. They said it took ten days to break a habit. The fact he hadn't tried to align any of the frames on the red wall behind the ratty couch in his uncle's office . . . the fact he was still here in Pennsylvania, proved he'd done more than break a single habit over the past few weeks.

He could use the excuse of having to go through his uncle's stuff for his lack of attention to neatness, order, and the future of his career. Sadly, that exercise hadn't taken more than a day. The boxes in the basement had contained an assortment of lawn toys, pool equipment, and the games and books that used to fill the shelves in the lounge. Otherwise, Robert had pared down his existence to an alarming degree after Madge had died. All that remained of him was the house, a misaligned collection of framed photos and prints, and the clothing hanging in his wardrobe.

Of course, the house was all Robert. Every stick of furniture, every coat of paint. And Frank was still here for something other than a collection of old stuff. He was here for Tom, which should have been obvious to both of them. Was obvious. But Tom was Tom and Tom deflected. Frank persisted. It made for an intense working relationship and that was what counted right now.

Keep telling yourself that, Frankie.

Telling himself this was what he wanted, this *project*, felt better. Truer.

Content with that, Frank slipped his phone into a pocket, stood, and stretched, bending toward the window as he did so. His eyebrows did a little stretch of their own as he recognized the car outside the lodge. Tucking in his shirt, he bent the other direction to check his reflection in the glass covering one of the prints. The glass wasn't much of a mirror, showing only a shadowy outline of his hair and shoulders. Frank fiddled with the shortened curls at his temples anyway, putting off the moment when he'd have to greet a person he simultaneously did and did not want to see.

By the time Frank made it outside, the visitor was leaning against the side of his car, arms folded, ankles crossed. The pose was one of relaxed nonchalance. Brian Kenway usually waited for the world to come to him, rather than deign to visit the world.

What had Simon ever seen in him?

That, Frank. Exactly that.

"Well look what the cat dragged up the mountain and left by the roadside," Frank said, stepping out of the shade of the porch. There was no sign of Tom. He'd shot another wedding that morning and was probably still in the cellar working on albums. For the moment, that suited Frank quite well.

"And what are you? The specimen left here last week? Last month?" Brian pushed away from the side of his car and met Frank halfway across the drive. He extended a hand and Frank took it. The shake was brief, barely cordial, and completely undermined by Brian's wide smile. "You don't seem pleased to see me," he said.

"Actually, I'm mostly surprised. I only spoke to Simon last week."

"So he mentioned when I was there yesterday."

"You were visiting Simon?"

"Why wouldn't I? We're in business together."

"You *were* in business together. He's working with someone else now." And sleeping with someone else, thank God.

Brian made a dismissive sound. "We still have a few projects in common. So, what's up with this place? It's a nice parcel of land."

"Why are you here?"

"Did you know your frowny face is an almost exact replica of Simon's?"

Frank hadn't known he was frowning. Now, however, he felt the wrinkles in his forehead deepening—and that annoyed him further because he'd always been the crayon version of Brian Kenway. Not quite as tall, not as attractively blond—the fact he'd been coloring his hair for years not withstanding—not as interestingly featured, and definitely not as charismatic.

"Simon and I have been friends for a long time."

A crease appeared between Brian's eyebrows. "Why do you dislike me so much?"

Because you broke Simon's heart. Not once, not twice, but at least once a year for the entire twelve you were together. "Not everyone is susceptible to your charms."

Brian waved a hand between them as though clearing the air. "Why don't we talk about the decrepit pile of stone behind you?"

Clenching his jaw, Frank turned to look at the . . . decrepit pile of stone. "Oh dear." He'd become quite used to the air of neglect. Seeing the lodge through Brian's eyes, he had to wonder if he and Tom had taken leave of their senses.

For the past week, they'd been sketching, researching, outlining, and planning. It had been stimulating work—and not only because of the time spent with Tom. Through this shared vision, they were rebuilding their friendship, and though Frank still wanted Tom with every cell of his being—his bathroom reeked of misspent semen—he'd willingly admit that they needed this. Needed time to just be together. They were relearning each other's quirks and becoming accustomed to each other's routines. So much had changed. So much hadn't. Like the lodge, their relationship needed a lot of work.

Frank considered the old building, which wasn't flattered by the midday sun. Morning began on the other side of the main house, only traveling around to the front by late afternoon. One might believe the original house had been planned that way so that arriving visitors would see the lodge lit up by the more golden light of afternoon, while guests were able to enjoy noon sunshine in the patio and pool areas. Now, the place simply looked much as it was: forlorn, forgotten, finished.

"It has seen better days," Frank said quietly.

"You're planning to knock it down, right?"

"What? No."

Brian frowned. "This is a great area for development. You could fit half a dozen nice houses here and quadruple any investment. Where are the boundaries? Is there much of a slope to the back lawn?"

"We don't want to knock it down."

"'We'?" Brian arched a single eyebrow. His mouth quirked at a matching, sardonic angle.

Frank's internal temperature rose by ten degrees. "Simon told you about Tom."

"He didn't mean to. Charlie was the one who mentioned him, and Simon picked up the slack."

"Charlie mentioned him? Wonderful. Terrific. My teenage love life is now the hot news item in Bethlehem."

"Don't we think a lot of ourselves?"

"I cannot believe he told Charlie what I shared with him in the strictest confidence." Actually, Frank could believe it. Simon might still be the soul of discretion when it counted, but when it came to Charlie, he had no secrets. They were just so damned couple-y.

Brian smiled. "He did look a mite uncomfortable, but you know what?"

"Oh, please enlighten me."

"I should have guessed."

"Guessed what?"

"You have just about everyone fooled. Simon most of all. But you're not what you pretend to be."

Frank opened and closed his mouth. Drew his eyebrows together. "You might as well be speaking Greek."

"You play at being the party boy, Franklin Tern. The out-and-proud journalist, posing for photographs with the sort of people most of us would give our left nut to meet. How many times have you been in Fairground?"

"You read *Vanity Fair*?"

"At the doctor's office."

"What is your point?"

"I've hooked up with some of your supposed lovers, Frank"—of course he had—"and you're just friends with all of them. In fact, there's a rumor about you."

"One I haven't heard?" His cheeks were not heating. The day had simply grown warmer, that was all.

Brian seemed poised to deliver his punch line and then he stopped. Refocused. Sorted his expression from cattiest to most genial. Frank turned, and yes, Tom had finally made it upstairs and was skipping down the steps from the front porch.

Dressed in his usual, casual manner—jeans and a T-shirt, flip-flops today instead of boots—Tom appeared lighter than he had the week before. That ghost-like quality continued to glimmer around him, but he seemed to step less carefully—in some respects. Tom was definitely here, with him, but the man still had secrets. Sometimes he looked so afraid. Frank didn't know how to ask why.

Extracting a hand from his jeans pocket, Tom extended it toward Brian. Lord, he was beautiful. All that dark, floppy hair. The silver threads could be highlights. Big, expressive eyes. A smile that was not quite tentative. "A friend of Frank's?" he asked.

"I'm Brian, and I suppose you could say that." Brian gave Frank a sideways smile, reminding him that they had been friends, once, even if the only thing they'd ever had in common was Simon. "You must be Tom."

Tom glanced at Frank as if asking for a cue.

"Brian works with Simon. My friend from Bethlehem."

"Oh, *that* Brian." Tom's dark eyebrows did a little dance.

Brian had the grace to look uncomfortable, but couldn't let a touch go without a riposte. "I see I'm not the only one who talks."

"Simon mentioned our plans for the lodge," Frank said, ignoring Brian's jab, "and Brian came to see the project."

"That's great!" The enthusiasm lighting Tom's face was heartbreaking. For all Frank wanted their venture to succeed, was prepared to invest in it—time and money—he didn't actually know if they could pull it off. "What can I show you?"

Tom was already walking back toward the lodge. Brian glanced at Frank, his expression so damned smug, Frank wanted to slap him. He snarled instead. Silently, pettily. And then fought the rising tide of embarrassment all the way to the front door.

Tom led the way inside, talking and gesturing. "We'd keep the entry way pretty much as it is, I think. The dimensions are good and with the window over the stairs at the back and above the foyer"— he indicated the large window set over the front door—"light isn't an issue. However we decide to decorate the place, this area works." He showed Brian a bashful smile. "Well, I'm no architect, but I think it does."

"I'm not an architect either. That's Simon's department. But I can see what you're saying. It's a good space. What's through here?" Brian indicated the archway leading toward the guest lounge.

Now that Tom was showing him around, Brian wanted to see the place? What the fuck? He'd been one step away from calling for demolition services when he arrived.

"This area I'm not sure about," Tom said. "Frank and I have discussed keeping it as it is, lounge and dining room, or maybe making it one larger space, like a great room. Advantages and disadvantages to both. One big space would be great for receptions, weddings, events. But would it still feel intimate enough for a smaller party? The wedding I shot this morning was only about thirty-five people. Really close-knit group. They'd have been lost in a space as big as all that."

Brian stood in the connecting doorway between the dining and lounge and looked back and forth. "I see what you mean." His forehead wrinkled, and he seemed to consider his next question before sharing it. "Have you thought about adding more outdoor space instead?"

Tom's expression shifted from bright to radiant as he gestured in the direction of the kitchen. "Let me show you the barn."

Not wanting to be left behind, Frank led the way. He noticed the smell as soon as he stepped outside the kitchen door. Not mold. Something sharper, like rotting meat or rancid garbage. He glanced at the cans lined up behind the garage, then back at the kitchen, seeing nothing amiss.

Behind him, Brian wrinkled his forehead and Tom stopped to do the same check as Frank. Kitchen, garage, garbage cans. "What is that smell?"

"Probably the leftovers from your attempt to cook last night," Frank quipped.

Mock scowling, Tom continued toward the patio.

Frank and Brian followed, and the fetid odor thickened.

"Any dead bodies you want to tell me about?" Brian asked.

"No." Tom was quiet, thoughtful, and then he strode to the edge of the empty swimming pool. Shock rippled across his face as he jerked back, covering his nose and mouth. He waved Frank and Brian away, saying something behind his palm.

"What is it?" Ignoring the wave, Frank approached the pool. The stink of rot was so heavy by the time he reached the edge, he could almost lean against it. He glanced toward the deep end, at the drifts of mulching leaves, small branches, and pile of fur and pink and . . . "Oh God."

Brian stalked toward the edge and leaned forward a little. "Are those raccoons?"

Not anymore.

Trying not to gag, Frank asked, "Could they have fallen in? Does that happen often?"

Tom shook his head and dropped his hand away from his mouth. "I'm going to go get some garbage bags." He disappeared in the direction of the laundry.

"Something or someone killed those raccoons and threw them into the pool," Brian said.

Frank nodded. He'd flirted with the same theory, in between trying to imagine how a corpse (or several) could bloat and explode without them noticing the smell long before this. "Kids, probably."

"I wonder if Patricia Nolan had anything to do with it," Tom said, returning with gloves and a wad of heavy black plastic.

"The woman from the Tinden Group?" Frank asked.

Brian's eyebrows rose. "They can play dirty, but isn't this a little juvenile?"

Tom shook his head, the gesture more thoughtful than outright denial. "She stopped to leave another business card about a week and a half ago. Had someone in the car with her. I was upstairs"—were Tom's cheeks reddening?—"and saw her through a window. I didn't feel like answering the door, so I just watched as she got out, knocked, left a card, and got back in the car. It was the same day that kid crossed the back lawn. They ran off when my cell phone rang."

"You think it's all connected?" Frank looked from the pool to the forest and back again.

"I don't know."

Frank blew out a breath. "Well, a few dead raccoons aren't going to put me off."

Tom held out the bags and gloves. "You want to clean them up, then, while I show Brian the barn?" His mouth was slanted in some sort of amused smirk, and Frank could feel the challenge in his gaze.

He snatched the bags and gloves. "If I die down there, please bury me in something other than black plastic. And not with the raccoons."

Laughing, Tom skipped back a step, then cocked his head at Brian. "C'mon."

"What? No, I want to watch Franklin Tern pick up dead animals."

Frank growled, and this time, he meant it.

Frank did not vomit, though he came close enough that he felt as though he'd earned every calorie that would pass his lips later that evening. And every ounce of wine.

After double bagging the ... remains, Frank stripped off his gloves and bagged them as well. He considered trashing his entire outfit, but decided a run through the laundry could delay that decision. Also, he wanted a shower. By the time he was cleaned up, Tom and Brian were sitting at the kitchen counter, chatting like old friends.

Tom glanced up as he entered and gave him a bright smile. "You survived!"

"Miracles will never cease."

Tom slid off his stool and hovered in front of Frank, looking for all the world as though he wanted to hug him.

Frank took a step back, half convinced he still smelled of rotting roadkill, the balance of his feelings centered around the fact Brian was regarding him and Tom with altogether too much interest. "Can I offer you something to drink, Brian? Water? Wine? Drano?"

"I'm going to go get our sketches," Tom said. "Don't kill him until after I get back?"

"Wouldn't dream of it."

Smiling, Tom slipped out of the kitchen.

Frank turned to Brian. "So, what do you think?"

"I think you're the saddest sack of testosterone ever to have drawn breath."

"Not following."

Brian hooked a thumb toward the door. "You're not sleeping with him, are you?"

"I would rather talk about the lodge."

"You know, I got why you never liked me. You saw through my bullshit pretty early on. What I never understood was why you didn't tell Simon what was going on. I guessed it was that you didn't want to be the messenger, but it still made no sense because I was convinced, one hundred percent, that your distaste for me was directly in proportion to your crush on Simon. I knew there was someone. A reason why none of your 'affairs'"—he made air quotes—"stuck. Why you bothered with the farce was a mystery, but again, I figured it was Simon. Always Simon."

"I wasn't jealous of you." Not a total lie. "I just didn't like the way you treated my friend. He was in love with you."

"And I loved him."

"And about a dozen other men at the same time."

"It wasn't like that."

"I don't care what it was like and I don't need any more of your insights, Brian. Stay out of my life." *And my head.*

"You're one sorry bastard, Frankie."

The nickname took a sour turn on Brian's tongue. The odd thing was, Frank could see Brian didn't mean it that way. In fact, if Frank thought about it, he might have been flattered that Brian was so invested in his . . . whatever this was. But at the moment, it felt like interference with a somewhat malicious intent.

"Did you come out here with the express purpose of insulting me?"

"No, I actually came to look at the property. As a favor to Simon, and to you."

"Why?"

"Because you're right. I'm an asshole."

"I never said—"

"You did, once. We were at a party, maybe four years ago—"

"Brian."

"Being able to work with Simon again is a gift. I won't say I owe him, owed him, but . . ." Brian sighed. "He asked me to come out here and so here I am."

Frank's thoughts stuttered, but he managed a quiet "Thank you."

"That's it?"

"I can be nice." Uncomfortable with the direction their conversation had taken, Frank started to move away.

Brian grasped Frank's upper arm, gently. "Listen, all asshole-ish-ness aside, I get it, okay. I don't know the whole story. Like I said, I always wondered who you were saving yourself for. I knew you weren't as easy as you made yourself out to be and it niggled at me. Maybe because I'm the easy one. Can't turn down—"

"You make a move on him and—"

"This time last year, I'd have done it. Now? I'm going to whup your ass if you don't."

"I cannot believe you are advising me on my love life." Frank tugged his arm, disengaging Brian's fingers. "But I'll take your suggestion under advisement." And not only because it aligned somewhat with his own plans.

Brian stood back and smiled, and for perhaps the first time in the fourteen or so years Frank had known him, there was no calculation in the curve of his mouth or in the gleam of his eyes.

Frank cleared his throat. "What can I get you to drink?"

Brian's smile widened. "Anything but Drano."

CHAPTER 19

For two weeks, Tom had been splitting his nights between a sleeping bag on the floor of the empty cottage where he kept his stuff, and the back seat of his car—which had been convenient to his mom for a few days, but once they'd released her to her room, it was just him sleeping with his pride. Leaning in the doorway of the office, he eyed the sofa with a pang of homesickness. Might not be much of a step up, but he could stretch his legs out all the way and it wasn't the freaking floor.

He was tired, sore, and needed a shower.

"Ready to go?" Frank turned away from the fancy laptop he had set up on the desk.

Lifting his shoulder from the edge of the doorway, Tom said, "I need a shower. Water tank at my place is on the fritz."

"Sure. Take your time." Frank held up his phone. "I've got a rough itinerary set up." He smiled. "I'm trying to see if any of the resorts we want to visit have a wedding planned. You'll be doing your usual Saturday thing."

Snorting, Tom left Frank to his plans and went to shower in Robert's bathroom. On the way back through the bedroom he eyed Robert's bed. A heavy dragging fatigue pulled him toward the edge, where he sat, smoothing his hand over the soft duvet cover. He'd been avoiding this part of the room—avoiding memories of the morning he'd found Robert. Robert's body. Ten o'clock had come and gone without Robert drifting into the office to grumble at the Keurig. He hadn't answered a polite knock at his door, not a call or a steady banging, and Tom had known he was gone the moment he opened the door and saw Robert's outline under the sheets—still, lifeless, and not peaceful. Just . . . empty.

He'd stood there for ten full minutes, not in and not out of the room, hovering in the doorway, trapped by the same fatigue that had him sitting here now. A need to not deal with whatever lay in front of him.

Scuffing footsteps drew his attention forward, back to the present and over to the door. Frank stood there, arms folded, expression solemn. "How's your mom?"

"Good. Getting better every day." And her improved health had come with a steady increase in messages from Mountain Manor. They were texting him now.

He should tell Frank he had nowhere else to stay. And maybe ask for a paycheck while he was at it. If he kept putting it off, Frank might think Tom was stringing him along for just that: money and a roof over his head—and rebuilding their friendship, angling toward *more*, was worth twice that. Being here with Frank, planning for a something he'd only ever considered a dream, was the only thing keeping him going right now—when he could balance it against the fear that Frank would decide this was all too hard.

That Frank wasn't going to stay this time.

Stop.

Tom put his hands to either side of him, flat against the quilt and pressed down. He'd visit the bank on Monday. Organize another loan. He had options. There were always options.

Gritting his teeth, Tom pushed up off the side of the bed.

"If you want to hang out today instead, we can do that," Frank said. "Try another swim. Talk about Robert?" The last was offered tentatively.

Tom forced a smile. "No, it's fine. I'm eager to check out the competition." Their supposed competition. "C'mon, we're wasting daylight."

"It's summer. Plenty of daylight to be had."

From the doorway, Tom cast a last quick look over his shoulder at the bed. Maybe he'd sneak in here tonight, get some proper rest. He'd need it if he was going to keep spending long June days with Frank.

Frank offered to drive. He'd finally collected his "precious" from the body shop, and Tom couldn't help his grin as he took in the softly gleaming black paint and sleek contours. It didn't surprise him that the car was twenty years old. Frank might like nice things, but once he had them, he kept them.

Frank turned the keys and depressed the accelerator gently. The BMW responded with a smooth purr. "All is right with the world again."

As they drove north, heading through the hills to the first resort on their list, Frank briefly outlined the history of his car. "I bought it with my first substantial pay check as a journalist. Well, made a down payment, anyway. I'd just been given a regular column and had sold my biggest story." His smile was boyish. "It was the best week of my life."

"And then you started winning awards. Getting spots on TV. Rubbing elbows with famous people."

"That was all quite some time after that."

"Are you really bored with it all?"

Frank tilted his head and shrugged. "I don't know if 'bored' is the right word. 'Jaded' might be better. 'Tired'? I started out looking for people to highlight, for the people who didn't have a name yet, but who should. That's how I made my name. I'm not sure when everything changed." He glanced over. "Life is like that, isn't it? One minute you're writing about a kid who invented a fabulous gizmo, the next you're writing puff pieces about people who don't need any more air up their asses, because no one wants to hear about new and interesting things anymore.

"Take this piece I was supposed to do in Puerto Rico. There are several billionaires down there throwing money at worthy causes, and a handful of other people just giving themselves. I went down to do a story on a woman who wants to help revolutionize electricity generation. Sadly, it's a clean slate down there. I never even got to meet her, because I couldn't get transport to the other side of the island. The most recent storm wasn't devastating in the manner of a hurricane, but to a country already picked apart and thrown back together, it might as well have been. So, I tried to cover that and . . ." His hands tightened on the wheel. "I discovered something I am not good at."

Tom swallowed his immediate desire to tease. He'd read the story Frank posted from Puerto Rico, and it had *not* been Frank's usual thing. The situation, the thinly veiled horror behind Frank's words, and that deeper tone. The sense of futility and worthlessness. Tom had supposed he'd imagined it until now. That maybe Frank had been trying for something he couldn't quite capture, because normally he wrote lighter pieces. Not fluff, but his interviews and perspectives always carried a tone of optimism. Joy, even. As though he felt privileged to have met the person he'd spoken to, and to have the opportunity to share their story.

"Could you go down again?"

Frank shrugged. "If I wanted to interview a billionaire, I could get a ticket tomorrow. If I wanted to cover an actor doling out smiles, I'd have several magazines bidding for the story."

"Have you tried contacting her directly?" Tom asked. He needn't have. He already knew the answer. Frank might project a carefree and somewhat frivolous manner, especially in the company of those who knew only that side of him, but he'd always been a deeply conscientious person.

"We've exchanged emails. Someone else is down there now, wading hip-deep through mud with her."

"Oh. I'm sorry, Frank."

"Don't be. It was too real for me."

Tom shook his head. "Don't say that. It just wasn't your kind of story, that's all."

"I have more frequent flyer miles than I'll ever get to spend, and all I want to do is stay home." Frank glanced over, the look in his eyes not insignificant. "I want to tell smaller stories again."

"Then that's what you should do."

Frank turned his attention back to the road. They were passing through the almost nonexistent township of Middle Smithfield. A supermarket, a tattoo parlor, take-out Chinese and pizza, a gas station, and a bar. "That's not the same supermarket you threw up in, is it?" he asked.

"Seriously? You haven't been along here in thirty years and that's what you remember?" As a change of subject, it was . . . It'd do.

"It's not every day you get to witness such a spectacular hurl."

Grinning, Tom ducked his head. "I'm going to say it was your fault. You bet I couldn't eat eight popsicles in a row, didn't you?"

"No, that was Matty." Frank's older brother. "And when you started saying you were going to be sick, he pulled in here so fast he nearly left his transmission out on Milford Road. Were we on our way home from Smithfield Beach?"

"Something like that. I could have just hung my head out the window."

"I seem to remember he was worried about his paint job."

Tom laughed. "God. My stomach's cramping just thinking about it."

"You gave a whole new meaning to the phrase 'taste the rainbow.'"

"Pretty sure no one was using that line back then."

The rest of the drive out to the first resort passed in a blur of similar memories: the time Frank had broken the plumbing at the Arby's, the time Tom had thrown up in gym class, the three or so fights they'd been involved in on the bus—the ones that ended with blood—and the time Tom had thrown up in the creek.

"I vomited a lot."

"It was weird, because you never ate enough. Still don't." Frank poked him in the ribs.

"I guess I had a nervous stomach."

"Heh. Okay, we should be close."

"Yeah, it's up on the left. I shot a wedding here about eight years ago. I think they've renovated since then."

Frank's eyes narrowed as he read the signs flanking either side of the resort driveway. "Did we slip through an interdimensional rift to Las Vegas?"

"I did mention it was all casino consortiums and water parks, didn't I?"

"I thought you were exaggerating."

"Not so much."

The Pocono Haven Resort had been renovated, and the new buildings were large and showy. Behind them, the old resort hotel brooded like a resentful cousin. Some effort had been made to bring it in line with the updated buildings, but paint couldn't hide architecture.

Frank parked in the sprawling lot beside the main building and they got out, stretching their legs. It hadn't been a long drive, but the Z3 was small, even for Tom.

"Want to wander around, or . . .?" Tom waved in the direction of the older part of the resort.

Frank nodded his head toward the main building. "Let's start there."

Once inside, Frank walked right up to the reception desk. A well-groomed woman greeted them with a friendly expression. "Good morning and welcome to the Pocono Haven Resort. What can I assist you with today?"

Frank grabbed Tom's hand and put on a brilliant smile. "My fiancé and I are up this weekend checking out wedding venues. I wondered if someone could give us a quick tour? And maybe a peek at one of the rooms?"

"Of course! Let me see who is available to show you around."

Tom spent about three seconds trying to figure out how to be a fiancé before simply "relaxing" into the stiff posture he was used to. Frank pretended to ignore him. A few moments later, a happy-looking guy dressed in a shiny suit walked up.

"Welcome to . . . Oh my God, Tom?"

"Riley?"

Riley reached for Tom's arm and wrapped his fingers around the biceps, squeezing gently. "I heard about Robert. I'm so sorry. How are you holding up?"

"Ah . . . Frank, this is Riley Blum. He used to work at Bossen Hill." About ten years ago. He'd . . . grown up. "Riley, this is Frank. Robert's nephew."

Riley glanced down at their joined hands, forehead wrinkling as his eyebrows jumped up. Tom had to try really, really hard not to extract his hand from Frank's warm grip.

Riley moved his hand to theirs, making what should have been an awkward, three-way shake sort-of thing. "Frank. So lovely to meet you. I don't know whether to express my condolences or congratulations first. Robert was a wonderful man."

Frank turned his hand, opening his fingers, until he escaped the pile of palms. Then he took Riley's hand in his and gave it a squeeze. "Thank you. It's nice of you to remember Robert."

"So when's the happy day?" Riley asked.

"We're thinking fall," Frank said, giving Tom a sappy smile.

Tom shoved his hands into his pockets, hoping to avoid any more holding and squeezing.

"Well, if it couldn't be me . . ." Riley all but sang.

Frank looked between them, one eyebrow arched.

"Oh, I was apparently too young for him," Riley said, interpreting the question. "Besides, he was on his girl kick around then. Sandra, was it? You were with her after Gerry, right?"

"Gerry, as in Sarah Street Grill Gerry?" Frank asked. "With the hot wings?"

Riley answered with a rapid chin bob. "Aren't they the best? No one makes a better sauce than Gerry."

If there'd been a background to fade into, Tom would have done it, even if it meant giving up his skin.

Frank shot him a gleeful smile. "I had a feeling about Gerry."

"Did you now?"

"Mm-hmm."

"Well, let me show you folks around!" Riley said.

They started their tour at the chapel (a little gaudy with all the marble and gold), moved on to the gardens (well maintained, but not particularly interesting), and then the reception areas—which, to be fair, were large and bland enough to carry any theme. Still, undecorated as the larger dining room was right then, it had the feeling of a ski lodge in the summertime: empty. Tom took pictures from every angle while Frank made notes—of how the tables and chairs could be arranged, the dimensions of the space, the proximity to the kitchens, the small stage against the far wall and, overhead, the lighting arrangement that could turn the room from anything into a romantic space for fifty to a dance club for an intimate hundred.

Lighting. Jeez. They hadn't even considered lighting.

Next were the rooms.

Riley opened a rather ordinary door on the ground floor of a rather ordinary building—white stucco with new columns to match the fancier building fronting the resort—and said, "This is our most popular room. We call it the Love Bubble Suite."

An immediate impression of "red" had Tom not so surreptitiously searching for a body. Red carpet, red curtains, a red sofa, and two chairs flanking a fireplace surrounded in brass. A crimson stripe followed the wall around to the bed, which was red and very, very round and set against a red accent wall. Before he could pass comment on the complementary color scheme, however, his gaze fell on the champagne glass. The freaking huge champagne glass set between two of the columns.

Next to him, Frank snickered and tugged on his hand. "Tom, look! A champagne-glass hot tub! I always wanted to fuck in one of these. It's my ultimate wedding fantasy come true."

Tom sucked in a breath and coughed. How was this even here? No one could live in the Poconos and not know about the tall champagne-glass hot tubs, but the fact they were real seemed a little ... unreal. The fact the place had been renovated, with someone making a decision to keep the glasses was more unreal.

Frank was under the glass now, pushing at the stem. "Oh, quite sturdy." He turned to glance at Riley. "Has one of these ever collapsed?"

"Not to my knowledge."

Frank was still grinning when he faced Tom. "How I love a challenge."

All Tom could think about was how unattractive his ass—anyone's ass—would look pressed up against the clear Perspex. And how many happy couples had done the deed inside the bowl. "So not happening."

"Aw, don't be like that." Frank pouted.

Riley looked charmed.

Ignoring them both, Tom toured the rest of the room. It was all red. Even the other tub. And the pool.

Frank met him in the bathroom. "If I know you, and I like to think I do, you're thinking there are three too many places for semen to collect in this room."

"I'm not a complete germaphobe, but there are three tubs in this place. Why three?"

"Because people love to fuck in water," Riley said, joining them. "Not my thing." He shuddered. "Lube and water, well ..."

Frank laughed.

"So what do you guys think? Do you want to see any of the other suites?"

"This gives us enough of an idea," Tom said. "Thanks, Riley."

"Sure, and if you decide to book, give me a call and I'll put a package together for you. As a friend."

They all shook hands with Riley trying to do the three-way clasp again—would his "package" include a similar option?—and then they were in the car, Tom working to stow his camera bags somewhere sensible, Frank's hands stuffed with brochures.

"You know when you hear about something, but you don't think it's actually a thing?" Tom asked.

Frank gave a dry chuckle. "I'm familiar with the process, yes."

"Seriously, those champagne-glass hot tubs. How are they still around?"

"What, you're not considering them for the Bossen Hill remodel?"

Tom shuddered. "No. And if I ever start to sound like I might? Drown me."

"Noted. Okay, what's next?"

"There's another resort just a little ways north of here."

"Is it going to be this same badly stitched quilt of past and present?"

"It was only built about ten years ago."

"Good, a modern comparison, then."

The newer resort was closed—as in shut down and boarded up behind overgrown walkways. "Holy shit, when did this happen?" Tom wondered aloud. "I drove up this way about six months ago to hike a section of the McDade Trail and this resort was open. They had snow tubing over there and ice skating on the pond."

"A last hurrah, perhaps," Frank mused.

"This is just depressing."

"In one way, yes. But in another, I can already see that there's a place for what we want to do. These resorts are large and gimmicky. Bossen Hill was never like that."

Tom could feel his eyebrows drawing together. He pushed his fingers into the crease between them in the hope of massaging away the beginning of a headache, or the deepening of his fatigue. "Shawnee is up next." He indicated the intersection at the top end of the abandoned resort. "Turn here. We can follow River Road back down toward the Water Gap."

The Shawnee Inn and the Skytop Lodge would be perhaps the stiffest competition to their plans. Shawnee all the more so because of its proximity to the interstate. It was a traditional inn that hadn't forgotten its roots, despite several renovations. The grounds were extensive, including river frontage and a championship golf course, which their guide pointed out several times from available windows. No champagne-glass hot tubs, but the rooms were nice, if a little bland.

Back in the car, Tom wrestled with his camera bags while Frank shuffled another batch of glossy brochures.

"It's a beautiful resort," Frank said.

"You haven't seen Skytop yet."

"I looked over their website. We'll have something neither Shawnee nor Skytop do, though."

"The pleasant aroma of mold and rancid raccoon?"

"I'm sure they've had a dead rodent or two behind their kitchens." Frank waved such thoughts away. "No, we're going to have intimacy. We won't be hosting golf tournaments and regattas. We'll be all about weddings."

Tom glanced over at Frank's profile and allowed himself to imagine—just for a minute—doing this tour for real. If he'd been able to . . . If he hadn't ripped Frank out of his life all those years ago, would they be married by now? Or would time have pulled them apart strand by strand?

How did you know when you'd found The One?

Was there such a concept? One single person who meant everything, who defined words such as *meaning*. A golden standard against whom all others paled. And what about second chances?

The past two weeks had been soft and hard. Every minute in Frank's company dissolved every objection Tom had had to . . . spending every minute in Frank's company. But though Frank sent a lot of long, lingering looks in his direction, touched him when he could, cooked for him, encouraged him to dream beyond conceivable boundaries just so they'd know what they could work toward, he had yet to make a move. To lean in and kiss him.

Did Tom's prickly shield serve as a deflector, or had Frank found a way to ignore the tension crackling between them?

Maybe he was simply waiting for Tom to make an invitation. What Tom couldn't figure out was whether he should. He wanted to. More and more each day. But if they couldn't figure out how to save the lodge, would Frank up and leave him behind?

The world wasn't as large as it used to be, though. Jersey City not so distant.

Tom swallowed and looked away, as he almost always did when long moments of silence settled between them. Even when Frank wasn't facing him.

How long could they string this out?

When did love fade?

Was that what this was?

If only he wasn't so tired.

CHAPTER 20

Tom started snoring three minutes after they left the Shawnee Inn. One minute he was giving directions, the next he fell silent. Then a soft snuffle drifted over from his side of the car. Frank glanced over and then turned his attention back to the road. Where it would stay, damn it, lest he wreck his car again. Having it fixed this once had been a miracle—and his insurance record was forever shot.

Of course, if he changed his primary residence to Pennsylvania, his premium would decrease.

He glanced over once more, quickly admiring the line of Tom's neck as he reclined back against the seat. His profile, turned slightly toward Frank. His sharp eyebrows, serious nose, and straight mouth. His skin was still darker than Frank's—not that age would wash him out—but a pallor existed beneath the perpetual tan that hadn't been there before. Had he not slept all week?

When he paid attention to the road again, Frank noted that he'd missed the turn off for East Stroudsburg and was about to pass under the interstate. A welcome center had been constructed on the left, enticing visitors who crossed the bridge into Pennsylvania to stop in for maps, refreshments, and a bathroom break. Frank drove past, following the river until he found himself in the small township of Delaware Water Gap.

Surprisingly, it hadn't changed—much. The park was still there, the old trolley. The diner had a neighbor, a farm stand/restaurant arrangement advertising fresh pie daily. The road dipped through the village, past the two inns, both popular with hikers on the Appalachian Trail, and Frank took the next right, following another memory up the hill toward the country club. Halfway up the steep incline, he turned into the parking lot for Lenape Lake, and slowed his vehicle to a crawl to account for the uneven pavement.

Being a Saturday afternoon, the lot was full. Hikers were coming and going, sweaty from the trail, sweaty from the drive across the river. His car stood out and if he stepped outside, he'd clash with the scenery. He wasn't dressed for this. Frank continued past the first lot and smiled as he noted the scrubby road angling away from the exit. It was still there. He drove past the Do Not Enter sign, following the ever-narrowing road until it started to feel like a bad idea. Just as he wondered if he'd have to reverse all the way to the first lot, the road widened into the circle of the overflow lot. A gate marked the continuation of the fire road, but Frank was content with the privacy he'd found.

He cut the engine and let his hands drop to his lap. Into the quiet floated warm air scented with birch and pine, encouraged through the open windows by a light breeze. The sweat on the back of his neck began to cool. Tom continued to snore.

Frank pulled out his phone. Surprised he had a signal, he dealt with a couple of messages, checked his social media accounts with less enthusiasm than he might muster for a colonoscopy, and began to question what he was doing. Parking in the middle of nature wasn't really his thing. He'd liked the woods as a boy, but had never taken to hiking or any outdoor pursuit that didn't include a pool bar as an adult. Yet here he was, parked at one of their old spots. He and Tom had been here a million times— Well, at least twenty if you counted each year of their friendship twice.

He indulged in another bout of Tom-gazing, feeling slightly guilty about his unabashed perving. Tom's arms caught his attention this time. Folded loosely in his lap, wrists crossed, his arms had the definition of a man who did more than peck at a keyboard. Frank could easily imagine Tom lifting slate tiles up to the roof, hammering nails, patching things, repairing them. Performing the manly sort of tasks Frank had left somewhere between high school and college. Not that he didn't know how to use a hammer, but he was sure he wouldn't swing one with the same focus as Tom.

Did Tom chop wood as well? Frank could easily imagine him stripped to the waist, lean back and broad shoulders flexing as he swung an axe up and down with precise force. Tom would chop neatly. He might dress like a bum, but he did everything neatly and with intent, which was probably why he was such a good photographer.

Perhaps staying in the Poconos suited Tom in a way. Maybe it hadn't been quite the sacrifice Frank had supposed it might.

Frank reached across the middle of the car and brushed his thumb over one of Tom's small, perfect ears. If it were even just a little pointed, he could be an elf. Frank smiled as he sifted his fingers through Tom's hair, moving it away from Tom's face. Tom shifted into his touch and Frank massaged his way over Tom's scalp.

Tom shifted again and opened his eyes. "What are you doing?"

Loving you.

Frank removed his hand, or tried to. Tom grabbed his wrist. Pressed their palms together and interlaced their fingers. Then he turned to look outside the car. "Where are we?"

"On the fire road behind Lenape Lake."

"Because . . ."

"I missed the turn back to East Stroudsburg and then decided to follow the river for a while."

Tom smiled. "I haven't been over here in a while. How long was I asleep?"

"Maybe an hour."

Covering a yawn, Tom said, "Sorry. It's been a long week."

"No trouble at all."

"Want to go for a walk?"

"Not really."

"Sunset is real pretty from Mount Minsi."

"That's a two-hour hike and we'd have to walk back in the dark. And I'm not wearing the right shoes."

Tom laughed. "Do you have the right shoes at home?"

"Probably. I seem to remember buying a pair of Merrell walking shoes when they were popular."

Tom lifted their hands and pressed his lips to Frank's knuckles. "Ah, Frankie. Don't ever change."

Ignoring the fact that his knuckles had just received the blessing his lips hoped for, Frank said, "But I have. I'm not the same boy who left." And never came back.

"Yes, you are. You've grown up is all."

Before Frank could lean in, cozy up the atmosphere a little, Tom was tugging on his hand again. "Let's go look at the lake, then. Be a shame to drive all the way out here and not at least do that."

Frank didn't want to look at the lake. He wanted to . . . not flirt, either. He wanted to move past that stage. He wanted to be inside Tom. His skin, his heart—every part of him. And his need made him awkward. He never had trouble talking to men. He was the life of every party. But every time he shared a quiet moment with Tom, his tongue stuck to the roof of his mouth and his palms sweated. It was like being fifteen all over again.

Tom had let go and was climbing out of the car. He didn't offer his hand again as they walked along the fire road.

Lenape Lake was more a pond than a lake. A green pond. Still, it was pretty in the late-afternoon light, lily pads outlined by discreet shadows extending end to end and overlapping the mossy shoreline. There was a small pebbled beach marked by two No Swimming signs. The green water wasn't very inviting. Also, there was an abundance of frogs and they were making a lot of noise.

Tom led him past the beach and onto a narrow trail that followed the shoreline for a while before angling away into the trees. The trail turned back toward the lake and spilled out onto a private beach of packed mud. A lopsided wooden bench offered a view across the lake. Tom sat and Frank perched carefully beside him, only settling his weight when the bench didn't sink beneath them.

The frogs weren't as loud on this side of the lake, and the air was still, as though the slight breeze couldn't be bothered reaching across the water. Frank sat and sweated and again questioned what he was doing. What they were doing. Then Tom took his hand, pulled it into his lap, and played with his fingers. Frank looked over to find Tom peeking up at him in a sort of sideways glance.

"What?" Frank prompted.

"Are you going to wait forever?"

"What are you talking about?"

"Us."

"Tom—"

"It's because of back then, isn't it? And the kiss at the creek."

Frank drew in a humid breath. "I think I made my position clear."

"So you *are* waiting for me."

Was Tom asking what he thought Tom was asking? "Y-yes."

"Ah, Frankie."

Tom closed his eyes and squeezed Frank's hand, and Frank wondered if this was it, the moment when Tom took what was left of his heart and shredded it into unrecognizable pieces. He gazed down at their hands, at the white edging around Tom's knuckles. At the lean arms he'd been admiring a short while ago. At the profile he'd never forgotten, the man he didn't know how not to love . . . and waited. He should get up and walk away, but a part of him wanted to know whether if he stayed for this final moment, if he let his heart be wrecked beyond repair, then maybe he could stop.

Tom opened his eyes. Reached up with his other hand, laying his palm against the side of Frank's face. Tears gathered behind Frank's eyes. But he wouldn't close them. He'd face this as he'd have to face every day after. He'd take it like a man and somehow figure out a way—

Reality blurred and Tom's face was next to his, lips next to his, touching his. Frank breathed. Tom breathed. Then Tom kissed him. Sweetly, tentatively. He moved back and Frank wanted to cry out. How cruel was Tom going to be? But then Tom was leaning in to kiss him again.

Pulling his fingers free, Frank set both his hands against Tom's shoulders and pushed him back. "Stop." Tom stopped. Met his gaze. "What are you doing?"

"I'm giving you what you want."

"What I . . . Don't be an ass."

"I'm not trying to be. I . . ." Tom flushed. "I want this too."

"This isn't a game, Tom. You can't kiss me and then try to drown yourself in the lake. I can't do that again. I can't—"

Tom touched two fingers to Frank's lips and shook his head. "I won't." He looked so damn sincere. Frightened too. And so much like his Tommy.

Frank didn't breathe and it seemed as if Tom didn't either. They remained locked in place, hands to shoulders, fingers to lips. Eye to eye. Perhaps a minute passed, Frank continued searching Tom's gaze for truth and found only what he felt: a desperate loneliness and crushing need. He broke the impasse, pulling Tom forward, nearly catching his fingers between them, and kissed him—hard and with no finesse. Mashing his lips against Tom's as though he had to seal them together, as though only fused like this could they withstand whatever might come next.

And he was crying. Could feel the ache of tears in his throat, the wetness of them against his cheeks. His chest heaved and his lips refused to move. His whole body was stiff, even the jerk of his shoulders as his lungs bellowed in and out with something that felt an awful lot like a sob.

Tom pulled away just enough to press his lips to Frank's cheek. Frank's eyes, closing each with a kiss. The other cheek, his temple, the side of his nose, his lips again. "Frankie," he whispered between kisses. "Don't cry."

Frank couldn't help it. He hated it, but couldn't stop. It hurt. His throat burned and his chest felt like it might burst. "I'm sorry," he croaked.

Tom shook his head. "Don't. This is my fault. I'm so sorry, Frank. If I could take it back, I would. If we could redo that night . . ." His breath was a quiet rasp. "I'd probably do the same thing, but I'd answer your letters. Tell you what went wrong."

"Tell me now."

Tom shook his head.

"Please, Tommy."

"It was so long ago and it doesn't matter. Not anymore."

Frank lifted his chin, defiance burning through this horrible combination of sorrow and hurt and love. He had to know, needed to know. He might not have wondered every day for the past thirty years, but he'd wondered often enough. That night had changed him. Kissing Tom and being rejected for that kiss had defined him for so long that letting the moment go felt impossible.

And yet . . .

Tom's brown eyes communicated more than sorrow. Regret pinched his brow, and the shadow of everything Frank felt underlined all of it. Confusion and old pain.

They couldn't undo the last thirty years. Time had marched on, folding over the hurt and turning it into scars. They couldn't change it. Best thing to do would be to let it go.

Could he?

CHAPTER 21

T om was about to open his mouth, to say it. To tell Frank why he'd hit him. To share his fears. Before he could, though, Frank cupped his cheeks and kissed him again, properly this time. Tom's heart heaved a happy sigh at the sweetness of that mouth pressed to his. At the brushes of lips, the almost chaste exchange as they learned the shape of each other, how their lips fit together. It was familiar and strange and wonderful, and when Frank parted his lips, Tom flicked his tongue between, just once in a quick tease.

He felt Frank's lips curve and couldn't help grinning in response. Their kisses became pecks and near misses as smiles interfered with their ability to connect more deeply, as they nipped, touched tongues, and played. Played.

Oh, this! Tom could cry for the joy of this. This was what their first kiss should have been. Light and happy, yet full of expectation. The knowledge that this led to everything else burned a blissful path down through his middle. Anticipation tightened his gut. Around them, the frogs continued to sing in praise of their reunion.

Lips still connected to Frank's, Tom got to his feet and straddled Frank's thighs, sliding into his lap. Frank welcomed him with a hand to either side, gripping his ass and pulling him forward. Now high enough to look down at the face he'd never forgotten, Tom took time to pay homage to each feature all over again. Pale-ginger eyebrows and lashes, Frank's almost button nose. His small, pink lips. Wide chin with a slight cleft between. The softening angle of his jaw. The pebble of one earlobe, then the other.

Frank's hands traveled up and down Tom's back. His hips seemed to undulate beneath him. Tom rode the wave, moving in with each crest until he was fused to Frank, until their mouths joined in the deeper kiss they both craved. Warmth touched Tom's back as Frank delved beneath his shirt. Tom sighed at the spread of a broad hand over his spine, the way Frank pressed his thumb just there, over Tom's hip, and traced up and down, as though he wanted to know every part of him.

Tom rocked forward, the heat in his groin hardening. The press of his zipper was uncomfortable, but pleasurably so. The strain over his thickening cock, another tease. He pushed a hand inside the collar of Frank's shirt. Then, trailing a kiss downward, unbuttoned from the top, baring Frank's chest while bending to kiss his collarbones. He scooted backward a little, opening a space between them. The hand at his back held him upright and steady. Tom left the rest of Frank's shirt buttoned, but pulled it out of his pants so he could touch Frank's hip, explore the softness of his stomach.

This was his Frank. Big and strong. Built for comfort, not speed. Tom wanted to be in bed with this man—enfolded in his arms and crushed up against his skin. His Frankie, his Frank.

Tom raised his chin, meeting Frank's lips, and inched his fingers downward over the hard ridge beneath Frank's belt and cupped Frank's erection, squeezing gently. Frank moaned into his mouth. The kiss deepened again, becoming frenzied and breathless. Tom could feel his hips moving as he stroked Frank's cock, catching the rhythm. He began tugging at Frank's belt.

"Wait." Frank's breath was warm against his cheek.

Tom stilled his hand. "What's up?" He hoped Frank wouldn't ask him to stop. Tom had denied himself—them—this for so long.

Frank glanced around Tom's shoulder, toward the water. "Someone might see us."

Tom touched the side of Frank's face and guided his gaze back to him. He smiled. Leaned in to kiss Frank's worried frown. "Why do you think I brought you back here?"

Frank grinned. "You brought me to your hookup spot? I'm beyond flattered."

"Fuck you."

"I wish you would, but not here."

Tom had Frank's belt undone. He reached inside Frank's pants, first tracing the outline of his cock through the cotton of his underwear, then easing the elastic away to expose him to the late-afternoon light. "Not here," he agreed as he shuffled backward.

Frank let him go and Tom stood for long enough to nudge Frank's legs apart.

"Pull your pants down a little," he said, kneeling between Frank's thighs.

"Oh God."

What he was about to do might be foolhardy, but Tom didn't care. He wanted this. Frank wanted it. And there was a certain poetry to doing it this way, out in the woods. As though he were making up for what he'd ruined. At eighteen, this might have been all they'd have managed. Furtive encounters somewhere off the beaten path. Quick and dirty fumbling behind locked doors. Their romance would have begun in secret and been all the more delicious for it.

Why not start that way now? Why not go back so they could go forward?

Tom licked his lips as Frank got his pants down to free a cock that was hard enough to poke a hole in the universe. Tom wrapped his hand around Frank's shaft and squeezed, reveling in the firmness of flesh and the sheer pleasure of having a cock in his hand. Pre-come glistened in the shallow divot at the top, beckoning his tongue, and Tom bent to savor his first taste of Frank as a man. He swiped his tongue across the swollen head and smiled as he felt the pulse of need travel down through Frank's cock and out into his thighs. The stiffening and relaxing that would soon become a roll of hips, then a thrust.

Frank put one hand on Tom's shoulder. He braced the other on the bench. "This is going to be over very quickly," he said, cheeks turning pink beneath his freckles.

"Been a while?" Tom murmured as he licked his way over the top and around the flare.

"Yes. And this might be a particular fantasy of mine."

"Being sucked off in the woods."

"By you."

A couple of weeks ago, that admission would have sent a jolt of panic through Tom's chest. Now he felt more of a thrill. Hadn't he always wanted to be Frank's fantasy?

Why did you let him go? a small voice whispered somewhere behind the spreading warmth of sex thoughts.

Not now, Tom chided. He bent to his task with enthusiasm and determination, wrapping his tongue around the glans before closing his lips and sucking downward, following his hand as far as he could. His fist nested into the folds of Frank's underwear and slacks, exposing a goodly length of firm, hot flesh. Tom savored his way down and up again. Down and up. It'd been a while since he'd given a blowjob, but he'd always liked doing it. Having a cock of his own made it easier. He knew where to squeeze, how to use his teeth—ever so gently—and what to do with his tongue.

After a short while, Frank's hips began to tremble. He didn't buck, though he used the hand at Tom's shoulder to keep pace, pushing as Tom sank down over his cock, gripping as Tom rose back up.

And he was making noise. Breathing harshly, muttering curses. Groaning, calling Tom's name in a soft patter of repetition: "Tom, Tom, Tom . . . Oh, God, Tommy." The sound of his voice joined that thrill seeping beneath Tom's skin. To know Frank wanted him this much. To know he wasn't just some random dude attached to the end of Frank's dick. This was him. This was them.

This was how it always should have been.

Inside his own pants, Tom's cock came along for the ride. The friction of his movement wasn't perfect, and he could do without a zip pressing into the side of his shaft, but . . . Man, he could come from this, without touching himself. By rubbing the inside of his boxers and jeans. By sucking Frank's cock.

Frank jerked forward, his hand tightening on Tom's shoulder. "So close," he hissed.

Nodding slightly, Tom sucked his way back down. He fumbled with the tangle of material beneath Frank's cock. Frank's balls were trapped in there. He'd loved to have sucked on them and played with them. Next time.

Frank stiffened, jerked, and stiffened again. He pushed at Tom's shoulder, but Tom remained where he was, resolute. He wanted all of

Frank. Hot semen hit the roof of his mouth and the back of his throat, and he swallowed reflexively and then eagerly. Felt the release in his own groin and the quick pulse of his climax.

Tom kept moving his hand, with the ebb and flow of Frank's peak, and grinned around his mouthful at the shout that echoed back across the lake, silencing the frogs for a single, golden moment. He sucked until Frank fell almost limp. Then Tom licked his lips, rocked back onto his heels, and glanced up.

Frank looked wrecked. As though he'd run a marathon only to fall across the finish line. His chest heaved, pushing his broad shoulders up and down. Sweat dampened the hair over his forehead, almost darkening it to orange. Almost. His eyes were closed, his cheeks pale but for a flush of pink. Grinning, Tom grabbed a hold of Frank's shoulders and hauled himself up high enough to kiss slack lips. Frank's eyes fluttered open. He focused on Tom, smiled loosely, and pulled Tom into his lap. Closer, then closer still, crushing Tom against his chest.

Where he belonged.

Tom put his head to Frank's shoulder. Could smell the sweat on his skin, feel the warmth of him beneath the damp linen of his shirt. The scent of semen and forest and Frank was so right, it put a lump in his throat.

Eventually, after a period of forever, Frank eased him backward. Hands to Tom's shoulders, he looked up into Tom's face. "How are you doing?"

"I came in my jeans."

Frank laughed. "Really?"

"Mm-hmm. I'd been waiting a long, long time."

Frank's smiled shortened into something sweet and light. "I can't believe we fooled around in the woods. At our age."

"You're only as old as you feel, and right now, I feel about twenty. Or I will until I stand up and remember I was on my knees for about half an hour."

"Not that long."

"Time passes quickly when you're having fun."

"You certainly were. You're, ah, very good at sucking cock."

Tom grinned. "I like doing it."

"Marry me."

Laughing softly against the fear squeezing his lungs, Tom eased himself out of Frank's lap. "Maybe we should see how the rest of it works first."

He cut a sideways glance at Frank and caught an expression that pretty much summed up how he felt. Frank's face showed the utter contentment that always followed a mind-blowing orgasm. His eyes glowed with fondness. Beneath all of that, though, was a sort of truth.

They weren't messing around here. They were, but not as teenagers. Sure, they might be recapturing their youth. But if the rest of it did work, then this could be it for them. A place to rest their forevers. The thought scared him spitless. But right now, as he gazed into Frank's light-brown eyes, Tom felt more welcome than scared, as though Frank had opened a door that only he had the key to and was saying, *Come on in. Stay a while.*

And Tom wanted to stay forever.

CHAPTER 22

Patricia Nolan had left another card tucked into the front door of the lodge. Frank could feel his jaw setting as he tucked the card into his pocket.

"What was that?" Tom asked.

"Nothing."

Because her campaign of harassment wasn't going to work. In fact, every card she left at the door only fueled Frank's resolve not to sell—whether she was responsible for the dead raccoons and stalkers or not. He and Tom might have just started their evaluation of the competition, but Frank could already see where Bossen Hill fit. Why it could work—*work* being a fairly operative word. They had a lot of it ahead of them.

Frank opened the door and stepped inside to the faint odor of mold and neglect. A hell of a lot of work.

He turned to Tom, who was holding two camera bags, one in each hand, and smiled. "Do you think we could sell the scent of mold as authenticity?"

Tom laughed. Shook his head and held up his bags. "Going to take these downstairs and then I need a shower before my shorts fuse permanently to my junk."

"I'll warm the water up for you."

Tom eyed him speculatively for a second, as though sorting through a collection of polite refusals. Then he grinned, shyly. The abashed smile threw Frank back across the years with dizzying speed, which he'd give as his reason for stumbling forward to press his lips to Tom's. He kissed that smile. Through it. Put his hands to either side of Tom's face and kissed the afternoon from his skin.

"Situation in my pants is getting more dire," Tom murmured between kisses.

Frank leaned away, dropped another quick benediction onto Tom's lips, and said, "Hurry back."

Tom was back upstairs and inside the door of Robert's bathroom before Frank even had time to finish undressing. The rest of his clothes, and half of Tom's, ended up in a messy pile on the floor. Then it was time to peel Tom's boxer shorts away.

"Ow, ow . . . hold on."

"Had you not come in about a year? Jesus."

Tom plucked Frank's fingers away from the elastic. "I had to sit in your tiny little car for about half an hour afterward. Not to mention the hike back to that tiny little car. Everything is squished everywhere."

"So I can see."

"I think I'm going to get into the shower with them on and unstick them that way."

"Probably for the best."

Frank followed him into the narrow shower and tried closing the door behind them. It bounced off his ass and swung back toward the wall. "Okay, new bathroom renovation note: showers big enough for two."

"And maybe those handheld showerhead thingies for rinsing down come-stuck underwear."

Frank grinned. "I'll be sure to put that in there."

Tom was peeling his shorts down with a wince, and while excitement tried to surge through Frank's veins—finally, he was seeing Tom naked—the ridiculousness of their situation dampened his arousal. His ass was getting cold, the spray from the shower kept stinging him in the eyes, and Tom's pubes were a mess.

"This isn't as sexy as I imagined it would be," Frank said.

Tom snorted. "Life rarely is." His shorts dropped to the floor with a wet *plop*.

Frank reached for the soap. "Let me."

He pumped a puddle of caustic yellow liquid into his hand and lathered it up into antiseptic bubbles. "What the hell is this? Carbolic or something?"

"Dial. Robert's favorite."

The sensation of being in the shower with a dead man only lasted a few seconds, but it was enough to ensure Frank wouldn't be getting hard for the next while. He began spreading soap down from Tom's navel, sweeping the bubbles toward his pubic hair before beginning to work the matted tangles apart.

"This isn't as sexy as I thought it'd be," Tom observed.

Frank started laughing. "Give me a minute."

"Here, just let me do this part. Pain is not my thing and you keep pulling on my pubes."

"I get to wash your dick."

"Yes, sir."

As soon as Tom was reasonably clean, Frank pumped out another handful of yellow bile, lathered it up, and took a handful of Tom's penis for the very first time. His ass still waved in the breeze and they were probably creating more mold issues, first floor to cellar this time. The soap smelled awful. But having Tom's dick in his hand was a moment of wonder. A memory he'd tuck away forever.

Frank stroked from root to tip, tugging as he did so, encouraging the shaft to thicken and lengthen. Groaning softly, Tom leaned in to drop his head to Frank's shoulder. His fingers caressed Frank's hips and stayed there, loosely attached. Frank could feel Tom's lips plucking at his wet skin. He concentrated on stroking and squeezing, learning the shape of Tom's cock. Enjoying the increasing weight as it plumped in his hand. Once it was hard, he began tracing the veins he could see, his index finger pushing against that all-important one along the underside.

Tom's groans deepened. He curled his fingers a little more tightly into Frank's hip.

Frank reached beneath to play with Tom's balls. Rolling and squeezing. He could almost feel them tightening beneath his fingers.

Tom gasped. "Fuck."

The water cascading over the back of Tom's shoulders, splashing onto Frank's chest, started to cool. "I'm going to make this quick," Frank said.

"It's going to be quick, either way."

Frank started stroking in earnest, pulling from the nest of curls at the base of Tom's happy cock, all the way to the head, twisting as he went. He paid attention to the upper half, circling his fingers, brushing his thumb over the slit. Pressing down and tugging. Tom shook against him and dug into Frank's skin. He started rocking. Mumbling.

"Yeah, yeah. Just like that."

"Like this?" Frank asked, circling and tugging the head again.

"Yeah. But longer. Squeeze harder."

Tom was ready for the coming-home strokes. Frank complied, lengthening the journey of his fingers, root to tip, squeezing the firm length in his hand with every stroke, making the passage of his fingers as tight as he could. Tom's hips bucked frantically. His breath rasped. His teeth came down against Frank's shoulder, a hook and a handle. He clutched at Frank's hips. Moaned and whimpered.

Then he yelled, the sound loud and almost mournful in the confined space of the shower, and shot against Frank's thigh, his semen warmer than the tepid water falling across their skin.

The water was cold by the time they'd washed off a second time. Tom was shivering as they toweled dry.

Frank kissed his temple. "It's the middle of summer. You shouldn't be cold."

"I can never get warm enough when I'm tired."

"You need to eat."

Tom lifted one shoulder. "I wouldn't turn down food."

"I'll fix us something."

The rest of the evening passed pleasantly. Frank had expected more awkwardness. He'd also expected more . . . more floating? More feet-off-the-ground excitement. Instead, deep contentment pulled at his limbs. The wine with dinner slowed his thoughts further, and as he nodded his way through the approximate thousand pictures Tom had taken that day, Frank could imagine doing this for the rest of his life.

He still wanted to write. He had most of a story fleshed out. Several articles had been published over the past few years about the failing resort industry in the Poconos. His story was going to be different. He had a local perspective and different questions. He also had something else to offer: himself and his plans for Bossen Hill.

"What are you thinking about?" Tom asked, pausing the slide show.

"My pillow, mostly."

"One blowjob and you're toast. That's not much of a refractory period."

"'Refractory period'?"

Smiling, Tom leaned in and kissed the corner of his mouth. "Want to go upstairs?" he murmured.

"I'm assuming the plan is not to tuck me in and sing me a lullaby."

"Is that your kink?"

A short laugh left him. "No, though it could be. Gah, why am I so tired?"

"Because I sucked you hard, baby. Also, you've drunk most of that bottle of wine."

"So I have." Frank tilted his head. "When you stay over, when you're keeping an eye on things, do you always sleep on the couch?"

Tom stiffened, seemingly surprised by the question. He drew back a little. His mouth opened and closed a couple of times before he finally said, "Ah, yeah. Why?"

"You should use Robert's room. If that's not weird?"

"I figured you'd . . ." Tom waved his hand weakly toward the wall.

"We could both stay in there tonight. The bed is larger."

Tom's posture relaxed a little. "Are you asking me to spend the night with you?"

"In the most awkward way possible, apparently."

Tom said nothing for a while. Sat looking at him, his brow lightly furrowed. Then, "When we were kids, I never quite got that you were shy. You were . . . different. You liked to talk and people liked to listen and you were always so bright and . . ."

"Noisy?"

"Yes. But when I think back now, it's like that noise was camouflage. Because I can remember you being social, but you spent every free afternoon and weekend with me." He held up a hand. "Not going to ask why, just trying to figure you out."

"I think you already have."

Tom shook his head. "Have you had a lot of . . ."

"Relationships, lovers?"

"I shouldn't have asked."

Frank shrugged. "Show me yours and I'll show you mine?"

A sideways grin pulled at Tom's mouth. "Well, you already know I was with Gerry, then Sandra. Both relationships died a natural death, I think. Gerry met someone else, and Sandra said she got tired of waiting. I always thought she meant for me to get down on one knee, but I think it had more to do with the situation with my mom. Nothing serious since then."

"Why?"

"Are you asking if I was pining for you?"

Yes. "No. I'm interested. Let's call it self-preservation. Are you boring in bed?" Frank was aware his tone wasn't quite as light as he'd hoped. Also, what the hell? As if Tom could ever be boring in bed. And so what if he was? Already this felt deeper than—

"I'll answer that if you tell me why you're not with someone. I've browsed your Twitter feed. You're always at openings and parties and dinners with interesting people. I've wanted to kill about twenty of them, mostly the ones who got to . . ." Tom looked down.

Heat rushed to Frank's cheeks. "Got to what?"

"Nothing. It's the wine talking."

"Your whole glass."

"You were hogging the bottle."

"Why do you stalk my Twitter feed?"

"Same reason you buy my prints and I buy your magazines. Only I'm one up on you on the pathetic scale."

Frank leaned back in the creaky office chair and folded his arms behind his head, stretching out his shoulders. He could feel a slight pull of muscle on the right side, the same side as the hand he'd used to pull an orgasm out of Tom in the shower. "I should have come home sooner." It wasn't with sadness he admitted this, but regret. "I thought about it, a number of times. More often over the past year when I started visiting Simon down in Bethlehem. But . . . I'm a stubborn fool, I suppose. You never answered my letters and I took that to heart."

"I'm sorry."

"It is what it is. And the truth about my Twitter feed . . . about me. I like to flirt, Tom. It's a game of words and you know how I've always loved words. But Twitter, Facebook, Instagram, the bio at the top of my columns, on the website my PA maintains, it's all the Frank people expect me to be. Underneath it all, it's just the same boring Frank who can think of no better way to spend the day than follow someone else around and tell their story."

"Meaning?"

"There hasn't been anyone else, Tom. Not since you."

"You're telling me you haven't had sex for—"

"God, no. No relationships, though. Not really. Just a handful of usually unsatisfactory encounters."

"That's . . ."

"Sad. I know. Which is why I pretend I'm someone else when I have to." Shrugging, Frank lifted his hands from behind his head. Placed them in his lap.

"What about Simon?"

"We slept together once. It was . . . I enjoyed it more than he did, I think."

"Ouch."

"If it had been mutual, yes, I think Simon could have been someone I— No. He is someone I love as a friend. He's been good to me. Loyal and kind. The best friend a man could ask for."

"Now I *am* jealous." Tom's smile was light, though.

Frank returned a similar smile. "Did you love them? Gerry and Sandra?"

"I guess. In an 'I enjoy coming home to you every night' kind of way."

"Still my beating heart."

Tom snorted. "I wasn't that cold. I did love them and care for both of them, even now. I don't think you can be intimate with someone you don't care about."

"You'd be surprised."

"I mean on a daily basis. When you're not having sex. But I'm not an easy person to be with. There's my mom for one thing." Tom's jaw clicked softly. "It's . . . If we do this, it's important you know that she's a priority. She hasn't always been there for me, I know. She was a shitty mother, but she could have quit that at any time. Up and abandoned me, left town, or fallen so far inside a bottle no one could get her out. It was a slim difference, sometimes, but she managed to keep a job and to keep just sober enough to get me through high school. She did that for me, Frank."

Frank could only nod. Tom's logic was twisted, but love did that, and in Tom's place, he'd probably feel the same. He'd seen Tom and Wendy together when Wendy had been sober, and the fact she loved her son had never been in doubt. He was her reason for being.

"I'd never come between you and your mother, Tom."

"I know. But am I going to keep you from everything else?"

"What do you mean?"

"The Frank who likes to talk, who is smiling in every single one of those photos, whose interest in every person he interviews bleeds through every word he writes—is he going to be content to stay here with a two-bit photographer who hasn't cut the apron strings?"

"You're an amazing photographer. You're also a successful businessman. I've trawled your website too and I've read the testimonials. Hell, I've bid on your prints in those charity auctions you put them up for. You're good at what you do, Tom, and I don't see you staying here as failure. You made that choice. Somehow you're balancing what you want with your mother's needs. There are very few who could do the same. And, on top of that, you kept this place *and* Robert going. You've been leading a remarkably full life."

Why was he only just realizing this now?

For weeks he'd been seeing Tom through the lens of his own guilt. Had assumed that because he'd left and followed their dream, Tom had been unhappy. Somehow, he'd discounted all Tom had done with his life and that . . . that had been extremely narrow-minded of him. Of *him*.

Question was, though, did Tom appreciate the fullness of his life? He must know what he had. Must understand what he'd accomplished.

"You didn't answer my question," Tom said.

"I didn't?" Frank thought back: Tom had been asking if he could stay. If he would. "Who says I can't have it all? That we can't? Yes, I want to stay, and no, I'm not going to resent you for needing to stay. But our situation is different now. I can take a day in the city and still come home. Hell, I need to go to Jersey next week. If a story comes up, one I want to write, I can fly out to nearly anywhere and be back in a day or two. Truth is, I don't travel as much as I used to, and . . ." *How to put this delicately.*

"My mother isn't going to be alive forever."

Frank winced. "Sorry."

"No, it's true and it's not as if I haven't made plans."

Frank thought about the notebook Tom had tucked into the bottom of a shelf in his basement office. Had he updated it? "Where would you go?"

Tom's laugh was short, but not bitter. "Probably nowhere because you're right. I'm overwhelmed at the moment. Taking care of Robert, keeping up with my mom, the photography, the lodge. I'm tired. I'm fucking tired. But . . . this is home. I love this house. I love the woods and the creek and the view from the top of Big Pocono and the damn frogs at Lenape Lake and even those stupid champagne-glass hot tubs, because when I see those things, I know I'm home."

Rather than feel sad that Tom's plans didn't include around-the-world tickets, a different emotion nudged Frank's chest. What Tom had described was exactly what Frank had been missing, and he recognized it with one of those cool, clear moments. Felt his chin lift and his heart move. Home. He'd been missing home.

He swallowed. Reached across the small space between them, the creaking of his chair another reminder of all of it. The mold he couldn't smell because he'd been sitting in it for three hours, drinking wine, and the simple fact of being here, with Tommy Benjamin.

But the moment was altogether too heavy. Frank smiled. "I think we're supposed to have this talk after we have significant sex."

"I'm going to say that handjob in the shower was pretty significant. Tangled pubes and all."

"Ditto on my blowjob."

Tom took Frank's hand. "Frank Sinatra just started singing in my head."

Frank blinked. "That's a little morbid."

"Not if you focus on the part where he did it all . . ." Tom hummed softly before singing, "My way."

Frank raised their joined hands and kissed the back of Tom's. "How about if we go to bed and have sex in the morning?"

"The way middle-aged people do?"

Frank laughed. "Just so."

CHAPTER 23

Tom squinted against the light streaming across the bed. It was on the wrong side of his face—and what was that lump digging into his left hip? He shifted, only to encounter a lump with his right foot. A curious flex of toes identified a small rise with a hard half circle at the top.

"It's a spring," Frank said. "I have three on my side and one under my pillow."

Tom turned his head. "Might be time for a new mattress."

"At least I know why you haven't been sleeping in here."

"I haven't been sleeping in here because Robert died in this bed."

Frank's upper lip curled. "Well, there goes my morning wood."

"Oh?" Smiling, Tom reached beneath the sheet, finding Frank's abdomen first—slightly furry and sleep warm. He skimmed his palm down toward the tented material at his crotch and squeezed the firmness he found there. "Feels good to me."

After last night, it shouldn't be such a marvel to touch Frank so freely. To be in bed beside him and know him this intimately—as a lover as well as a friend. Still, Tom's thoughts wanted to take a little spin and he let them. It had been a while since he lived for the moment and every moment spent with Frank should be *lived*.

Frank moved into his touch, hips and body navigating the sea of lumps and broken springs until they were pressed together, locked in a kiss that should have been disgusting. Were they already past the morning-breath phase? Or was the insistent grope of Frank's fingers between them, that incidental brush and squeeze as he found Tom's cock, just more important than the slightly bitter odor of Frank's breath?

Stupid question.

Tom thrust his thickening erection into Frank's hand and continued his own ministrations—stroking and tugging. He slipped his fingers inside Frank's pajama pants, his lips pulling from the kiss at the memory of those pants: a concoction of silk, pale blue, and paired with a matching monogramed pajama shirt.

"What are you grinning about?" Frank murmured.

"Your pajamas."

Frank huffed. "They were a gift."

"Of course they were. You'd never buy monogrammed pajamas for yourself."

Frank laughed, his breath just warm now, familiar, and bent to kiss him again. "Stop it," he said between small pecks. "Can't kiss you while I'm laughing."

"Can I have a pair for Christmas?"

As his laughter rose in pitch, Frank continued dropping small kisses on Tom's lips. "How about a pair in red and green flannel?"

"As long as I never have to answer the door in them."

"That's what robes are for."

"Oh my God. You have a satin robe, don't you?"

"I have several robes. They're quite the sensible garment."

Tom caught Frank's moving mouth, kissed him deeply. Their hips synced, rocking forward together, drawing back in time. "Do you have one with you?" His question was breathless.

"Yes."

He was so close—closer than he'd be this quickly from his hand alone. The smell of Frank's skin, musky from sleep. The lingering scent of soap and sex from the night before. The warmth of his skin and that steady rhythm. His balls were tight, his spine tingling. His heart pounding—

And nearly stopping as someone rapped on the window, calling out, "Frank? Tom?"

"Holy fuck." Tom fell away from Frank, pressing his palm flat to his chest as though the pressure of his hand would keep his heart from leaping through skin and bone.

Beside him, Frank was cursing and fighting with the sheet, which had become twisted around his legs. He rolled to the side of the bed and disappeared with a thump, another curse, and a cry of pain.

"Are you okay?"

"No, I'm not okay. I fell on my dick."

Tom swallowed the urge to laugh, coughing instead.

"I heard that." Frank's head appeared over the edge of the bed, cheeks flushed, eyes bright with pain.

A voice sounded outside the window. "Frank? You in there?"

Frank was shaking his head. "Fucking Brian." He raised his voice. "Go sit on the porch, Brian. We'll be out in a minute."

Cackling was heard through the glass, and an exchange of voices.

"He has someone else out there with him," Tom observed. His heart had stopped trying to push through his ribs, but his chest felt sore. Also, his dick refused to deflate. *So this is what a fear erection feels like.* And at that thought, he felt the shift as blood began to redistribute itself throughout his body. He sat up, pulling his boxers up at the same time, and crawled toward the side of the bed.

Frank was sitting with his back pressed to the side, his legs spread out in front of him. His pajama pants were down around his knees and he was pulling gently on his half-flaccid penis.

Tom put his chin on Frank's shoulder. "Can't see any blood."

"Thank God."

Pressing a kiss to Frank's cheek, Tom murmured, "I'll suck it all better later. Why is Brian here?"

"He sent me a text saying he might stop by this weekend. I didn't expect it to be Sunday morning, though. And we really need to stop talking about Brian while I have my cock in my hand."

"He's a good-looking guy." Like, seriously good-looking. Tall and blond with gorgeous eyes, a classically square jaw, and the sort of build that usually weakened Tom's knees.

"Don't make me cry," Frank said.

Tom gifted him with another kiss, this time catching the side of Frank's mouth. "He's not you." No one could compete with his Frankie.

Dimly, they could hear a banging on the front door. "He's just fucking with us now," Frank said.

"I'll go let them in. Take your time. Sure everything's okay?"

Frank raised one eyebrow. "We'll find out tonight, hmm?"

"We'll either have the best sex ever or a funeral for Little Frankie."

"Who're you calling little?" Frank said with an expression of mock hurt.

Laughing, Tom slid off the bed, picked his shirt up off the floor and went to answer the front door. It was Brian and another tall, handsome man with eyes the most fabulous shade of blue—like cut and polished sapphires. And though the god-among-men had friendly lines at his mouth and eyes, his dark wavy hair held not a strand of gray. He was built too.

Were all of Frank's friends this gorgeous?

"Good morning," Brian boomed. He gave Tom a quick up-and-down inspection and grinned. "Hope we didn't interrupt anything."

Tom scowled. "I'm beginning to see why Frank doesn't like you." He looked pointedly toward the other man.

"I'm Simon," the guy said, extending a hand. "I stopped apologizing for Brian about eighteen months ago."

"Heh." So this was Simon. Forcing a smile, Tom took Simon's hand. "I've heard a lot about you."

Simon's smile was gracious and seemed genuine. It was hard not to like him immediately, damn it.

"Come on in." Tom stepped back and gestured toward the office. "Make yourselves comfortable. Brian knows where the coffee maker is. Have you had breakfast?"

"We thought you guys might like to get breakfast out with us. I texted Frank last night and this morning," Simon said.

"Oh." Why was he blushing? Tom pressed a not-cool-enough hand to the side of his face. "Um, we, ah, had a long day. Went to bed early."

Brian was giving him the once-over again.

Tom backed away slowly. "I'm going to get a shower. Frank will probably be up for breakfast."

Leaving Brian and Simon to confer quietly behind him, Tom fled to Robert's bedroom. His bedroom? His and Frank's room? The room they'd slept in last night! He pushed through the door and slammed it shut behind him. Frank was in the shower.

"You need to check your messages," Tom called into the bathroom.

"I just did. Would it have hurt them to call?"

Tom pulled his T-shirt back over his head. "Honestly, I think Brian was too enamored of the idea of catching us out like this."

"He didn't even know we were sleeping together."

"He sure looked like he knew something." Tom paused in the bathroom doorway to admire Frank's shape through the misted shower enclosure.

As though sensing his gaze, Frank turned. "Well, you did answer the door in boxer shorts."

"Would a robe have been more appropriate?"

"Yes!" Frank turned back around, ducking his head under the water to rinse his hair.

Grinning, Tom stepped out of his shorts and slipped into the shower behind Frank.

Frank groaned. "We don't have time."

"I know. Pass me the soap. I'll do your back, you do my cock, and we'll be done."

Frank bent to kiss him, wetly and noisily. "I adore you."

"Right back at you."

Tom took them to a local diner for breakfast. Some part of him wanted to discombobulate the fabulous Brian and Simon. He'd liked Brian when they'd first met. Less so this time—mostly because he was embarrassed. He didn't want to like Simon. He was too goddamned stunning and put together. Cultured in a way Tom would never be. He could see why Frank spoke so well of him. Neither man seemed discomfited by the orange vinyl booths, cheap brown coffee mugs, and creased plastic menus, though.

"I'm going to have The Duke," Brian said, putting his menu aside.

"Have you ever eaten sausage gravy before?" Simon asked.

"Just because I grew up in Jersey City doesn't mean I don't know how to country. If you'll remember, Morristown is in the actual garden part of the state. We eat biscuits all the time."

Snorting softly, Simon put his menu aside.

Frank watched the pair with a bemused expression.

Tom squirmed in his seat.

A server took their order and Brian leaned back, draping an arm casually behind Simon's shoulders.

Simon shot him a look.

"Sorry, sorry. Forgot you're all but married now." Pulling his arm away, Brian lifted his chin toward Frank. "And don't you two make another happy shiny couple?"

"Jealous?" Frank asked.

"I told you I'd have him if you didn't want him."

Tom cleared his throat.

"Don't be an ass," Simon said.

"Where's Charlie?" Frank asked.

"Keeping vigil. It could be any day, any second." Simon checked his phone. "If I get a text, I'm gone."

"Any day?" Tom quirked an eyebrow in Frank's direction.

"Charlie's daughter is very, very pregnant."

"Ah." He vaguely remembered Frank mentioning it. "Um, congratulations?"

Simon's return smile was strange—a mixture of pride and confusion. It made him seem more human in some way. No less handsome, but maybe a touch more approachable. "I'll pass that on. Charlie will appreciate it."

"He will," Frank agreed. "He's that kind of guy."

Everyone but Brian was smiling now.

"So what's the occasion?" Frank asked.

Simon spoke up. "Brian showed me the pictures he took last week, caught me up on your plans. He wanted my opinion on a refit, and I wanted to see the place for myself, if you don't mind." He turned to Tom. "It's a gorgeous example of Dutch Colonial architecture. Do you know when it was built?"

"It belongs to Frank. It was in Frank's family," Tom said, trying not to squirm.

"You know more about it than me," Frank said.

Simon was still smiling in Tom's direction. "From what Brian told me, I got that impression too."

Tom glanced at Frank and Frank gave him a small nod. He took a deep breath. "It was built by Robert and William's father, Harold Tern, in 1932. It was modeled after Groeneveld Castle, in extreme miniature." He laughed. "Only twenty guest rooms, all with private bathrooms, which was pretty forward thinking of him. Harold valued comfort, though, which is why the first thing you see when you come inside is the lounge—which is another hallmark of the style."

Simon's impossibly blue eyes brightened, and really, he shouldn't have been able to become *more* handsome, but he did. Jesus. "You've studied the style! That will be so very handy when we draw up plans."

"Plans?"

The server interrupted them, laying out breakfasts: Brian's overflowing plate of biscuits topped with chipped beef and sausage gravy, home fries, and some sort of relish on the side. Tom secretly wished him heartburn, then took it back as he acknowledged the gift Brian had brought them. Simon was sketching an outline on the back of his paper placemat, which he moved out of the way for his two eggs, poached, and whole wheat toast.

Frank was having eggs Benedict, because of course he was. Tom had ordered his usual: a short stack and hot maple syrup.

"Brian mentioned adding outdoor space and showed me pictures of the barn. It appears in remarkably good condition," Simon was saying. "I've not suggested a renovation for a barn before, but we recently designed a neighborhood based on a Moravian farm and we did all of the outbuildings, garages, sheds, and whatnot, in a similar style."

And on it went. Pausing only to eat his eggs before they got cold, Simon filled the back of four placemats with rough sketches of ideas he'd been percolating. "I'd like to walk through the house. See the barn, take more precise measurements. Brian has given me an idea of the larger scope of the project. I can tell you about the individual buildings. What did you want to do with the cottages?"

Brian chipped in with a vague outline of the business model Tom had proposed during his visit. Tom glanced at Frank. Could Frank afford this? He supposed they'd have to decide that after Simon and Brian told them what it all might cost. Would there be a point where Frank weighed the apparent cost of repairs against their new relationship? He and Frank were older now. Supposedly wiser.

Was there harm in allowing everyone to dream up until that point?

Beneath the table, Frank took his hand and squeezed it, and Tom took that as his answer.

No. No, there wasn't.

CHAPTER 24

With breakfast a heavy lump in his stomach—questioning why he'd had eggs Benedict did him little better than wondering why he'd eaten both muffins and then snagged a piece of Simon's toast to mop up the rest of the hollandaise sauce—Frank followed Simon's trim damn ass around the upper floor of the main house. Simon ducked into each room, hummed softly to himself, made notes, and snapped pictures with his phone. Then on to the next one.

When he reached the end of the hall, he turned around, seemingly prepared to peek behind every door on the way back. Instead, he stopped and smiled at Frank. "Looks good on you," he said.

"What?"

"Happiness."

Frank made a rude noise in his throat and then ruined it all by asking, "What makes you think I'm happy?" Scowling, he tried again. "What makes you think I'm any happier today than I am on any other day? I live a charmed life, after all."

Simon's mouth quirked gently into an annoying half smile.

Straightening his spine did little to lessen the weight in Frank's gut. He did it anyway. "I'm not the one who has turned all domestic in his old age."

"Only because your house is about to fall down around your ears."

"It's not that bad."

"Close. Why have you never brought me here before? We've been to Cape May at least a dozen times."

"We've been to Cape May six times. Anyway, Cape May is quaint. This place is a disaster."

"A beautiful disaster." Simon made a note on his phone. "It's not going to be cheap, what you and Tom want to do here."

"I know."

Simon looked up and . . . just looked. Pinned Frank to the wall with intense scrutiny. "How did I never know you had a secret self?"

"What?"

"Tom, this house."

"You knew about both."

"I didn't know how much you still cared. You seemed happy, Frank. You were always smiling, flirting. The life of every party. You were the wind that blew through my doldrums more times than I can count."

"Listen to you getting all poetic."

"Frank."

"What? My happiness has never been your job."

"Of course it has."

"I have no regrets, Simon. I've achieved all I set out to achieve. More, even. I've been writing my own ticket in the most literal sense for the past ten years."

"And yet you're prepared to give all of that up to renovate a family resort in the Poconos. What about your writing, Frank? The travel, the parties."

"What about this much-vaunted happiness you were just flapping about?"

"I know how seriously you take your career." Simon's consternation deepened. "I wish I knew how to advise you."

"Tell me what you're thinking, because on the one hand you're warbling on about how happy I seem, while on the other you seem worried about my career."

"Has he told you what happened that night? Why he punched you?"

Ah . . . Sucking in a short breath, Frank held it until his lungs ached lightly with the expansion. Then he let it go, his chin dipping into a quick nod.

"What did he say?" Simon asked.

"He hasn't. I wondered what you were getting at, was all."

"Frank . . ."

Frank held up his hands. "Does it really matter? After all these years?"

"Is that what he asked you?"

Damn it.

"Frank, he's asking you to put—"

"He's not. I offered. This is my inheritance, and this is what I want to do with it."

"Are you sure?"

"You said I looked happy!"

"Not at the moment, you don't."

Frank backed up a step, shaking his head, and went to turn away. Simon caught his shoulder, halting his progress, and wrapped his hand around the back of Frank's neck. Then he was right there, pulling Frank into—

"Is this a hug?"

"I know it's not a thing we generally do."

Bewildered, Frank shifted slightly so that the loose embrace was less sideways and more natural. "Why are you hugging me?"

"Because I love you, you idiot, and because I don't know how else to tell you."

"Words would have been fine." Frank extricated himself from Simon's odd little hug, but kept a hold of Simon's hands. "Should we talk about you?"

"I'm fine. You've been there every time I needed you, Frank. I'm trying to do the same for you."

Frank exhaled slowly. Squeezed Simon's hands and let go. "Remember when you moved to Pennsylvania and I went on about how brave you were, upping sticks and crossing a border? Starting again on your own. A new business, a new town. I was so envious." He felt a wistful smile edge across his mouth. "I love my work. I love what I do. But I'm tired of the travel and I'm tired of pleasing other people. This is my opportunity to please myself, and the best part is I can do this and keep writing. I can write about this and plan to. And if this fails, I can write about that. But in the meantime, I get to actually do something instead of watching other people and . . ."

And that was it, Frank realized. He hadn't put the notion into words until now, but that was exactly why he wanted to do this. A part of it was for Tom, another for Robert, who had left him this gift. But mostly, it was for him.

Frank let his smile widen, and what he felt inside must have finally reflected outward, because Simon's eyes lit up. His own hesitant smile stretched to full.

"Okay," Simon said, his chin bobbing up and down. "Okay."

"So I have your permission to fuck up my life now?"

"As if you needed it."

Frank snorted. Then, sobering, he leaned in and lowered his voice. "Brian is the one we should be talking about. He's—"

"I know."

"Is he making a nuisance of himself?"

"Not really and Charlie likes him, which is not as bewildering as it should be."

"We're not going to have to find him a boyfriend, are we?"

Simon barked out a laugh. He patted Frank's arm. "Brian can take care of himself. He always has."

Frank wasn't so sure about that, and he wasn't even sure why he cared—except for the fact that Brian obviously wasn't over Simon. It made little sense, but it also made a lot of sense. Sometimes it was hard to appreciate just what you had until it was gone. He glanced toward the middle of the upstairs hallway, to where the grand staircase descended to the main level. To where Tom and Brian were firming up an outline of their plans.

Was that how Tom felt? Was that why he was receptive now? Frank knew Tom still had secrets, but didn't they all? They weren't teenagers anymore. What mattered now was what they chose to share, and how—and the fact Frank wouldn't allow himself to be so easy to dismiss this time.

Frank started at the soft touch on his shoulder. He'd dragged a chair out onto the front porch to think back on the day while watching color bleed from the sky. Sunset was burning a ragged line behind the trees, and when he blinked and looked up at Tom, he was surprised at the darkness gathered around him. Night truly fell here in a way it never did in the city, where streetlights threw back the dark as though denying every day its end.

Tom moved around to the front of the chair, and guided by Frank's hand, straddled his lap again. Frank found he enjoyed the weight of Tom across his thighs and the manner in which the seat evened out their height so that their faces were almost level. He also liked that this wasn't something they'd done before. It was a new habit, one for now.

He touched the side of Tom's face, laying his palm against Tom's cheek. With the sun all but set behind him, Tom's face was a mystery of dark shadow, but the tilt of his head so he could press his cheek into Frank's hand more than made up for it. He turned, touching his lips to Frank's palm, then leaned forward to kiss him lightly.

"You've been quiet this evening," he said, resting his forehead against Frank's for a second before lifting his chin to press a kiss there.

"Just tired. Long day with an abrupt start."

Tom shifted in his lap. "How's Little Frank?"

Frank wrapped his hands around the back of Tom's hips. "Probably fine."

"Didn't hurt to piss or anything today?"

"This is not quite the conversation I envisaged us having after dinner."

Tom bent down to kiss his lips. "Mmm?"

"Mmm."

Frank let himself be drawn into a deeper kiss and the further he drifted, the less important his thoughts became. Questions faded into the warm night air, replaced by a happy thrum of blood as his body came alive. Tom's kisses already felt familiar—the tease of his tongue now anticipated as he flicked it back and forth, inviting Frank to give chase, and the small, pleased sounds he made, as though kissing was the most joyful act.

Which it was.

Before they could get carried away on an old chair on an even older porch, Frank wrapped his hands around Tom's buttocks and stood, easily lifting him out of the chair. Walking proved a little less easy, though Frank thought pressing Tom against the porch post and kissing him harder well made up for his slight stumble.

Tom pulled out of the kiss. "Nice save."

"Humph." Frank backed them away from the post and carried Tom inside, dropping little kisses onto his face along the way. His arms were sore by the time he got to the stairs, but he persisted until they arrived at the first landing. There, Tom wriggled out of his arms and jumped down, only to grab Frank's hand and drag him up the rest of the stairs. "Are we going to your room because you have supplies?"

"That and I'm not sure sex on the mattress downstairs would be advisable."

Laughing, Tom led the way to room 206, kicked open the door, and dragged Frank toward the bed, where he immediately began tugging Frank's shirt upward.

Frank caught his hands and looked down into Tom's face. He wasn't sure why he'd pressed pause, and a quick study of Tom's expression revealed no clues. Tom's dark eyes were full of want and desire. His quick mouth was crooked into a genuine smile.

Now wasn't the time for thought. Frank had waited too long for this.

Mentally backing down from the moment, Frank let go of Tom's hands and reached for his shirt, helping Tom pull it over his head. Then he dispensed with Tom's. Pants came next. Neither of them was wearing shoes, which should have been disturbing; Frank never went without shoes. He hadn't been wearing a belt, either. Boxers and briefs followed, and Frank stepped away from the mess of clothes on the floor, determined not to be the man who took the time to fold everything before having sex.

One glance at Tom, naked, crawling back across the bed, was enough to distract him. Frank put his knees to the bed and followed, pinning Tom down as soon as he caught him, reveling in the full press of flesh to flesh. Oh to feel Tom's skin against his own. The hot, hard length of Tom's cock against his thigh. Tom's hands were everywhere, fingers caressing Frank's back, groping his ass, fondling the nape of his neck, skimming up over his ribs, and finally grasping his erection. Frank did the same. Bracing himself over Tom with one knee and one elbow, he explored the tightly packed body beneath him. Tom's neat little pecs, the dark nest of chest hair between. The lean line down between his ribs. The enviably flat abdomen. His skin was a study in contrasts. Soft and rough at the same time. Tanned darkly along his arms and around his neck, and the color of washed stone across his torso.

Frank kissed both nipples until they pebbled. Tom's hiss as he bit each point made him smile. He kissed a path to Tom's lean cock, thoughts of teasing his way around that no doubt aching point disappearing as soon as he caught the scent of arousal. He circled the head with his tongue, taking his first taste, then swallowed Tom down, lips parting noisily over his delicious mouthful at Tom's short, sharp shout.

The blowjob was inelegant. Frank was too turned on to think about how to make it good—and he didn't want Tom to come like this. Not tonight. They'd been fooling around for two days. Now he wanted more.

He let Tom's dick slide out of his mouth and pressed a kiss to each hip bone. Then he crawled back up to kiss Tom's mouth.

"Why did you stop?" Tom asked, though the answer seemed to shine from his eyes.

"Because I want you inside me," Frank said.

Tom's smile widened. "I hoped you'd say that."

Grinning, Frank went in search of supplies. Nothing in his suitcase. When he turned toward the bathroom, he noticed Tom had propped himself up on his elbows and was watching him move about the room. Frank ducked into the bathroom to find his kit bag. Tom was still watching him as he returned to the bed.

"What are you looking at?" Frank asked.

"Something I've wanted for a very long time."

"My ass?"

"You, Frank."

Frank's heart gave a little leap. Tom's words felt true and Frank wanted them to be. So why was he still standing here? Chalking up the small interlude to the fact he was naked, vulnerable, and very turned on, Frank dropped the bag on the nightstand and crawled back into the bed, condom and lube in hand. "How do you want me?"

"On your back. I . . ." A flush unfurled across Tom's cheeks. "I want to make love to you."

"I want that too."

Settled on his back, a pillow beneath his hips, Frank watched as Tom uncapped the lube and slicked up his fingers. It was weirdly clinical and intimate. He hadn't let a lot of men go there. In fact, he could count on one hand the number of times he'd bottomed. Any anxiety fell away as soon as Tom put the bottle aside and looked up, though. The wonderment on his face stole Frank's breath, and when Tom leaned forward, not aiming for his ass but coming up to kiss him, Frank was back on that damn bench beside Lenape Lake. Full of emotions he couldn't contain. On the verge of tears and so damn scared that his hands shook as he lifted them to wrap around Tom's shoulders.

Then they were fully involved in the kiss, and the thrum of his pulse changed, picking up, sending tingles down his spine. The first touch of Tom's cool fingers to his hole was electric and wonderful. Fucking necessary. Frank's entire self seemed to slip down to that one place, and though the metaphor was crude, as Tom worked him open, he felt parts of himself giving way. One finger was the past, two was the hurt and fear. The soft rhythm, in and out, the pace of their newness. The brush across his prostate the spark—the core of everything that had always been between them.

By the time Tom pressed the sheathed head of his cock to Frank's entrance, first a nudge, a breath, then a quiet easing inside, Frank felt as though they'd done this a hundred times. More than. It was always meant to be this easy between them, this splendid. He wanted to be joined with Tom. To feel Tom move inside him. Wished only that they'd been together long enough to dispense with that last barrier.

Tom paused once he was fully seated. His narrow hips a perfect fit between Frank's upraised thighs, his arms straight out before him, a hand planted to either side of Frank's ribs. He smiled. Frank smiled back up at him, at the halo of dark, floppy hair, the large dark eyes, that pixie smile.

"You ready for this?" Tom asked, his voice quiet, almost reverent.

"Bit late to ask, isn't it?"

Tom chuckled. Rocked his hips forward a little.

Frank felt his smile winnowing. He fought it, then said, "I didn't know I was still waiting."

"Neither did I." Tom's voice was the barest whisper.

Frank touched the side of Tom's face. "Love me."

He only realized what he'd been asking, what he could have been asking, when Tom answered: "I never stopped."

Tom started to move then, as though he knew the moment would swell too wide if he didn't do something. Frank closed his eyes and tipped his head back into the pillows. He let his hands fall where they would, both loosely folding around Tom's hips. And for a while he simply breathed and experienced. Lived the burning path of pleasure Tom wove inside him. In and out with a slight rock at the end. Images of Tom's face passed across the blackness behind his lids. Tom's smile and brightness. Tom as he was now. Tom the man. The man inside him, making love to him.

"Frank."

Frank opened his eyes. Tom leaned forward, and they kissed in that frantic and breathless way—their lips just catching, their need pulling them together, making their lips cling between kisses as Tom moved harder, faster, his breath puffing against Frank's cheek.

"You feel so good," Tom said, and the bland comment was the most wonderful compliment.

Frank gripped Tom's hips. "So do you." But he wanted more, he wanted . . . more. He pressed his hands to the front of Tom's hips. "Can I turn around? I want it harder. I want you to fuck me, Tom."

The pixie smile widened to feral proportions. Tom pulled out and Frank got to his knees. Tom wasted no time, spreading Frank wide before pushing back in. The stretch was just what Frank needed. He gasped and groaned, ground back into Tom's thrusts. Immediately the soft tingle that had been gathering with agonizing slowness at the base of his spine began to pulse forward, squeezing his balls into a tight knot. He reached for his dick and met Tom's hand there. Together, they jacked him in time to Tom's thrusts.

"Harder, Tom."

"Oh God."

The slap of skin became a pleasant sting as Tom drove into him from behind. Balls-deep with every thrust, skewering him, turning him inside out. The angle struck his prostate, sending electricity through his veins. It was the most delicious sort of burn. The pain of being alive.

Tom picked up the pace, thrusting faster. Leaving Frank the care of his own cock, Tom put one hand on the back of Frank's hip and the other hand flat against his spine. When those fingers curled, pressing nails into Frank's skin, Frank knew Tom's peak must be close. He arched back, meeting the next few thrusts with near bone-jarring force.

Tom cried out and stiffened. Then he jackhammered into Frank, his frenzied pace and misfiring thrusts so damn Tom that Frank nearly laughed. Instead he groaned at the feel of his lover coming inside him, thin skin of the condom notwithstanding. He squeezed his cock harder. Stroked up and back, pleading for his own release.

When it came half a minute later, the bedroom disappeared. Noise ceased battering his eardrums—Tom's shouts and moans, the creak of the bed, his own ragged breath. His body went numb and white light blotted out his sight. Then everything returned on a cymbal crash, and Frank fell forward. His cock jerked in his hand, and he had just enough presence of mind to protect his precious before landing flat on his face, Tom sprawled across his back.

Time ebbed and flowed and finally steadied.

The sheet beneath him was cold and wet and his balls felt empty. "Holy fuck."

Sliding off him and to the side, Tom echoed the sentiment in his own way. "Jeez."

"Thirty years, Tom."

"Huh?"

"We could've—" No. They couldn't go back. Forward was the only way, but his thoughts were a broken jigsaw puzzle. Pieces scattered everywhere. "Just wondering if that's why."

Tom cuddled up next to him. "Why it was so good?"

Frank had to get off his stomach. If he fell asleep this way, his neck would hurt all day tomorrow. And they'd have to peel the sheet away from him with acetone. Also, his hand was already tingling. He shouldn't sleep with his fingers wrapped around his cock.

"Yeah." Frank made the effort to roll onto his side, facing Tom. "Not sure we can top that."

"But we're going to try?"

Frank's answering grin felt stiff. His face hadn't quite recovered from that weird bout of numbness. "Further exploration is going to have to wait until morning. I can't feel half my face, and I think my hand is stuck to my cock."

Tom started laughing and his mirth was infectious. Laughing in his current position wasn't the most comfortable thing, but Frank gave in. And though the orgasm had been amazing—better than— this might be the best part. Lying wrecked in a puddle of spilt joy, laughing with Tom.

CHAPTER 25

Sandra: *Tom? We have returned mail from your address. What gives?*

Sandra: *I'm worried about you. Please call.*

Sandra: *Call me, Tom!*

Sandra: *Don't make me track you down.*

Sandra: *Tom, they're talking debt collection. Please call me.*

After reading Sandra's last text, Tom silenced his phone and tucked it under a pile of papers on the edge of the desk. The slight lump kept drawing his attention, though, and every time he glanced over, invisible hands squeezed his stomach and rolled it.

He looked back at the laptop screen, but failed to immerse himself in Brian's preliminary proposal. He checked the time. Maybe an hour in the cellar would clear his head. He had two albums to assemble and cell signal was spotty down there. And he could start compiling a list of what he had to sell to make up what he owed Mountain Manor.

The printer wouldn't get him much, and he did need that for the proofs. Maybe the camera he kept in the car? He could get a couple hundred for that. Use his phone for "life happens" shots for a while. He had to keep the car; the bus didn't stop anywhere convenient and how would he get to weddings otherwise? Could he trade it in for an older model?

"Penny for your thoughts."

Tom jumped half a mile—or half a foot—landing with a whoosh of breath and a curious burn of guilt, as though Frank had caught him listing Bossen Hill property to sell. Or figuring out how long he could coast on his hospitality—not that Frank knew he was keeping Tom at the moment. Tom checked the laptop screen and the pile of papers covering his phone and then looked up, reaching for a Wednesday morning sort of expression. What that might be, he truly didn't know.

Frank stood over him, smiling laconically. "Maybe those thoughts need more. A silver dollar, perhaps?"

Four thousand of them would do nicely. Then you can tell me where I can get another two for next month.

He should just ask Frank for a paycheck. One wouldn't make much of a difference, but he'd at least be able to stop the calls from Mountain Manor. Of greater concern was what he was going to do for money if they went ahead with this project. Maybe he could introduce the subject by hinting at how many hours he could put in beside any contractors.

Of course, if Frank was anything like him, he'd see their time as a bill they didn't have to pay. Then there was the complicated ball of crap involved with asking the man he was sleeping with—

"Tom?"

"Sorry. I was reading over Brian's proposal and daydreaming."

Frank smiled. "Yeah? Has he given us a figure yet?"

"He's waiting on Simon for that. Right now we're building stages, so we can price out each one in case we don't want to do everything all at once. Like, obviously the house itself is the first stage." Tom turned back to the laptop and scrolled down a little. "He's divided the garden into three other stages: barn renovation, patio refurbishment, and the guest cottages. We need to prioritize those."

Frank grabbed a chair. "Okay, so let's talk it out."

They did that for about half an hour, and finally had a rough plan based on the season each stage could be complete.

While Tom made notes for Brian, Frank pulled out his phone. "I have to go to Jersey for a couple of days. If I go tomorrow, I can be home by the weekend."

Home. Tom smiled.

"Want to come with?"

Tom glanced up. "To New Jersey? Why would I do that?"

"You could see my place. I've got a great view of Manhattan." Frank grinned. "You can tell me if I've hung your prints well. See that

I actually have hung them. We could have sex in a bed that doesn't threaten to collapse beneath us at every turn."

Tom laughed. Then he shrugged. "I dunno. I . . ." He looked around the cozy office, oddly reluctant to leave. Would the lodge collapse the moment he stepped away? Obviously not: he left nearly every day.

Would he collapse without the lodge to . . . what? Without this project?

"Everything okay over there?" Frank's pale-ginger eyebrows were drawn down and together. He touched Tom's hand. "You've been quiet the past couple of days. Anything you want to talk about?"

Shaking his head was automatic. "No." Tom forced a smile. "We've been busy at night, is all."

"And most mornings, I know. My balls are working overtime to keep up. I even found myself researching sperm production to see if there was something I could eat or drink to refill the well."

Tom laughed again. "Only you, Frank."

"Tell me you're not interested in this elixir of youth I'm researching."

"I can't say that, but I am hoping we remember that we're not eighteen sometime soon. Even my legs are sore this morning."

"I can think of worse ways to go."

"Mmm."

The familiar crunch of gravel distracted them. Frank glanced toward the office window. "Are we expecting someone?"

"Not that I know of."

"I hope it's not that annoying Nolan woman again. She managed to get my cell phone number. Did I tell you?"

"You did not."

Frank stood, pulling his phone out of his pocket. "I'm not above suing her for harassment if she doesn't stop leaving messages."

"You should." Tom leaned forward to peer through the window. His pulse jerked up at the outline of the car approaching the circle. "It's the police."

"Huh?" Frank looked up from his phone. "Did you say police?"

"Yeah." Tom stood.

They opened the door before the officer knocked, and Tom eased the scowl away from his face before it could lay permanent lines. The police force had always seemed like a weird choice for Neil Crook. Then again, the guy was weird. And stalkerish. After learning that Tom and Gerry were no longer dating, Neil had pursued him with single-minded purpose for nearly two years. Sandra had found it amusing. Tom, not so much.

Neil's eyebrows shot toward his hairline as he spotted Frank. "Franklin Tern! Long time no see."

Frank plainly didn't recognize Neil, so Tom made introductions. "Frank, you remember Neil Crook?"

Frank's mouth dropped open. He hurriedly shut it, only to open it again as he stuck out a hand. "Neil! It's great to see you."

They exchanged a quick shake with Neil smiling and bobbing his head. "Likewise. I didn't realize you were back. We were all wondering what might become of this place with Robert gone." Neil cleared his throat. "Ah, and my condolences."

"Thank you. What brings you out?"

Neil pulled a small notebook from his pocket. "Oh, a complaint, actually."

"A complaint?" Tom glanced at Frank only to meet a flirtatious wink. Were they both thinking of bedsprings and creaky posts? Had to be.

Neil traced a finger across his notepad. "Suspicious activity, people in the woods, coming and going."

"I walk the trails regularly," Tom said. "For maintenance and just when the weather is nice."

"At night?"

"What? No." Had someone else seen that kid ducking through the woods after skulking around the cottages? "Who's complaining?"

"I don't have that information." Neil closed his pad. "Mind if I take a look around?"

"For what?" Frank asked.

"Intruders. Vagrants. Squatters. A cache of illegal substances. Have you been up here for long?"

"Close to a month and I've seen no sign of any—" Frank's brow furrowed. "Wait, the first week I was here someone came into the house. Right through the front door. I thought it was Tom, but he was still in the garage, I think."

Ghostly fingers crept across the back of Tom's neck. "And there was the kid that crossed the back lawn one afternoon. A couple of weeks ago. And the raccoons, Frank."

"I'm hardly likely to forget those."

"Raccoons?" Neil asked.

"Three dead and badly decomposed raccoons dumped in the pool," Tom said.

"And you didn't report them?"

"They were just dead raccoons."

"We supposed it was a prank," Frank put in. His expression suggested he thought it was something more now, however.

"Is it possible you have someone squatting out back somewhere? Kids using the barn or old guest cottages as a hideout?" Neil asked.

"I don't—" Tom began.

"Could we?" Frank interrupted, directing his furrowed brow at Tom.

Tom quickly shook his head, even though he didn't know for sure. Not about the barn, anyway. What he *did* know was that if they started going through the guest cottages, they'd find his stuff and he'd have a lot to explain.

"I'd be happy to check them out for you, since I'm here," Neil said. He smiled and it was not a disarming expression. "It'll give us a chance to catch up some more."

"I'm sure we can take a look ourselves," Frank said.

"Not sure if you're aware, Frank, but we've got a lot of problems up here with the younger generation. Heroin, crack cocaine. It's not just weed anymore."

"Was it ever?" Frank murmured.

"Well, you see, with reports of young people running back and forth through your property, I could insist on taking a look at your outbuildings. Seeing as we're all old friends, I figured we could do this . . . friendly-like."

Frank seemed to consider this a moment, then nodded. "Oh, fine. Let's get it over with. Tom?"

Tom pressed his hands to his sides to prevent them from betraying the panic building in his chest. "I'll get the keys to the cottages."

"We'll meet you there. I'll take Neil through the garage first."

Damn it. He wouldn't manage to shift more than a box or two before Frank and Neil were finished in the garage, so he might as well stop thinking about it. The idea was tempting, though. As was just disappearing down the driveway. Or misplacing the keys. But making Neil come back out here with a warrant probably wasn't the friendly thing to do, and causing difficulties now would only reflect badly on him once Frank got an eyeful of the boxes stacked in cottage number one.

Shit.

Tom went to get the keys and then met them in the garage, where Neil was inspecting every corner, and finding nothing—until he checked Tom's car.

"Could someone be living in here?" he asked, indicating the blanket and pillow on the back seat.

Tom's pulse thrummed in his throat. "I use them to cover my camera bags."

Frank gave him an odd look.

Neil took his time poking through the rear garden, all the while explaining where these kids were hiding their drugs. Tom formed the impression that he didn't often have a captive audience and was taking full advantage. They inspected the barn next and even Neil agreed that the roof was in such poor condition that no one would risk sleeping in there. Finally, they came to the pair of intact cottages.

Tom unlocked the doors for One and Two and gestured toward Three and Four. "The doors are locked, but with the state of the roofs"—it was always the roofs—"I'm not sure I need to bother."

"Agreed." Neil opened the door to Cottage Number Two and poked his head in. "Lights?" he asked.

"Just flip the switch. These two are still powered. No water, though." Tom cracked open the door to Number One. "I'll check in here."

Frank's phone rang. He pulled it out of his pocket, scowling. His expression cleared when he looked at the screen, though. Accepting the call, he lifted the phone to his ear. "What's up, Lucas?

His PA. Tom ducked into the cottage and stood there, scrutinizing the three stacks of boxes that represented his life up to this point. What was he going to tell Frank? That his apartment was being fumigated? No, he'd have mentioned that before now. That he'd made an arrangement with Robert would be better. That he was just using the place as storage.

Frank pushed through the door, pocketing his phone. "How is Neil Crook with the police?" He eyed the stacked boxes and frowned. "What's all this?"

"I can explain."

"Eureka!" came a curiously joyful shout from the cottage next door.

Tom scrambled outside where Neil met them, holding up a tackle box.

"Paraphernalia," he explained.

"Para-what?" Frank asked.

Neil flipped open the box to reveal a bong, a small pipe, empty baggies, not empty baggies, and a small supply of white powder.

Well, hell.

CHAPTER 26

Ignoring the prickle at the back of his neck, the sense of premonition regarding what he'd seen in Cottage One, Frank peered into the box as Neil sorted through the contents. The pipe and bong had a grimy and suspect appearance. They were also familiar, as was the box. The bags of weed and powder couldn't possibly be as old as the *paraphernalia*, though.

Tom was regarding the box with an expression close to shock that quickly faded as apparent anger surged to the fore, coloring his cheeks a darker shade of tan. "I had no idea this was here."

"This could be an issue with you lecturing the kids and all," Neil said.

Neil thought the drugs were Tom's? And what was this about lectures? "Tom?"

Tom made an irritated gesture. "I've talked to the students at the high school about what addiction looks like." He glared at Neil. "What are you implying?"

"That box doesn't belong to Tom," Frank said. "It's my brother's. The box and the pipes are about forty years old, Neil. The drugs might be new, but someone found Matty's box and is putting it to use." And it wasn't Tom. He could be a moody bastard, but knowing his history gave Frank all the more reason to believe Tom would never touch the stuff in the box.

Beside him, Tom deflated a little, though his face remained flushed.

"Seems pretty convenient to me," Neil drawled. "Might have to get the state police in on this one."

"For a couple baggies?" Tom just sounded disgusted now. "C'mon, Neil, it's not mine—and even if it was, I wouldn't be running around the woods at night with it." He looked up, focusing on the distant line of trees, then frowned in Frank's direction. "I think we've definitely got some kids sneaking around here, though."

"Place looks abandoned enough," Frank agreed.

"I'm gonna take this in," Neil said, hefting the box. "Start an investigation. Either of you got plans to leave town? I might have to call you in for questioning."

Was he serious?

The idea of being in an interrogation room with Neil wasn't simply annoying, but disturbing. Did he still suck his Twizzlers? An absurd image flittered across Frank's thoughts—Neil leaning a hip against the table in an interrogation room, busily shoving a Twizzler in and out of his mouth, and Frank loudly admitting to everything just to get him to stop. Frank quickly pressed his lips together over the ridiculous smile that wanted to take over his mouth. So not the time. Besides, he had other concerns—such as all the boxes stacked inside Cottage One.

Frank pulled his wallet from his pocket and extracted a business card. "Here. I can be reached on this number. I'll be sure to remain in the country until you close your investigation."

Neil took the card. Then he narrowed his eyes at Tom. "And I always know where to find you."

Tom answered with a weak smile and, "Want to poke around some more? Might find a container of coke or something in the cellar."

"Don't be coy with me, Benjamin."

"You don't really think that box is mine?"

Neil moved pursed lips back and forth, looking like a Mr. Potato Head with a wonky mouth, before letting go a sigh. "Probably not. Just don't go anywhere, all right?"

"If it is kids, you're not going to find them," Tom said. "They'll come looking for their stash and when it's gone, they'll disappear."

"Maybe I could stake out—"

Frank tapped the business card in Neil's hand. "Call me and I'll give you the number of my lawyer." It was becoming increasingly obvious why Neil was still a small-town cop with no apparent rank—not to consider the Stroud Township Police Department unkindly.

"I'll do that," Neil said, pocketing the card.

Then, thankfully, he took the tackle box and left the premises.

After watching the taillights disappear down the drive, Frank turned and started back toward the cottages at a determined pace.

Tom caught up with him a few seconds later, falling into step. "I'm going to see what else is in Cottage Two," he said. "Clean it up and figure out how they were getting in. The lock wasn't touched. Might serve to change the locks on both doors anyway. Not quite sure what we can do about security out back, though—"

"What about all the boxes in Cottage One?" Frank asked.

Tom looked up, cheeks aflame once more. "Storage."

"Uh-huh." Lengthening his stride, Frank pulled ahead. He could hear Tom practically scrambling to keep up, and in other circumstances, might have laughed at the game. It wasn't a game, though. He wanted to know why there were three not-so-neat stacks of boxes in the first cottage.

He pushed through the door and into the middle of the almost empty cottage. A lone chair nestled in one corner, a rolled-up sleeping bag tucked into one side, a yoga mat poking out of the other. Farther down on that side, the closet doors stood half-folded like a broken fan. Frank moved past the boxes, peered into the closet, at the neat row of hanging polo shirts, and closed his eyes.

Tom stepped quietly to his side. "I can explain."

Frank shook his head—not because he didn't want to hear Tom's explanation. More to clear thoughts he didn't want to acknowledge. *Why now?* He'd asked himself that question repeatedly over the past couple of weeks. Why, after thirty years of silence, was Tom willing to be with him now? He touched two fingers to his nose, squeezing the bridge carefully between, feeling for the knot Tom had left there that night.

His sinuses burned.

He didn't want to believe that all Tom had wanted from him was somewhere to live, but the evidence almost shouted into the silence battering his ears. And if there was one thing Frank hated—well, a thing—it was being made to feel a fool.

"Frank?"

"Do you actually have a place in town?" Frank jerked his chin toward the chair as he asked. There was no obvious outline for the mat and sleeping bag on the floor, and of course there wasn't. He'd had Tom with him every night for the past few days. Where had he slept before that? Not here, unless he'd gone to all the trouble of sneaking his car out before dawn only to arrive back as the sun rose. He turned around. "Where did you sleep last week?"

Tom's hands formed a complicated knot in front of his stomach. "In my car."

"In your car!"

Flinching, Tom stepped backward.

"What the actual fuck, Tom?"

Tom pulled his hands apart and squared his shoulders. "I had to give my place up to pay for Mom's care at Mountain Manor."

"But you're busy nearly every weekend. And Robert was paying you as well."

"Was. I haven't been paid since two weeks before he died."

"What?"

Tom started patting his pockets, then interlaced his fingers again. "Look, it doesn't matter, does it? I don't work here anymore, not really. My job died with Robert." He took another step back and turned toward the door. "I'll start loading up my car. Call Gerry or something. I can get my stuff out—"

With one stride, Frank was beside him, grabbing his shoulder. "I don't want you to leave."

"Then what do you want?"

"I want you to tell me what's going on."

"I'm homeless, Frank! I'm a bum who can't support himself, let alone his mother." With each shouted word, Tom seemed to break a little, his shoulder becoming less and less steady beneath Frank's hand. He was trembling, Frank realized.

"How long?" he asked.

Tom shook his head.

"How long, Tom?"

"Just let me go. Please. I'll go."

"Why do you want to go? Where will you go? God, where do you even sleep when you're in your car? Did you do that while Robert was alive?"

Another head shake.

"Did Robert know?"

More sorry side-to-side action.

"Talk to me, Tom. Please. Help me understand what's happening here." *Tell me it's not what it looks like.*

Tom had never been the mercenary type. The idea that he might be now didn't mesh with the man who lectured at schools, took pictures of kids and weddings, and maintained a website of soulful photography that practically sold itself. The man mortgaging his happiness against his mother's future.

Tom couldn't hear his thoughts, though, and whatever Frank's face said obviously spelled out something else entirely, because Tom kept shaking his head and backing away, his shoulder slipping from beneath Frank's grasp.

Frank's pocket buzzed. Ignoring his phone, he started after Tom who wasn't running, but walking quickly toward the garage.

"Tom, wait. We have to talk about this."

Frank's phone kept ringing.

Tom kept walking.

Frank pulled out his phone, ready to tell Lucas that whatever it was, it had to wait. A glance at the screen showed Simon's brooding face. He swiped Accept and raised the phone to his ear. "Now's not really a good time. Can I call you back?"

"Liv had her baby."

Frank stopped walking. "What?"

"The baby. It's a girl, Frank. A little girl."

"Ah, congratulations?"

"Can you not be an ass for five seconds and celebrate this miracle with me?"

"I'll celebrate with you tomorrow. Or maybe later this afternoon, after I finish collaring Tom."

"Uh-oh."

"He . . . It's too much to tell you right now, but . . . Fuck it." Tom had disappeared inside the garage, and Frank could hear his car starting up. "Goddamn it." He started running.

"What happened?"

"He's homeless, Simon. He's been living . . . God, I don't know where. On the sofa in the office. On the floor in one of the cottages. He's been sleeping in the back seat of his car for the past two weeks because I was here and he didn't want me to know!" The shock of it finally hit, piercing Frank's chest with a jagged spear.

Panting, he crossed the garage floor in time to see Tom's car turn out of the side drive.

How had he not known what was going on? He was a journalist, for Christ's sake. He was supposed to notice details—like how often Tom turned up wearing the same clothes as the day before. The fact he always seemed to need a shower when he got to the lodge. The Mello fucking Yello supply in the kitchen.

Though, he could have had another stash at his place of residence. Except he didn't.

Just how much did the care for his mother cost and . . .

"Shit."

"What?" Simon asked.

"He hasn't been paid in nearly two months. I . . . God. Why didn't he ask me for a check?"

"Would you have, in his position?"

"No." Of course he wouldn't have—because they'd let this damn wound fester for way too long. Frank massaged his chest. His poor heart. "What's her name?"

"What?"

"Liv's baby. I assume mother and daughter are well?"

Simon laughed, and even through the phone, his emotional state was clear. This was a big moment for him—and Frank had nearly ruined it. "Liv named her Meredith, and they're both well."

Frank let a smile creep across his mouth—the barest lift of his lips, but an easing of the pain in his chest nonetheless. "Give her my best, will you? I'm . . . Thanks for calling and telling me."

"You're welcome. Now go sort things out with Tom."

Frank massaged his forehead. "I don't know if that's possible."

"You're the one who schooled me in the art of grand gestures."

"Charlie wasn't homeless and lying about it."

"It's a different situation, but the same solution should still apply."

"That's the thing, Simon. It's really not that different."

"What do you mean?"

"This is exactly what happened thirty years ago."

"He *hit* you?"

"No. No." The second no was much quieter than the first and the cell phone felt heavy in Frank's hand. "He doesn't trust me, Simon." Quieter still, "He never did."

CHAPTER 27

August 1987

Didn't matter whether Tom moved enough to cause a slight breeze or sat still. Sweat continued to creep from his hairline, making his face itch. The back of his neck was a grease trap, and he was pretty sure his hair was clinging to his scalp like a wet rag.

The sun had set about an hour ago. It shouldn't be this hot.

Down on the patio, two stories below, kids splashed in the lit-up pool. Tom wasn't the best swimmer, but now that he could touch his toes to the bottom, he didn't mind the pool. He liked the creek better. The water was colder, crisper. It smelled good too. Like air and leaves and summer. And now that he and Frank had finished shifting the boulders that formed the edge of what could be a small pool, they had a spot to wallow in without the current threatening to drag them all the way to Stroudsburg.

A scuff higher up drew Tom's attention to the slope of the roof where it joined the flat part over the second-floor balcony. Frank was pushing a wrapped bundle over the lip. Tom crawled over to meet him, pulling on the wadded-up towels. They were probably full of Tupperware. Frank couldn't go anywhere without a snack.

"It's hot up here," Tom said. "Want to go to the creek instead?"

"And break my ankle again in the dark? No, thank you. Besides, now that Matty is gone, we've got the roof all to ourselves."

"He's been gone for five years."

"And not likely to come back. Did I tell you his wife was pregnant?"

"All right, Matty!" Of all the people to settle down and start a family, Frank's older brother would have been Tom's last pick. But he could see it. Beneath the weed-smoking, prank-playing façade, Matt had always been the practical sort. Hell, he was going to be a doctor just like his dad.

A light depression pressed down on Tom's shoulders. Matt had gone off to be a doctor. Frank's sister, Annabelle, was teaching, and Frank would be leaving for college tomorrow, where he'd no doubt get his degree in journalism and go on to shape the world through his words. Would he want to take their notebook with him? Would Frank alone be the one to achieve their dreams?

Probably, because Tom would be staying here in Pennsylvania. He was grateful for his partial scholarship to Marywood up in Scranton, but knew that'd be as far from home as he was likely to get, and only for a few hours a day. In between his studies and the commute, Tom had to work. Keep working. Some folk had exciting futures. Some didn't.

The second bundle of towel clanked oddly. Tom unwrapped it to reveal two six-packs of beer. He didn't really drink and neither did Frank, but tonight they'd both make an exception. It was going to be the last bit of time they had together for a while. He yanked a can out of the plastic loop and had it open before he'd even settled back onto the roof.

"Take one of the towels," Frank said.

Tom raised his can in a toast. "I'm good."

Frank fussed a bit more, laying out the towels and snacks, and then he helped himself to a beer and sat next to Tom. Knocking their cans together, he said, "Cheers."

Tom grunted and swigged. The beer was warm. "Where did you get this?"

"From Matty's stash in the cellar. His tackle box was down there too. Should I have brought that up as well?"

"Nah, this is fine." Neither of them smoked. Next year, that might change. Frank would have all sorts of adventures in the city. "All packed?"

"Yeah."

"What time are you leaving?"

"Not until late. Won't be much traffic on a Sunday and it's only eighty miles."

Eighty-eight, actually, from Bossen Hill to Columbia University. It could be worse—he could have headed west like Matty had.

Frank elbowed him gently. "I'll be home on weekends."

"No, you won't."

"You can come to the city."

Tom gave him a flat look, which probably failed under the vague light of the moon.

Frank sipped his beer. "This is disgusting."

"It's beer."

"Let's drink up, then. I don't want our last night to be swallowed by melancholy."

"Better to drink warm beer, make plans we won't keep, and then vomit up the memories."

"Aren't you feeling jolly?"

"Sorry." Tom drained his first can, crushed it, and stopped just before he pitched it over the roof. There were still guests in the pool, and throwing beer cans from the roof was more a sixteen-year-old thing. He grabbed another beer and popped it open. Frank finished his first with a loud burp. Tom passed the open can over and pulled another from the rings.

For a while they did nothing but sit and drink. The first six-pack disappeared, but the snacks stayed untouched, which was unusual. Frank was always eating—unless he was nervous.

"Are you worried about school?" Tom asked.

"What?"

"You're not eating."

"Oh."

"You're going to do great." Tom willed a smile into being and found he didn't have to try hard to sustain it. Thoughts of Frank's future made him happy, even if he knew he wouldn't be a part of it. Not the way they'd planned. Frank had a generous soul and it showed in his writing—even when he thought he was being witty. He liked people and he liked telling their stories. He was going to make it big, and that made Tom proud.

"We're both going to do great, Tommy. The world had better watch out."

Beer swimming happy laps in his blood stream, Tom found it easy to agree. Maybe they would. Tucking an arm beneath his head, he reclined onto the towel Frank had laid out behind him and gazed up at the stars. He'd tried photographing the night sky, with little success. He had worked the problem over in his mind, though. What he needed was a longer exposure and a way to stabilize his camera so it didn't move. Something kept knocking his tripod on previous attempts. Wild animals, probably. Raccoons out hunting for a midnight snack.

Frank settled beside him, the warmth of his shoulder welcome despite the sweat still dampening Tom's skin. He rolled his head to the side. Frankie was looking at him with a half-drunk smile. Jeez, he'd miss that smile. He'd miss Frankie. He'd become just *Frank* at school, no doubt. Someone other than this freckle-cheeked, ginger-haired man-boy who was still smiling at him.

"What'cha thinking about?" Frankie asked.

"Your name."

"How's that?"

"Will you go by Frankie or Frank at school?"

"Why not Franklin? I'll want to begin as I intend to continue."

Franklin. Tom snorted.

"What?"

"You don't look like a Franklin."

"What do I look like?"

Mine. "You'll always be Frankie to me."

"And you'll always be Tommy to me."

"Tom."

Frank grinned. "Tommy."

"Tom!"

Frank made to grab him, apparently forgetting he had a beer can in his hand. Liquid sloshed over the lip, some catching Tom in the eye. Squeezing it shut, he massaged the lid as if that would make a difference.

"You okay?"

"Yeah, just blinking beer out of my eye." He opened his eye and peered through the blurry darkness. "Frankie? You there?"

"Can you see?"

"No!" Tom injected as much panic into his voice as he could. "How'm I going to take pictures with only one eye?"

"Oh, Jesus." Frank was flipping through his snack collection. "I think I've got some water here. Hold on. Keep blinking. Or . . . don't. Shit. I don't know what to do with an eye injury."

Tom sat up, legs folding up at the knee, and bent forward, rubbing at his temple. "It stings, Frankie!" It was hard not to laugh.

Then Frankie was kneeling in front of him, a tin cup in his hand. "From the Thermos."

"You're going to wash my eye out with hot chocolate?"

"No. It's hot water. I brought tea bags up." Of course he had. "Let me see."

Tom moved his hands away from his face and blinked a few times. His eye should be nice and bloodshot from the beer and all the rubbing. Unfortunately, his mouth wouldn't stay in a grim line.

"Are you— Oh, you little shit."

Frankie dropped his cup and wrestled Tom backward, down to the roof. Tom rolled them, digging his fingers into Frankie's ribs while fending off the hand burrowing into his armpit. The bulk of Frank beneath him brought other thoughts to mind. Of skin instead of damp cotton. Frankie's beery breath called into question the probable taste of his mouth. The powerful thighs beneath him hid who knew what treasures. And, oh, to feel those arms around him in an embrace instead of a tussle.

It'd been a while since they'd wrestled and this was why. Tom couldn't think straight when he was this entwined with Frank. Couldn't keep to the promise he'd made himself and the one he'd extracted from his best friend. They weren't allowed to do this. They weren't allowed to be in love, or to explore each other this way. It wouldn't end well. Couldn't.

Tom's blood plunged south in a dizzying rush, and an invisible band tightened around his lungs. Still, he dug his fingers into Frank's side as though pretending this was all in innocence would save him.

Frank rolled them the other way, pinning Tom to the roof. Tom groaned as he felt the weight of another man against his hips and the telltale hardness nudging his thigh. If Frank brought his hips down, the game would be up. He'd feel what Tom wanted to hide. Frank caught one of Tom's hands and raised it over his head, pressing it to the warm tile. Tom slid his fingers under Frank's T-shirt, skating across his ribs. Frank gasped. His hips bucked forward and he gasped again, more purposefully this time.

The pressure against Tom's cock was wonderful and awful. Mostly awful. No, mostly . . . *Shit.*

Frank pushed his hips down, mashing their thighs and erections together. "Tom," he whispered.

"We can't." Swallowing a moan, Tom willed his fingers to remain still. To stop tracing over Frank's sides.

Frank leaned down and kissed him, the softest brush of lips. "Why not?"

Tom closed his eyes. Felt his mouth change shape as he sought another kiss. *As he kissed Frank back.* Frank's groan reverberated through his body, making Tom's skin tingle and his chest ache. He arched and Frank was right there, moving into him. Their lips parted on the same note and their tongues touched. An invisible spark leaped between them, tingling at the lip and buzzing by the time it struck Tom's chest. The world seemed to quake.

Oh God.

No.

Tom rolled them to the side, all the while trying to find the will to pull his mouth from Frank's. They couldn't do this. Shouldn't. Couldn't. Frank was preparing to leave him. College in New York City would only be the beginning of Frank's new life. A better life—everything Frank had ever wanted.

Could he take just one more kiss before Frank left? Just one. It already hurt, as though Frank was halfway to the city. Tom leaned in instead of away, diving his now free hand into Frank's hair, tugging at orange curls. A last kiss and it set his heart on fire. He was going to explode from the heat of it. As if not directed by him, his other hand was drifting lower to the hardness tenting Frank's shorts. He felt something bounce off his foot, but paid it no mind. The struggle between his head and heart had all his attention. He had to let go. He didn't want to let go!

Then there was a shout. Several shouts. Heart pounding, Tom reared back, away from Frank. He panted into the darkness, listening. Had that been his subconscious warning him away from the thing he wanted most in the world? Reminding him of why he couldn't have it?

No, it was people down by the pool. Talking, yelling.

"I think we knocked a can off the roof," Frank said. Smiling, he leaned forward, lips already pursed for another kiss.

Something inside Tom's head clicked, and his hand, the one at Frank's waist, came up and back. His fingers curled. He tried to stop it, but it was as though he'd lost control of his limbs. No, he'd lost his grip on the world. Frank's kisses were as dangerous as he'd known they would be.

Suddenly Frank was reeling away from him, hands cupped over his nose. Tom's knuckles hurt. He looked down, mystified, to find he'd made a fist. Oh shit.

"Frankie?"

"What the fuck. Why did you hit me?"

Swallowing tightly, Tom eased himself backward across the roof. He should apologize. No . . . No, it was best to leave it this way. It'd be easier all round if Frank thought he'd meant to hit him. He had meant to, hadn't he? It was the only way to stop what was happening. To halt the headlong flight into a complication neither of them was prepared for. Into everything they couldn't have. Frank was leaving. Tom couldn't. It'd been naïve to pretend that he might.

But Frank had to go. He was too bright to stay cooped up in this small town, hampered by the weight of love. Frank had to be the one who fulfilled their promises for both of them. He had to be the one to go out there and see the world.

"Because you promised." Tom tried to keep the desperate note out of his voice. "You promised we wouldn't do this."

"You kissed me back!" Frank's voice was muffled and nasally. Jeez, was that blood?

What had he done? Oh God. He'd broken them. He'd broken everything.

Go! Go now. "You promised!"

Heart pounding hard enough to leave a bruise on the inside of his chest cavity, Tom crawled to the edge of the roof and slid down the slope toward the window.

"Tommy. Stop. Let's talk about this. Tommy. Fuck! Tommy!"

Ignoring Frank's broken cries, he slid inside the window and disappeared.

CHAPTER 28

Present Day

"MR. Benjamin?"

Ignoring the situation never made it disappear. He should know that by now. Tom changed course and approached the reception desk with what he hoped was a politely curious expression.

The receptionist clearly wasn't buying it. She turned the flat-screen monitor to face him and tapped the display with a long, curved fingernail. "Your account is two months overdue, Mr. Benjamin. Plus there's an extra bill outstanding for the clinic visit, oxygen service, and maintenance fees—"

"Maintenance fees?"

With her other hand, she moused over the maintenance fees and clicked. A bill unfolded across the screen listing a broken toilet.

"What happened to the toilet?" He really didn't want to know.

"I'd say we had to call a plumber."

"That's not covered?"

"Not when it happens more than once in a reasonable period, or when the, er, blockage is deliberate."

His mother was flushing shit . . . no, something other than shit down the toilet. What the ever loving . . .

"Okay, anything else?"

"There's a substantial late fee. You could talk to the office about that. They wanted to talk to you about leaving your car in the lot all night as well. We have a strict policy about the guest lot."

Could his day get any worse?

Tom tapped the top of the desk, then stopped as his fingers began to shake. "I'm going to go visit my mom. I'll stop back past—"

"We'd prefer if you made arrangements regarding your outstanding account before you visited, Mr. Benjamin."

"Are you saying I can't visit my mom?"

The receptionist's polite expression hardened. "What I'm saying is that if you don't pay your bill, you might be visiting your mom in the street."

"You can't do that. She was sick only three weeks ago."

"All of our residents require some level of care, and that costs money."

"Right, right." Tom sighed and it was as though all the air had left his lungs. Not just the used-up portion. Did he have to do this now? "Is Sandra Chen working today?"

"She is."

"Can I talk to her? We go back and she knows about, um, stuff. And maybe she can help me make some arrangements."

The receptionist obviously didn't believe that one of the nurses could help him arrange anything other than treatment for his mother, but still she paged Sandra, who strode into the lobby a short while later, her fixed smile promising more problems than solutions.

Grabbing his arm, she led him to the far corner of the lounge and through a door he hadn't noticed before. Immediately, they were in a smaller sitting room, decorated in somber tones. The single window looked out over the fountain set at the top corner of the gardens. Tom glanced between the sofa and two chairs before moving toward a chair.

Sandra pulled him toward the sofa and sat. He sat next to her. "Why do you have another lounge next to the lounge?"

"This is the bereavement room."

That explained all the tissue boxes. Tom's heart stopped. "Is Mom—"

Sandra put a hand on his arm. "She's fine, Tom. It's you I'm worried about."

"Why?"

"Where are you living?"

Tom spoke to the fingers curling around his forearm. "Up at the lodge."

"There's no phone up there and you haven't been answering your cell. Last week your car was in the lot four nights running." Sandra's grip tightened. "You weren't sleeping in it, were you?"

"Why would I—"

"Goddamn it, Tom. We're supposed to be friends!"

"We are."

She let go of his arm and leaned back a little. "Then tell me what's going on. Is this about Robert? Do you still have your job up there?"

"I . . ." Tom's throat closed. He didn't know. Not after today.

Taking a cautious breath, Tom scrubbed a hand across his face before pushing his fingers into his hair. His too-long hair. He looked down at his knees, noting the way the denim thinned across the knees, and then caught a whiff of himself. His throat convulsed again, threatening to cut off his air.

He hadn't showered yet that morning, but not because he'd had nowhere to go. For the past several nights he'd slept in Frank's bed and showered in Frank's shower. It had been nice to be in one place for that many nights and mornings in a row. He'd missed that—had missed his sofa in the office. Realistically, though, he'd known he couldn't camp there forever. That Robert hadn't figured out what was going on had been a miracle.

God, he should have just asked Robert for a room. He'd have said yes even if they'd been booking guests. And that would have been a whole lot easier to explain to Frank.

Would have—

Damn his pride for getting in the way of, well, everything.

"Tom?"

Tom winced, then shook his head. "I gave up my place about five months ago. I couldn't afford that and the fees here. Things have been picking up—it's wedding season. But I had to renew my software licenses and recertify for the school photography, and I haven't sold a print in a while and . . ." There was insurance on his car, the medical bills for his mom not covered by Medicare, and payments on the debt consolidation loan his mother had been carrying for fifteen years.

"Why didn't you say something?"

"Really?" Tom scoffed. "'Hey, Sandy, I just lost my house.'"

"You couldn't arrange something with the bank?"

"I tried. Now that Robert's gone, I'm self-employed, and not showing enough income to make any payments."

"You should have called me."

"Would you? If you were in my position."

Sandra leaned forward. "Yes! I helped you get your mom into this place, remember?"

"And that's favor enough."

She shook her head. "Jesus, Tom. This is exactly why we broke up."

"We broke up because I didn't want to get married."

"Is that what you thought?"

"Ah . . . yeah?"

"Let's just say we broke up because your head is so far up your own ass it's a wonder you don't have a permanent migraine."

"Maybe I do." Tom pushed his hands through his too-long hair again and massaged his head.

Sandra didn't say anything for a minute, and all he could hear was the rasp of his nails against his scalp. It was almost soothing, except for the looming sense of defeat at his back. The feeling he was about to be crushed—by everything.

"Okay." Sandra spoke softly. "What are we going to do about your account here? Can you pay for even one month?"

Tom dropped his hands. "What good is that going to do? I'd still be a month behind, and I don't have the money for next month."

"Why not?"

"Because my job pretty much died with Robert."

"There isn't a provision in the estate? Can't you write yourself a check? I know you were practically running that place."

Tom hitched his shoulders upward and spread his hands. "Would you write yourself a check from a dead man's checkbook?"

"Stop asking what I would have done, Tom. Jesus. This isn't some kind of game. We worked hard to get your mom in here, and you're about to lose her place because you can't adult up."

"I've been adulting up for forty-eight goddamned years. I'm fucking tired of adulting up. Which is not a thing people say, by the way. What the fuck?"

Sandra glowered at him. "Your pride is going to be the end of you one day. It's going to grow so big, so heavy, it will push you into the ground. Smother you. Bury you."

Today was shaping up to be that day.

Suddenly boneless, Tom slid off the couch and onto the floor. The movement was familiar, the same slip and slide he'd done that day by the creek to escape the claustrophobic complications of having kissed Frank. The duck and cover from the roof thirty years ago. The sinuous way he'd negotiated his finances for the past decade, always staying one step ahead . . . until now.

He'd been running, weaving between obstacles for so long, he didn't even know how not to do it. How not to slide under something instead of facing it. Now, here he was, sitting on the floor, back pressed into the couch, knees pulled up, head thrust between. And the world hadn't stopped spinning yet.

"Tom?"

Sandra's hand was warm on his. He looked up at her and croaked. His throat ached.

"Tom, what happened? Why are you crying?"

He was crying?

"Tom . . ." She was down on the floor next to him now, tucking an arm around his shoulders. "Oh, Tommy. What's wrong? What's happening?"

"I don't think I can do this anymore."

"What do you mean?"

"This. Me. My mom."

"We'll figure it out. I can talk to the director—"

"It's not just the money. I . . ." He shook his head.

"What?"

"I found something I really want to do, Sandy. Someone I wanted to do it with. And this—" he swept his arm out "—this is always going to hold me back. I've spent my whole life telling myself I was happy here and I believed that I was. But I'm not. Not without . . ."

"Without what?"

His heart hurt so bad, it might collapse in his chest. Fall inward and pull the rest of his soul through the hole into nothingness. "Not a what, a who."

Sandra's elegant eyebrows rose. "Who?"

"F-Frank."

"Who's Frank?"

"He's . . ." The one who got away? The one Tom let go? The one he pushed away. The one he'd loved nearly all his life. The one he never forgot. The one he craved with every piece of himself. The one who, for a handful of weeks, helped him dream again.

"He's everything. Always has been, always will be."

Sandra's expression softened. She nodded—once, then a couple of times. "Now I get it."

"What?"

"Jesus Christ, Tom."

Could he ask what again?

Sandra got to her feet and then bent to grab his arm. "You need to go get him."

Tom tugged free. "I can't."

"Why not?"

"Because of this . . ." He indicated the room.

Sandra set her hands on her hips. "Bull. Shit. Write me a check. I don't care if it's for five fucking dollars. I'll talk to the directors, see what we can arrange. Then go find this Frank. If anyone deserves to be happy, it's you."

"But what if—"

"What if you have to live forever wondering why not?"

Tom stiffened. His mouth dropped open. Oh God. Wasn't that exactly what he'd been doing for the past thirty years?

Hadn't he dwelled beneath a cloud of *why not* for long enough?

Sandra was grabbing his arm again. "C'mon. Up you get."

Tom stood. He wrote out a check for five dollars. Then he ran to his car. Sandra was right. More than that, though, Tom was done with letting things go and believing there were things he couldn't have. It was time to set his life straight. He'd come clean with Frank. Tell him everything. Apologize first—grovel if he had to. For back then, and for now.

Frank was a fair man. Even if they couldn't work stuff out, he'd pay Tom for the hours he'd put in before and after Robert's death. Then Tom could figure out his next steps.

What? No. Why was he thinking that way? The whole reason he was in his car right now was to go get what he wanted, wasn't it? To run toward instead of away.

The sign for Snow Hill Road registered in the periphery of his vision. Tom punched the brakes and yanked at the wheel, making it around the corner to a chorus of squealing tires and horns. He powered up the road with a new determination beating behind his breastbone. This time he wouldn't give up as easily. He'd convince Frank that what they had was worth . . . everything. It couldn't be about the money. It had to be about them.

Gravel clinked against the underside of the car as Tom swerved into the bottom of the driveway. The lodge rose up from the ground, bathed in afternoon sunlight, and Tom's breath hitched as he noted both the empty presence of the building—*it always looks like that*—and the absence of Frank's car.

He's parked in the garage.

Frank's car wasn't in the garage.

His bag wasn't upstairs in room 206.

Even though he knew it wouldn't be there, Tom checked the office for Frank's laptop. Gone.

Frank was gone. He'd left. And there was no note.

Would you answer it if he had left one?

Sick and tired in the truest sense, Tom slumped onto the couch and pulled out his phone—but stopped before dialing a single digit. *That's not how you fix this.* Putting his phone away, he approached the desk again. There was only one way to do this now: the right way.

CHAPTER 29

Why was he listening to Sinatra? He should be throwing things or sulking in a corner of the couch with a tub of Coconuts for Caramel Core. Drinking. Surely he should be drinking. Instead, Frank was sitting at the desk in his Jersey City apartment, oblivious to the glorious view of the Manhattan skyline at sunset, wondering if he should read a proposal from Brian fucking Kenway. And listening to the song Tom had sung, just two words at first, then the rest of it as they lay in the dark, thinking about sex and sleep.

Since when was Tom the sort of man who sang?

Frank slapped his laptop closed, cutting Sinatra off mid-croon, and spun his chair around. The red-gold vista of buildings across the river blurred into a rippled reflection until the window ended and wall began. The chair stopped, and he was facing his favorite of Tom's photographs: Boulder Field. The eighteen-acre enigma of Hickory Run State Park.

He remembered hiking out there when they were kids, both of them wondering aloud at how all those rocks had gotten there. What they were for. Tom taking pictures that, to Frank, all seemed the same. Rocks, big and small, in varying colors of stone. When he'd first seen the photo featured on Tom's website, the stark, otherworldly landscape called to him, as a memory and another enigma. Did Tom think about him when he went out there? Did the picture contain a message? Or was the field simply representative of Tom? Stone. Immovable. Broken?

Frank had searched for patterns in the light, the shadow, and the rocks themselves. He'd pondered the significance of the one tree at the far corner. The slim band of slate-colored sky.

A harsh buzz interrupted his latest attempt to solve the puzzle. Frank pushed out of his chair and crossed to the panel mounted on the wall by the door, depressing the Talk button as he glanced at the fuzzy little video screen. His finger slipped off the button and he watched, dumbly, as Tom's mouth moved, making no sound.

He pushed the button again. "Tom?"

"Frank."

"What are you doing here?"

"Delivering something I should have sent a long, long time ago."

Frank shook his head. No. Nope. No way. It was too late for this. Yesterday, Tom had walked away from him one too many times. Opening his door now would only invite eighteen acres of rocks to spread across his living-room floor, and he was so fucking tired of trying to pick them up.

"Go home, Tom."

"Please let me in."

"Why? So you can tell me why I should renovate the lodge?"

"I don't give a shit about the lodge."

Then why had he never left? Frowning, Frank stabbed the button again. "Then why are you here?"

"For you, Frank. I'm here for you."

Frank's heart performed ill-advised calisthenics in his chest. He believed in love. Despite having his heart broken before he grew proper chest hair, he still believed it could happen. Not for him, maybe. But for every lord and lady in the sometimes ridiculous, always worthwhile romances he read.

He'd lived his life hoping for a moment like this. For a man to be on his doorstep, heart in hand.

He'd never dared to hope it might be Tom.

His doorbell rang. What the actual . . .? Frank stared dumbly at his finger, which was still pressing the door release, the buzz of it hissing through the speaker. "Traitor." Scowling, Frank turned to survey his apartment, looking for . . . somewhere to hide. "Dear God."

The doorbell sounded again. Then Tom knocked.

"Go home, Tom!"

"For fuck's sake," echoed through the door.

Frank hauled the door open and pulled Tom inside. Then he found himself scanning the apartment again, still looking for somewhere to hide. This was too real. Tom was in his space.

Trembling, Frank took a step back.

Tom held up his hands. "Frankie. Fuck." He rubbed at his face and tugged his hair. Panted slightly, as though he'd taken the stairs to the top floor. "Okay, hold on." Reaching into a pocket, he extracted a sheet of paper, then set about unfolding it, smoothing the creases against his denim-clad thigh. "I spent all night writing this. Please let me read it, and then if you want me to go, I'll go."

"What is it?"

Tom's throat moved as he apparently swallowed with difficulty. "My confession."

His what?

Tom lifted the sheet. "Dear Frank."

"You started a confession with 'Dear Frank'?"

"Are you going to let me read this or not?"

Frank motioned for him to continue.

"Dear Frank, I . . ." His eyebrows crooked together. "Hold on, I scratched out a lot up here."

Frank repressed a sigh.

"Okay. Here goes. Dear Frank, I made a terrible mistake thirty-two years ago—"

"Don't you mean thirty years?"

Tom glanced up. "No," he said softly. "I mean the day we sat on your bed and told each other we liked looking at boys." He glanced back down at his sheet. "I told you we couldn't be together, ever, and at the time I thought I was being selfless. Heroic, even. I thought I was saving you from a joyless future." He scanned downward, sighed, and started reading again. "I was being selfish. Because I knew, even then, before then, that I couldn't keep you, even though that was what I wanted most in the world. To be with you every day. To spend my whole life with you. But I knew I'd never amount to much, and so I figured I'd do the brave thing and let you go." He looked up. "Or push you away."

"Tom—"

"Let me finish." Tom studied his paper again, then his hand fall to his side, the sheet rustling gently against his leg. "I wanted to tell you I'd made a mistake, from the day after until the day you kissed me. But I couldn't figure out how to go with you, do all we'd planned, and the last thing I wanted to do was ask you to stay. Or hold you back."

The paper crumpled as Tom curled his fingers around it.

"No, that's a lie. Fuck. I was afraid, Frank. I kept telling myself I let you go, but the truth is, I pushed you away because I was afraid you'd leave me. I knew you'd have to go. For college and then after. To live the life you'd always planned. I couldn't go with you, and I didn't want to be left behind, so I . . . Goddamn it. I didn't mean to punch you. I don't know why I did that, except I was scared and angry and that kiss was everything, Frankie. I'd wanted you for so long and then for you to do that on the last night. To kiss me right before you went away. You broke my fucking heart with that kiss, and I hated you for it and I hated that I had to let you go."

"We made those plans together," Frank all but whispered.

"What?"

"This life you thought you had to let me go and lead. It was supposed to be our life. Benjamin and Franklin, remember?" Frank had no idea how he could say this so calmly. Inside, his voice tripped over the uneven beat of his heart, and he was reasonably sure his legs were going to give out at any moment.

"You must have known I couldn't go." Tom sounded as though he was barely holding himself together.

"I didn't. Call me a fool, but I never thought for one second that we might not go together." Not until that night. He'd known college would be a separate journey for both of them, but after that? They'd meet up, tuck their respective degrees into the back of the notebook carrying their final itinerary, and set off.

Had he really been that naïve?

Testing one knee and finding it less than stable, Frank gestured toward the interior of his apartment. It was basically one large room. One very large room with a couple of bathrooms and bedrooms attached. As he crossed the seemingly endless space to the couch, Frank wondered why he'd chosen to live in such an expansive place.

Tom remained by the door. Fitting. He'd said his piece. "You can disappear now," Frank said. "Don't mind me." *I'm old and I need to sit.* God, his chest hurt. Why did this hurt so much?

"I'm not finished."

Half turning, Frank eyed the crumpled paper clutched to the side of Tom's leg and raised a single eyebrow. Tom looked down and retrieved his . . . letter. Tom had written him a letter. Finally. After ignoring every one Frank had sent that first year, he'd finally replied. And the awful thing was . . . Frank already knew everything Tom had just said. Deep down, he'd always known.

Frank sank onto the couch and Tom appeared in front of him. Dropped to his knees, wincing, then settling at the edge of the thick rug. "Can I read the rest?"

"I can't imagine what else there is to say. You were afraid and you pushed me away. Done and done."

"That's . . ." Tom's chin dipped. "Should I just go?"

"It's what you do best, isn't it?"

"Fair point and I deserved that, but there's more. There's . . . I thought there might be an 'us.'"

I thought so too.

Tom scanned his letter, then crumpled it again. Sucked in air and let go a rush of words. "I didn't tell you I was out of money and hope and all that shit because I didn't want you to feel obligated. I didn't want you to think I was using you to keep my job, or for a place to live. I know I went about everything the wrong way, but I really, really didn't want you to think that what was happening between us was a convenience thing. I just wanted to love you, Frank. I wanted you back, and I wanted you in my life, and it was a dream come true to have you there, talking about a future for us, and I didn't want to . . . I didn't . . ."

His chin dipped lower and he took a long, but curiously shallow-sounding breath.

Frank wanted to lean forward, but held himself back with a force of will he hadn't suspected he had. Well, unless he counted the stubbornness that had kept him from visiting the Pocono Mountains for twenty-nine years too long.

Were they both a field of rocks?

Tom looked up. "I was embarrassed and scared. Again. I've been running on ice for the past six months. I've lost two houses, Frank. I bought one for my mom in that neighborhood across the creek.

Where we used to live. I thought it would make her happy to live in a nice house on top of the crappy place where we used to be. And it did, for maybe a year. Then I found out she'd borrowed against the house and that she was not only drinking, but pushing all kinds of shit into her veins."

A bitter expression rippled across Tom's delicate features.

"The house was a mess. I had to put her in care. Then clean the place up and sell it at a loss. Then I had to sell my house to keep paying her bills. I don't have anything left, Frank, and I didn't know how to tell you that. I'm a bad bet. I always have been and probably always will be. But, God, you were there, and it was like you still loved me and I wanted that. I wanted it so much."

Though sympathy overlapped the pool in his heart for all of Tom's struggles, a small part of Frank lay in reserve. A dry patch, perhaps, that asked, *What about me?* He wanted with every fiber of his being to pull Tom into his arms and tell him they would be okay. But could he fix everything that was wrong? This wasn't about a kiss gone awry thirty years before. This . . . This was so much more.

God, this *was* so much more, and Frank had never considered himself strong. Harder emotions were not his purview. He was a marshmallow covered in chocolate.

Giving up any pretense of remaining dry and untouched, Frank allowed the flood. "Jesus fucking Christ."

He pulled Tom up off the floor and onto his lap, and Tom leaned into him, shuddering.

They stayed that way for a long, long time. Breathing. Existing together in a warm, moist bubble of tears held in check and something that felt an awful lot like regret. Questions finally began to filter through, big and little and in varying shades of stone. Frank almost asked the most obscure: *What does it mean?* He meant the photo above them and suspected Tom would know what he was talking about, because wasn't that how it had always been?

Except for this.

Except for their feelings.

He asked a different question. Half a question. Whispered it over Tom's ear. "Do you . . ."

Tom looked up, his face both tragic and beautiful. "Do I want you to come back? Yes. Do I love you? More than you could possibly ever understand."

"Will you . . ." God, what was wrong with him?

"Frankie," Tom murmured.

Frank swallowed. Tried again. "You wrote me a letter."

Tom nodded. "It sucked, but I finally wrote you a letter. And delivered it."

"Tom . . ." Emotion choked him. Frank forced his way past it. "I'm sorry." The weight in his lap shifted as Tom stiffened. Frank shook his head. "I didn't see it. I . . . I didn't see it. I should have come back for you. I should have taken you with me. I didn't know I was supposed to be the knight. I . . . God. I spent all this time waiting for you, when you were . . ."

"Don't say that. You spent your life doing amazing things. As you were meant to do. We were kids. We didn't know how to do shit."

"I'm so sorry."

"I'm the sorry one. I let my pride get in the way of everything."

"No, you were being loyal."

"I was being a self-righteous fucking prick."

"Not self-righteous. Never that. Tom, why didn't you . . . You could have asked Robert for help."

"I did. Now and again. But he had problems enough of his own."

Frank felt his spine straighten. He put his hand between them, flattening his palm over Tom's heart. "Ask me."

"Ask what?"

"Ask me to help you."

"What? No."

"If we're going to do this, if we're going to pick up that old notebook, even in the most metaphorical sense, then we're going to do it as equal partners."

"We'll never be equal, Frank."

"If that's how you really feel, then we'll never work."

"What do I have to give?"

"Yourself, Tom. God, how can you not see that? Your passion, your drive, your need to make others happy, to care for people, to give them what they want. Your years of service to a house that always was home to everyone who visited it. Your friendship. Your love."

"Love doesn't pay bills."

"Tom, love has paid your bills all your life. Your love for your mother."

Tom shifted in his lap, a backward shuffle. Then he closed his eyes. "I . . ." The twist of his features was awful to watch. Worse than tears. Far, far more terrible than listening to his confession, his letter. As Frank watched, Tom fought with himself. Became a solid and lonely pillar, and trembled until he should come apart. He hissed and ground his teeth. He shifted backward twice, as though considering flight.

Then he turned and faced Frank and pushed the words out past what had to be a tight throat. "I need help."

Frank nodded.

Tom swallowed. "Help me, Frankie. Help me put it all back together."

Frank pulled him close. Back into his arms. Tucked a hand behind his soft, dark hair and hugged him. "Always, Tommy. Always. Never going to leave you alone again."

CHAPTER 30

Tom gave a start as Frank lifted him away from the couch. Then he wrapped himself around his man, his Frankie, and let himself be carried, hoping it was toward a bed. Confessions were exhausting.

As Frank dropped him onto a large, neatly made king-size, Tom took note of the framed photograph above the headboard. The view from the top of Mount Tammany. It was his, as was the opposing view from the summit of Mount Minsi on the opposite wall. The realization that he'd been here all along, a part of Frank's life, was somewhat surreal. Or maybe the aftermath of intense emotional overload lent more significance to what were, essentially, just a couple of prints. Nice views. Nothing special.

Frank was looking at him with that single eyebrow raised in a questioning arc.

Tom pulled him down. Kissed him. "Thank you."

"Whatever for?"

"For being you."

Tom pushed Frank sideways, encouraging him to sit on the bed. Then he climbed around so that he was in control, nudging Frank backward, putting one knee between Frank's legs and his hands to Frank's shoulders. He gave Frank a push before covering him like an inefficient blanket and kissing him—hopefully senseless.

He quite liked the idea of Frank senseless.

Could it really be this easy to move on? Beneath him, Frank moaned softly. His big body seemed to mold around Tom, pulling him down with attractive magnetism. He wrapped his hands around Tom's back, his palms warm, and enticed Tom's tongue into his mouth and sucked on it. Tom's cock hardened in a teenage instant. Yes, it could be this easy. Should always have been. He pressed down and Frank pressed up. The groan passing between their mouths was a combination of hot breath and want.

Once started, the grinding between their hips continued, Tom rocking into Frank, and Frank arching up. As Frank hardened beneath him, Tom shifted so their cocks rubbed together. Constrained cocks, the fabric of his jeans and Frank's tidy slacks working both for and against. The friction was nice, the constriction something he could work with as a method to line up and press. Nothing equaled the feel of hot flesh to hot flesh, though.

But before they went there, Tom needed to express the emotions swirling through his body. To find the words to finally put the past where it belonged so that he could make love to his future.

"I'm—"

Frank kissed his lips closed. "Unless you're going to tell me you want me, we're done talking for now."

"Of course I want you. Frank—"

Another kiss. "I know. We'll talk about it tomorrow. Then get on with living the rest of our lives." Frank smiled up at him.

That sounded . . . so good. Tom kissed Frank's smile. Then kissed him again. He dropped one more kiss to Frank's lips, openmouthed and light, and sucked Frank's lower lip between his. Caught the flesh with his teeth. He let go and nipped Frank's jaw, licking across the nearly smooth skin beneath. The remnants of Frank's aftershave numbed the tip of his tongue. Tom licked lower, enjoying the quiver of Frank's throat. Pushing up to an elbow, he started undoing the buttons of Frank's shirt, dipping down to kiss newly exposed skin. He sucked on the just-visible rise of Frank's collarbone, and finally, spread his hands across Frank's bared chest.

Frank didn't have a lot of body hair. His pale, freckled skin seemed to discourage it, which suited Tom quite well. He rubbed his cheek to Frank's pecs, feeling dense muscle beneath the softness of Frank's outer "self."

Fingers tangled with Tom's hair. Frank massaging his head—no, pulling him away from a nipple. "You're killing me."

Tom tugged free and bit the rosy little nipple right beneath his lips. "Never."

Frank shifted his hips sideways and rolled, the movement swift enough to catch Tom by surprise. He landed on his back, Frank hovering over him. Frank dipped down to kiss him, then began tugging his shirt upward.

Lazy minutes, hours, nights passed as clothes were shed, nipples tortured, belly buttons explored, ribs tickled, lips trailed across miles of skin. Tom lifted his face from an affectionate burrow in the side of Frank's hip to discover Frank—on his back, with his head propped up on folded arms—smiling at him, and realized the urgency had passed. Somehow they'd progressed from "toss down and fuck" to "roll around naked and lick every inch of skin" stage. After unpacking and dumping so much emotion in such a short time, it was ...

"This is nice." Yep, he'd just referred to their foreplay as *nice*.

Uttering a short laugh, Frank grabbed Tom by the shoulders and hauled him upward. Tom grinned the whole way, sure he'd never get tired of Frank's big strength. Frank kissed him. "This *is* nice."

Tom landed on his back again, and Frank went directly from *nice* to *hell yes* by crouching between Tom's legs and slurping up his dick. Tom's erection plumped an extra degree as Frank swallowed him down. He could feel Frank's throat around the head of his cock. Tom's hips bumped up involuntarily. Frank pushed them back down, moving his mouth along Tom's length at the same time, the ring of his lips tight, the flat of his tongue tracing contours that hadn't been explored by anything other than a hand in far, far too long.

The groan building in Tom's chest felt like the precursor to an orgasm. It almost hurt to let it free, and then he had to figure out how to suck air into his lungs as Frank sucked his way to heaven.

Tom groaned again. "Oh my God. So good."

Way better than the fantasy he'd conjured while standing over the bed in room 206, Frank's pillow clutched to his face.

Frank murmured something, the vibration traveling along Tom's shaft. Tom wrapped his hands around Frank's head and ... didn't pull. Didn't pump, didn't fuck Frank's face. Oh, he wanted to, though, and it was damn hard to keep his hips still and let Frank do the work.

With every suck, Tom's self edged through his body, burning through arteries and veins, dragging against his skin. His spine became a highway of sensation, his lower back a collection of tingling nerves. His groin ached and his balls drew up high and tight. When Frank nudged a finger backward, beneath his sac, stroking, beckoning, Tom raised his knees and flung them apart, making his invitation obvious. He hadn't been fucked in a long, long time, but if that was what Frank wanted, that was what Frank would get.

That first touch to his hole sent a lightning bolt up his spine, halting the downward flow of pleasure. Tom hissed and bucked. Frank stroked him again, gently, and the electric touch restarted that downward pulse. Abruptly, Tom wanted to come—quite badly. Putting a restraining hand to Frank's shoulder, Tom stiffened and drew back.

Frank lifted his head, letting Tom's cock pull from his mouth. Tom nearly yelled at the loss of hot suction. He nearly lost it too, which would have been strange and embarrassing. Climaxing with a finger on his hole and a wet mouth hovering over his harder-than-hard cock? Squeezing his eyes shut, Tom fought his way back from the edge. He breathed slow sips of air until the tide turned. Frank shifted above him, removing his finger and stroking the top of his thigh instead.

When Tom opened his eyes, Frank wore a troubled expression.

"I'm okay," he said before Frank could ask.

"You sure about that?"

"I didn't want to come yet. God, Frank. One touch and I was ready to explode."

Frank let his hand drift back between Tom's thighs, down toward the crease of his ass. "One touch, huh?"

"Don't. Not yet." Tom clenched. He aimed a grimace-grin at Frank. "How are you so incredibly hot?"

"It's a talent." Frank dipped down to kiss his lips, then rubbed their noses together. "Do you bottom much?" The whisper was quiet, warm, curious.

Tom shook his head. "It's been a while. That's why I'm so sensitive."

Frank nosed his cheek. "Would you, for me?"

"In a heartbeat."

Frank kissed him again, longingly, but with a languid heat that suited the shift from must-fuck to roll-around-and-talk. Frank kissed his eyes, his nose, his lips. His jaw. When he got to Tom's ear, he whispered, "Can I fuck you?"

"Yes, please."

Frank rolled away, probably to collect supplies.

When he rolled back, Tom put a hand on his. "Do you test regularly?"

"I do."

"Me too."

Frank looked at him for a long moment, his gaze searching. Then he nodded, and the gift of his trust felt more momentous than Frank hearing out his confession and accepting it. Frank tossed the condom back toward the nightstand and uncapped the lube. Prep became a competition between the dazzling allure of Frank's mouth over his cock and the sweet press of fingers. Tom learning again—and why did it always feel like the first time?—to unclench more than one muscle. To open his self. To let go. To ask for a pause when he needed one. And, above all else, to be able to give voice to the pleasure of it all, to let Frank in and tell him how good it felt. How raw and real.

By the time Frank hovered between Tom's knees, the blunt tip of his cock pressed to Tom's hole, Tom felt as though he'd come twenty times. Exhaustion and elation combined to press his limbs into sharp angles. His skin stretched taut between. In the middle, in the center of his chest, he lay loose, however. Open and ready.

Frank inched inside Tom, the pleasure of feeling him—truly feeling him in the way he couldn't have with even the thinnest layer of latex between them—far outstripping any discomfort. Frank was careful, pausing when Tom would have told him to continue. Then he was inside and Tom could only lie there, breathing shallowly.

"So full," he moaned.

"So good, Tommy. You feel so damn good." Frank moved his hips.

Tom moaned again and closed his eyes. Tipped his head back. Frank bent forward to skim his lips over Tom's throat, the motion shifting everything down there once more. Warm breath touched Tom's jaw, floating up toward his ear. "Ready?"

"Yes."

Frank started to thrust and Tom's world ended. Everything he'd known up to that point disappeared in a rush of sensation. Stars collapsed, black holes expanded, devouring the stuff of life. The universe died . . . and was reborn, surging into being with a dizzying pop.

"Frank!" Tom drew in a ragged breath. His first of a new existence. He clutched at Frank's hips. Smoothed one hand around Frank's ribs and up his back. Rocked with him, with the gentle in-and-out motion. Contemplated moving his hips.

"Shh." Frank's lips grazed his temple. "Ah, Tommy."

"I'm having an is-this-real moment," Tom admitted.

"Me too."

"We should have been doing this forever."

Frank grinned down at him. "Yes, we should."

The laugh felt good, sparking nerve endings in his newly born body, and that shift of self began all over again. The downward motion of sensation—the gathering in his groin. The imminence of orgasm. Only the slight pinch kept everything in check . . . until Tom acknowledged that small pain as an essential part of the whole. Wrapped it into the ball of everything settling low in his back.

"You're so beautiful, Tom."

Tom opened his eyes. When had he closed them? He gazed up at Frank. "So are you." Not just a rote response. Frank was radiant. "You were always golden. Still are."

"Like brass, you mean."

"Stop that, and fuck me harder. I want to feel you tomorrow."

"Darling, you already will."

"More, Frankie. More."

Tom grabbed his cock. He barely needed to stroke it, but the feel of his fingers notched everything a single note higher. Frank moved, and now every stroke hit that perfect spot inside. Tom clenched and let his eyes cross. He could hear Frank laughing softly. He smacked Frank's side. "Keep going. So close."

"Mmm."

Hard, faster. Skin slapping. The scent of sex rising between them, intermingled with the now familiar whiff of Frank and sweat. Their skin and their selves. Frank's breath washed across his face in rhythmic pants. Tom nipped at Frank's lower lip. Their lips brushed and parted. Breath turned into grunts and the world became a twisted pendulum, the shorter swings coming faster and faster, knocking, almost breaking.

Tom came with a shout, his body stiffening without permission as control ripped through his fingers and balls, shooting out the end of his cock. The wild stroke of his hand became slippery, fast, and completely unnecessary. But to not touch himself right now was unthinkable. He bucked and writhed. Could feel his ass tightening over Frank's cock. Could hear Frank wheezing over him and then he was yelling too. Frank's cries were deeper and a little hoarse, as if his orgasm had been long buried, then suddenly unearthed. He slammed into Tom in a way Tom would feel for more than a day. Tom didn't protest. This was giving himself to Frank. Giving Frank something no one else could. Because even through the cotton wool stretched between real thought and orgasm thought—or perhaps because of it—this was a moment only they could share. This was theirs, uniquely. A climax held off for thirty years. It was love—long and deeply held. It was their future. And it was every second in between.

Also, it was sex, and sex with someone you wanted this much could only ever remake the world.

Frank eased off and out of him and flopped onto his back. Lying beside him, utterly wrecked, Tom breathed until fingers tangled with his. He rolled his head to the side and met Frank's light-brown gaze. After a mutual stare that lasted a few breaths, Tom let his own gaze roam, taking in the faint freckles gathering across Frank's cheek. With as much time as they'd been spending outside, he'd be speckled by summer's end. Tom traced the ginger arc of each eyebrow in turn, studied Frank's nose and lips. Looked up toward his hairline and frowned at the slightly darker color framing his face. Lit only by a lamp, Frank appeared much as he had all those years ago, even to the color of his hair.

"Was I worth the wait?" Frank asked.

Tom squeezed Frank's hand and shook his head.

Frank opened his mouth, and Tom leaned in to kiss it shut, gently, before whispering over his lips. "More than, Frank. More than worth it."

Frank pulled him close, and Tom let himself melt into his lover's arms. He might never have left the place where he'd been born, but now he felt as if he was truly where he belonged. Nestled in against Frank's chest, he was finally home.

CHAPTER 31

Not displaying a visible reaction to the changes time had wrought on Wendy Benjamin was perhaps the hardest thing Frank had ever done. Surely Tom had brought him to the wrong room? He checked the number on the door even though a whisper inside his head reminded him that he had no idea which room number was supposed to be hers.

Wendy had always been a small woman. Now she embodied the cliché: frail as a bird. Her white hair resembled the fluff atop a new chick's head, pink skin just visible beneath. Her eyes had faded from blue to gray, and beneath the parchment hue, her skin held an unhealthy pallor. Liver failure, Tom had said. And she'd apparently had several intestinal surgeries as well as cancer. And a broken neck. And a coma of some sort, the last of which had left her grappling with reality in a way no alcoholic stupor ever had.

No wonder Tom lectured the kids about addiction.

No wonder he'd never left Pennsylvania.

Rather than stand by the door and cry, Frank slipped inside the room, softening his footfalls by touching his toe down before lowering his heels. Tom was crouched in front of Wendy, holding her hands and speaking in a low voice.

"I've brought someone to see you, Mom. You were asking about Frank a little while ago."

Tom continued talking, and Frank noticed he didn't speak as one might to an invalid or someone who'd lost as much as Wendy had. He spoke as any doting son might.

Oh, Tom.

Frank's chest tightened.

After wrapping up a report on his week—thankfully leaving out the part about them fucking in an utterly proverbial manner since their return from Jersey City—Tom asked Wendy if she wanted to go for a walk. When she gave no reaction, he checked her shoes, then turned to look over his shoulder. "Can you bring the wheelchair over?"

Realizing he'd not moved much past the doorway, Frank jolted himself out of the trance he'd fallen into, claimed the chair from the corner, and pushed it across the room until he had it positioned just behind Tom.

"Is it okay if we take her out?"

"She likes the garden," Tom said. "She might, um, become responsive if we take her outside."

"Do you want to be alone with her?"

"Only if that would make you more comfortable."

"No. I . . ." He couldn't say he was exactly glad to be here. He'd experienced perhaps his most cowardly moment when Tom had first asked if he wanted to visit. But he was here, and he was here because Wendy was as much a part of his life as Tom.

Taking a deep breath, Frank turned to Wendy—who remained still and unfocused in her chair—and said, "It's so good to see you again, Wendy. I'm looking forward to touring your garden."

She made no answer, but Tom's smile was worth the small pantomime.

Tom lifted his mother and settled her in the chair, fussing over her pant legs and shirt until he was sure she was comfortable. Then they wheeled her out of the room, down the hall, and out into the summer sunshine.

Wendy did brighten as they toured the garden. Frank would never have taken her as one who enjoyed the outdoors; Wendy always had seemed to be working when they'd been kids. But Tom must have inherited his love of nature and hiking from someone. They rolled to a stop in front of a flower bed. Behind, a short lawn ended at a line of trees over which the sound of the highway rippled almost like a stream. If Frank squinted—eyes and ears and never mind how he got his ears to squint—he could almost imagine he was near the creek at home.

When had he started thinking of Bossen Hill as home?

Tom sat on the convenient bench beside the chair, took his mother's hand in his, and started telling her more about his week. Frank stood there feeling awkward until she seemed to glance up at him. Her head moved, anyway. Then her gaze sharpened and she was looking right at him. Frank tried for a smile.

"Frankie."

His smile widened out of perfunctory and into astonished. "Hello, Wendy."

"You sure did get tall, didn't you?"

She not only knew who he was, but that he was grown? Frank shook his head, then nodded. "I was always on the large side."

Wendy produced a dry cackle. "Yes, you were. Did you come back to get Tommy? He missed you, you know."

Beside her, Tom scowled lightly.

"I did," Frank said.

She lifted a shaking hand. It dropped back into her lap. Frank reached down to clasp it and Wendy smiled. "You take good care of my boy." The squeeze she gave his fingers was feeble, but beneath it, Frank could feel the strength that had kept her alive this long. Say what you wanted about Wendy's choices, but something had kept her here, and Frank didn't have to think about what . . . who that might be.

He squeezed back, gently. "I will."

Wendy faded then, leaving Frank wondering if he'd dreamed the entire exchange. But her hand still rested loosely in his. He crouched beside her chair and held on until Tom said they could take her back inside.

"Why don't you get her settled?" Frank said. "I need to"—he pulled his phone from his pocket—"make a call."

Tom's eyebrows quirked in different directions, but he nodded and wheeled Wendy back toward the building. Frank followed at a slower pace, changing direction at the fountain and reentering the building through the lobby area. He strode directly toward the desk and greeted the receptionist with a smile.

"How do I go about paying Wendy Benjamin's account?"

"I asked for help, not a handout!"

Frank had expected this. He might be in love, but he hadn't lost all sense. He watched as Tom paced the short length of the office, past the sofa he'd apparently called home for the past five months and up to the bureau housing the evil little coffee maker. He spun on his heel and turned back again.

Should he wait for Tom to wear a hole in the floor or simply wear himself out? The couch was *right there*. If and when Tom did collapse, however, he'd only wake in the same mood. A more stubborn man had yet to be born.

Frank let him complete another two grumbling circuits before he held up a hand. "Can I say just two things?"

Tom stopped and glared at him. "Just two?"

"I'll start with two."

Tom folded his arms.

"Technically, you are now my employee. As such, you're entitled to certain benefits."

"I'm not in a full-time care facility."

"No, but your family is. A good portion of Wendy's care should be covered by your benefits."

Tom scoffed. "My benefits? You do realize I don't have any, right?"

"Isn't that illegal?"

"Seriously, Frank?"

Frank waved his hands. "Okay, let's move on to the second point. If Robert had required long-term care, would you have arranged it?"

"Yes."

Frank spread the hands he still had in the air and shrugged.

Growling, Tom unfolded his arms and resumed his pacing. Frank let him go. The floor would give way soon. Before that happened, however, Tom angled himself toward the couch and flopped into an angry bundle, arms and legs tucked in, head bend forward. He growled again, muttered something, tugged on his hair a little, and finally breathed out.

Had the storm passed? And was this what Frank had to look forward to for the next forty or so years? Of course it was, and he'd known that.

Now would be a bad time to smile, wouldn't it? Shit, Tom was looking up. Frank pressed his lips together.

Tom narrowed his eyes. "Fuck you, Tern."

"Yes, please."

"Am I really your employee?"

"I don't know how it works when ownership of a business changes hands, but I would assume so." The thick envelope of paperwork he'd only skimmed, should have fucking read, would likely have documentation to that effect. "Either way, we need to renegotiate your contract."

"What if I don't want to work for you?"

"Then don't. Be my business partner instead."

Tom scowled. "I have nothing, Frank."

"You are vital to this project. I wouldn't have thought of it without you, and while I tidy up some of my writing commitments, you'll be the man on the ground, so to speak." Frank leaned forward in the office chair. "I already considered us partners in this deal."

"What if we fail?"

"Then we move on to the next thing."

"Failure means debt, Frank. It means not being able to buy new mattresses and silk pajamas."

"*Quelle horreur!*" Frank put his flapping hands back in his lap and took a more serious tone. "How long have you been making that work for you?"

Tom arched a single eyebrow. "What, my lack of silk pajamas?"

"Exactly that."

"Frank, being poor isn't a joke. It's not an adventure."

"I don't imagine it would be, and I'm not going to say I wouldn't care because you'd be at my side. I might prefer tailored shirts and the feel of silk against my skin, but I'm not all fluff and nonsense. And I don't intend to fail. I'm not going to devote two years of my life renovating this resort while expecting to fail. We're going to build something wonderful here, Tommy. You and I. And while we're building our dream, I'll write about it and you can take the pictures, just as we always planned."

Tom started shaking his head.

Frank pointed a finger at him. "Don't scoff, but there's a book in this. There are stories here"—he circled his finger through the air—"and don't forget, I've been selling stories for the past thirty years.

I have more than a few loyal readers, and a number of people who want me to make them sound more interesting than they are. So we're going to make this work."

"And all I have to do is take pictures? Come on, Frank. We're not teenagers anymore."

Frank set his jaw. "I'm going to say this one last time." Oh who was he kidding? This was Tom. He was going to have to say this every day for about a year and then probably weekly ever after. "I cannot do this without you and not because I need someone here to supervise construction. But because this is your dream too. Your home. This house is as much yours as it is mine. More so, maybe. And if that's too idealistic for you, I have no fucking idea how to run a resort. You do. You know the history of this place and you have a firm idea of the direction you'd like to take it in. You're the intellectual half of this venture, Tom. I'm just the one taking out the loan." Sure, it was a large loan, but he had invested wisely over the years. He could afford the payments. When it came to money, Frank was nothing if not practical.

Tom was scowling again. "I know what you're doing."

"Good."

"God, you're infuriating."

"Even better."

"So..."

"So." Frank turned on his most charming smile.

Rather than relax back into the couch, Tom leaned forward, grasping his knees. "We're really doing this."

"Simon might cry if we don't."

Tom snickered, then lifted his head as the driveway announced a visitor.

Without looking around, Frank said, "We should keep the gravel driveway. Early detection system."

"Bitch to plow in winter, though."

"Think anyone will get married in winter?"

"The way we'll have this place set up? Absolutely."

Grinning, Frank pushed to his feet and bent to peer through the front window. The car was vaguely familiar. Tom was already stalking toward the door and Frank followed. It was Patricia Nolan. The woman was relentless!

Tom was down the steps and in her face before she'd even closed the door on her car. "Was it you?"

"Excuse me?" Patricia eased away from Tom, but didn't close the car door. Good move. She might need to make a quick getaway.

"How much did you pay that kid to throw a bunch of dead raccoons into the pool? And what about the kids that have been sneaking around the property? And the drugs. Did you plant them there and call the police?"

Patricia rocked back, but her apparent indignation had a rehearsed look to it, as if she'd practiced in front of a mirror. "I have no idea what you are talking about."

Frank joined the party. "Ms. Nolan." He offered a tightlipped smile.

"Mr. Tern." Her return smile tried harder than his. "Have you—"

"You are a nuisance. If I find you on our property again, without an invitation, I will not only call the police, but begin legal proceedings."

Her smile faltered, then simply vacated her face, leaving her mouth in a mild gape. "Excuse me?"

"I have no interest in selling this property. But even if I did, it would not be to the Tinden Group. I'm not a fan of their business practices. You, in particular, should consider another line of work."

"But—"

"I'd like you to leave."

"Mr.—"

Frank held up a hand. "Stop. I'm not interested in anything you have to say. You can leave now, or wait for the police to arrive. Your choice."

She looked between them two more times. Back and forth, lips still parted as though she couldn't decide whether to speak or not. Then, snapping her mouth shut, she got into her car, slammed the door, and spun her tires on the gravel in a clear attempt to drive away in a furious rush.

"We should definitely keep the gravel," Frank said.

Tom bumped into him from the side, hands wrapping around Frank's torso. "Fuck that was hot."

"What?"

"You being all Mr. Tern."

"Whatever do you mean?" Once more, Frank tried to instruct his mouth to do other than express his actual mood.

Grinning, Tom lifted to his toes and pressed a hard kiss to Frank's recalcitrant lips. "Let's go upstairs," he murmured before kissing Frank again.

"Best idea you've had all day."

"Frank?"

"Mmm."

"You know I love you, right?"

"And I love you. Always have. Always will."

Tom seemed to settle then. Not exactly inside his skin—more inside himself, as though the rightness of what they were doing finally made sense. Or he'd simply accepted that it did. He smiled, and his smile was like the sunshine on a spring afternoon: warm and full of promise. "I like the sound of that."

EPILOGUE

About a year later, or thirty-one years later.

T om smoothed his palm over the warm slate, pausing as he reached the edge of one roof tile, before floating his hand over the next.

"It's going to take me another year to get used to this pattern," Frank said.

"I think it's beautiful."

"You would." Settling next to him, Frank nuzzled his temple before leaning back with a sigh. "I approve of it in principle, of course."

Of course. Frank was a deeply practical man. Even his frivolity was planned. Therefore, reclaiming and restoring as much of the original slate roofing as they could hadn't been a tough sell—until he'd seen the end result.

The mixture of grays evened out when viewed from afar, but up here on the roof, you could tell the new from the old. Tom loved the effect. It suited the history of the lodge, particularly in light of the recently completed restoration. It suited them, reminding him of their boyhood friendship and how that was a part of their newer, deeper relationship.

And the roof made for extraordinarily beautiful photographs. Tom couldn't wait for fall.

Beside him, Frank was fiddling with the bag he'd dragged up there with them. He'd brought blankets too. Bright, colorful rugs with knotted tassels he'd found in the marketplace of some country Tom had never heard of. Tom pulled one off the stack and started spreading it across the tile. In his pocket, something pressed into his thigh.

"What are you smiling about?" Frank asked.

Tom glanced over, unaware he'd been smiling. Straightening a tassel, he shrugged. "I dunno. The fact you still think we need to sit on something other than tile?"

"Comfort is never out of style."

"That should be our tagline or whatever."

Frank chuckled. "If we were running a simple bed and breakfast, I'd consider it."

Blankets spread, Tom settled back next to Frank and leaned into his shoulder. "So what's in the bag?" As always, Frank had packed snacks and drinks for a trip that would take them no more than five minutes from a fully stocked refrigerator. Tom had come to understand the practice went far beyond a constant need to eat, however. Or maybe he'd always known that. Frank just liked to have opportunities. He liked to surround himself with small choices. It gave him a sense of being prepared for any venture.

Frank flipped open the soft-sided cooler to reveal a cold, sweaty bottle of champagne, flutes wrapped in linen napkins, plates, silverware, and several neatly stacked Tupperware containers.

"Is this dinner?" Tom checked the sky. The August sun had dipped toward the horizon and would be making its exit soon.

"It's 'Oh my God the lodge is finished, except for Mount Trash between the laundry and garage, and we're halfway done with this project and I'm exhausted and so it totally makes sense to eat on the roof.'"

Tom laughed. "Okay."

"It makes no sense whatsoever to eat on the roof, by the way."

Tom nudged Frank's shoulder with his. "It's a thing we do. That's all anyone needs to know."

Frank kissed his cheek. "Mmm."

"So did you hear back from Lucas?" Sometimes Tom felt sorry for Frank's PA. He'd had a lot to handle this past year.

"Regarding the latest Twitter storm or—"

"Don't be coy, it doesn't suit you. The book, Frank. Does he have the contract from your agent?"

Frank tried to purse his lips and then tipped his head toward the bottle of champagne nestled in the side of the cooler. "He has the contract."

Jubilation exploded inside Tom's chest. Frank had been uncharacteristically nervous about pitching his book, which was part memoir, part history of the resort industry in the Poconos. Tom had known he'd get an offer, though. Frank's style of interviewing translated perfectly to writing about not only himself, but what he hoped to accomplish with Bossen Hill.

"Proud of you," Tom murmured, leaning in for a proper kiss.

Frank met him halfway, his lips already soft and welcoming, and the kiss was one of Tom's favorites: the sort that lingered without becoming too heated because they each had the time to sit there, breathing in the scent of the man they loved.

Pulling back, Frank said, "I could tell you your photos clinched the deal."

Tom scoffed. "Whatever."

"I couldn't have put together the proposal without you, and we're going to write it together. You know that, right?"

Tom swallowed a lump that got smaller every time he had to deal with it. Every time he realized, all over again, that Frank was here, sitting next to him, loving him. "Okay."

"So let's celebrate!"

The cork flew, the bubbly flowed, the food served and picked over. The sun set over talk of inconsequential things, including what color they'd paint the bedroom in the small apartment they'd made out of Robert's bedroom and bathroom, the workroom, and unused space at the end of that hallway.

Frank had sold his apartment in Jersey City late the year before and they'd been "camping" in whichever room had the least amount of dust while work went forward on the lodge. Frank had complained about their living situation almost daily, but Tom had quickly come to appreciate that Frank mostly did so because he felt he should. The only time he'd suggested they leave and stay somewhere else for a few days was the trip they'd taken shortly after Tom's mom had passed away. Frank had taken him to Cape May, and they'd given most of his mom's ashes to the sea. The rest were in a small urn next to Robert and Madge.

"*She's family*," Frank had said.

Whether Frank's father and mother had agreed or not, they'd made Tom feel welcome in their B&B, where Tom and Frank had been the only guests on that cold and blustery week in January. When Annabelle arrived with all of her family, Tom had truly felt a part of something for the first time in a long, long while, even though that something had involved saying goodbye to his mom.

He'd been glad to get home, though. Back to Pennsylvania, the lodge, and his future with Frank. Back where he truly belonged.

Frank burped softly and rubbed his stomach. "Not sure those stuffed peppers were such a good idea."

Chuckling, Tom rolled over to pat Frank's belly. "But you'll try anything once, right?"

"Absolutely." Frank turned to face him. "Or more than once, if required. Some things take a while to work." His forehead wrinkled. "I'm trying to come up with some sort of metaphor about flavors developing and marinating, but it all sounds so sticky."

"And someone is paying you to write a book."

"It's a silly old world, isn't it?"

"Mmm."

Frank studied him in silence for a beat. "You're quiet tonight. Not that you're ever loud."

"I can be loud in bed."

"You can."

Tom smiled.

"What's up?" Frank asked, his eyebrows twitching together.

Tom reached over to smooth the crease in the middle of Frank's forehead. "Know what today is?"

"The day we tore down the dust sheets and declared an end to the war on our sinuses?"

"Think back a little farther."

Frank frowned. "Hmm . . ."

"About thirty—no, thirty-one years."

"Oh." Frank got it instantly. "Really? Today's the day you broke my nose?"

"I actually broke it?"

"Yes! There was blood everywhere, and I had to go to college with a black eye."

"Shit."

"Why are you laughing?"

"I'm not . . ." Tom pressed a hand to his side and sat up. "I'm . . . Okay, I'm laughing."

Frank was too. "I don't know why it's funny. It hurt. Then there was the whole broken-heart deal."

"And the letters I never answered."

"And thirty years of us being the most stubborn people ever conceived. Truly, Tom, why did we never come find each other? Why did we wait so long?"

The lump in Tom's throat swelled. "I don't know," he croaked.

Frank sat up and leaned forward, touching his forehead to Tom's. "Shh. Don't. I'm sorry."

"Don't be. I'm sorry."

"Are we going to set this day aside as our annual day of apology?" Frank moved back a little, putting some breathing space between them. "We could save up all the apologies of the year and deal with them all on one day. Sounds marvelously efficient, don't you think?"

Tom shook his head. "No, it sounds terrible. I'm not going to sit on shit like this, or anything, for even a day anymore. If I do something that requires apology, I'm making good there and then, even if I have to write a letter on my arm."

"You and this obsession with letters. You know I really don't require a handwritten note explaining why you didn't replace the toilet paper."

"That was a joke. I did it once!" Tom patted the pocket of his jeans and reached inside for the paper he had folded there and the small book tucked in beside it, and pulled them both out.

"What's this, then?" Frank asked, touching the book.

Tom handed it to him. This was the easy part. "Our new notebook."

Brow creasing, Frank flipped open the cover and scanned the first page, where Tom had written: *The New Adventures of Benjamin and Franklin.* He glanced up with glassy eyes, and turned the page to find Tom had already recorded their trip to Cape May. Frank touched the words and smiled. "It's a good start."

"Mm-hmm."

Smile widening, Frank nodded toward the note in Tom's hand. "And that? Is it about the muddy footprints you tracked across the kitchen floor?"

Tom coughed out a laugh. "What? No. That wasn't me."

"I'll be glad when all the outdoor work is completed."

"Another year and you'll only have me to blame for muddy tracks."

Frank sat up straighter. "Then we'll have guests."

"We'll have guests before then."

"We will?"

Tom unfolded his piece of paper. "I hope so." He glanced down and all the blood in his body ran backward in a loud rush, getting stuck and abandoning vital processes. His head seemed to swell and sway and the sound of the crickets and frogs dialed upward.

"Tom? Are you feeling okay?"

Tom ran his thumb across the first words on his page. "'Dear Frankie.'" He looked up.

Frank had his quizzical expression on. A half smile, his brow lightly furrowed.

Tom showed him the letter, and together they read the rest of it: *You are the best of me, know the worst of me, all that is me. I have loved and will love you forever. Marry me. Please. Yours always, Tommy.*

"You signed it 'Tommy.'"

"I was always Tommy to you, from that very first day."

"Tom . . ." Frank's eyes glinted in the twilight.

"I know—"

Frank put a finger to Tom's lips. "No."

Tom's heart stopped. "No?"

"I mean no excuses. No qualifiers. No explanation. No apologies. Just . . . yes. Yes, Tommy, I will marry you."

Frank's arms were around him, and Tom leaned into the crushing hug, surprised they were hugging and not kissing, which was how he'd imagined this moment progressing—when not torturing himself with dark fantasies of Frank laughing, Frank tearing up his letter, Frank telling him he didn't believe in marriage, or that it wasn't for them, Frank . . .

Oh, Frank.

The letter fluttered from Tom's fingers, skimmed along the tiles, old and new, and drifted over the edge of the roof. No one yelled from below. Nothing but the loud buzz of a summer night celebrated with them. But for Tom, the moment rewrote an entire chapter of history.

They couldn't go back. They both knew that. Thing was, he didn't want to. Because what he had now was bigger, better, and more complete than he could ever have imagined. A life, lived. And now a life he planned to share with the man he'd always loved.

The man who had just promised him forever.

"Love you, Tommy."

Tom nestled that impossible inch closer. "Love you too."

Explore more of the *This Time Forever* series:
riptidepublishing.com/collections/series-this-time-forever

Dear Reader,

Thank you for reading Kelly Jensen's *Renewing Forever*!

We know your time is precious and you have many, many entertainment options, so it means a lot that you've chosen to spend your time reading. We really hope you enjoyed it.

We'd be honored if you'd consider posting a review—good or bad—on sites like **Amazon, Barnes & Noble, Kobo, Goodreads, Twitter, Facebook, Tumblr,** and your blog or website. We'd also be honored if you told your friends and family about this book. Word of mouth is a book's lifeblood!

For more information on upcoming releases, author interviews, blog tours, contests, giveaways, and more, please sign up for our weekly, spam-free newsletter and visit us around the web:

Newsletter: riptidepublishing.com/newsletter
Twitter: twitter.com/RiptideBooks
Facebook: facebook.com/RiptidePublishing
Goodreads: tinyurl.com/RiptideOnGoodreads
Tumblr: riptidepublishing.tumblr.com

Thank you so much for Reading the Rainbow!

RiptidePublishing.com

Acknowledgments

I have a Big Book of Ideas. My "book" is actually scattered across several notebooks and my ideas are sandwiched between outline sketches, snippets of dialogue, pages of brainstorming for plot points, and journal entries. There is no order to any of it—but I always know which book to grab when I'm looking for my notes about a specific idea.

Frank and Tom's story happened in two separate notebooks. I had an idea for a story about an abandoned resort and the guy who was living in one of the broken-down cottages. And then I had a character sketch for Frank, who one of my beta readers had loved and wanted me to write a book for. When I married those two ideas together, this story was born. So my first thanks go to Laura, who asked for Frank's story.

As always, I owe tremendous thanks to my first-round readers: Jenn, who told me this was the best book I've written yet, and Eli, who told me how to make it even better.

All the thanks to my editor, Caz, for helping me define and polish, and to the rest of the team at Riptide for their outstanding attention to detail.

Thank you to the readers who love my characters as much as I do!

Finally, thank you to my family, who accompanied me on several visits to local resorts while I conducted research, and to the Lady Writers for the friendship, feedback, and lessons in local history. Not all of the geographical details herein are correct. I moved the Stroud Township line, and Spanky's is actually south of town. Otherwise, this book is the Poconos as I know and love them.

On the subject of historical accuracy, Mello Yello wasn't actually introduced until 1979, so Tom's love affair with my favorite soda begins about six months early. At least I didn't say he invented it!

ALSO BY
Kelly Jensen

This Time Forever series
Building Forever
Chasing Forever (coming soon)

To See the Sun
Out in the Blue
Wrong Direction
When Was the Last Time
Best in Show
Block and Strike

The Counting series
Counting Fence Posts
Counting Down
Counting on You

The Chaos Station series, with Jenn Burke
Chaos Station
Lonely Shore
Skip Trace
Inversion Point
Phase Shift

The Aliens in New York series
Uncommon Ground
Purple Haze

ABOUT THE
Author

If aliens ever do land on Earth, Kelly will not be prepared, despite having read over a hundred stories of the apocalypse. Still, she will pack her precious books into a box and carry them with her as she strives to survive. It's what bibliophiles do.

Kelly is the author of a number of novels, novellas, and short stories, including the Chaos Station series, cowritten with Jenn Burke. Some of what she writes is speculative in nature, but mostly it's just about a guy losing his socks and/or burning dinner. Because life isn't all conquering aliens and mountain peaks. Sometimes finding a happy ever after is all the adventure we need.

Connect with Kelly:
Newsletter: eepurl.com/czGhYz
Website: kellyjensenwrites.com
Facebook: facebook.com/kellyjensenwrites
Twitter: twitter.com/kmkjensen